Mad 'Cause She Ain't You

Mad 'Cause She Ain't You

YOSHE

URBAN
BOOKS

www.urbanbooks.net

Urban Books, LLC
78 East Industry Court
Deer Park, NY 11729

ISBN 13: 978-1-60162-532-8
ISBN 10: 1-60162-532-4

First Printing January 2013
Printed in the United States of America

10 9 8 7 6 5 4 3 2 1

This is a work of fiction. Any references or similarities to actual events, real people, living or dead, or to real locales are intended to give the novel a sense of reality. Any similarity in other names, characters, places, and incidents is entirely coincidental.

Distributed by Kensington Publishing Corp.
Submit Wholesale Orders to:
Kensington Publishing Corp.
C/O Penguin Group (USA) Inc.
Attention: Order Processing
405 Murray Hill Parkway
East Rutherford, NJ 07073-2316
Phone: 1-800-526-0275
Fax: 1-800-227-9604

Chapter 1

You Remind Me

Ebony

As the giant clock on my living room wall ticked on, I was getting more and more impatient with my son's father, Shah. He was supposed to be picking up our son for the weekend and he was running late. I was already aggravated because my so-called boyfriend, Drayton, had been promising to return my phone calls for almost a week and I hadn't heard from him. I was just a bundle of nerves all across the board.

As of late, Dray had been giving me the brush-off. His attention was waning and we weren't spending as much time with each other as we used to. That was when I came to the conclusion that our on-again, off-again relationship was finally at the end of its road. It was quite obvious that my man of three years was cheating. It didn't take a rocket scientist to figure that one out. And poor me. I had been hanging on to Dray's scrotum for dear life, even though I knew damn well that our relationship had been a wrap for the past year.

I probably had more experience in dealing with cheating-ass men than I had in a quality relationship. Even Shah had cheated on me when we were together. So sad. And it wasn't hard for me to detect the signs—my female instincts never steered me wrong. I mean, come on, man, did these guys really think that I was stupid?

What was wrong with me? I had asked myself the question that I think every woman may have asked themselves at least once in their lifetime. And that wasn't the only question I asked. Why did it seem as if I was always dating the same type of guy? Was it the creeps I chose to get involved with the problem or was it something about me that led them astray?

There were over a hundred answers and a thousand books written as to why men cheat but I didn't need any of those. All I needed was one answer to that one nagging question. All I wanted to know was why did my boyfriends keep cheating on me?

The problems between Dray and I began shortly after our two-year anniversary in September, 2010. Dray had been complaining about every little thing I did and insisted on picking arguments with me. That was when the light bulb went off in my head.

It's another woman, I told myself. *Please don't tell me that this shit is happening to me again.*

Instead of confronting Dray about my fears, I did my emotional suffering in silence. Plus, I wanted to play fair. I did not want to outright accuse the man without any physical evidence because of a gut feeling that I had. Another reason I chose to keep quiet was because I was almost pretty sure that Dray would have used these reservations as a platform to sever the ties with me. I figured that he was just looking for a way out and I wasn't about to make it easy for him. Yes, there was always this nagging insecurity that had me thinking that Dray would be the one to leave me. And truthfully, I didn't want to lose him. What I really wanted was for us to work on our relationship.

I found myself daydreaming, thinking back to the good old days when Dray and I first got together. I met Dray in March of 2006. He was a transit police officer, and I a station agent for the Metropolitan Transit Authority. In the beginning, there wasn't much dialogue between us and it damn sure wasn't any love at first sight. Before I actually got to know Dray, I truly thought that he was just another self-absorbed, conceited jackass. At least, that was the impression that he gave me. He had this standoffish attitude that I didn't like and I didn't bother to speak to his ass because of it.

A few months after we met, I began noticing the flirtatious glances that Dray was giving me. I didn't entertain it, though because, honestly, he was so strikingly handsome that I was actually intimidated by the guy. Not to mention, I couldn't help but wonder, why was he trying to flirt with me? What was he up to?

When the flirting became too much for me to bear, we ended up exchanging phone numbers with each other. But instead of getting romantically involved right away, Dray and I became really good friends. Although the sexual chemistry was what eventually sealed the deal between us two, our friendship was what initially made me fall in love with Drayton Jackson.

On the afternoon of September 25, 2008, after two and a half years of a strictly platonic friendship, we took things to a whole 'nother level. I was stationed at the A train Jay Street subway station in Brooklyn and Dray was on patrol duty at the Hoyt-Schemerhorn station, one train stop away. He had taken it upon himself to make a special trip to my post to take me out to lunch that day.

My face lit up when I saw Dray walking toward me. I opened the door to let him inside the booth.

"What's up, Mr. Bestie?" I said, giving him a friendly hug.

Dray hugged me back then gave me a nod of approval. "You're looking mighty good in that uniform

*today, girl!" he said, biting his bottom lip. I playfully
slapped his arm. "Now, where are we going to eat?"
he asked.*

*I shrugged my shoulders. "It doesn't matter where
we eat. I'm just happy that you're treating your old
buddy, old pal to a meal," I replied, patting his shoulder in the process.*

*Dray smiled at me. "Anything for my girl," he said
with a wink.*

*It was about 12:30 P.M. when my coworker came to
relieve me for lunch. I gathered up my belongings and
told Dray to wait for me while I went to use the rest-
room. But instead of waiting for me near the booth,
Dray followed closely behind me.*

*I didn't think that anything was strange about him
following me until I unlocked the door to the bathroom. Dray quickly pushed me inside, locking the
door behind us.*

(I just stood there, in complete shock. I didn't know
what was about to happen, but at the same time I knew
what was about to happen, if you know what I mean.
The way that I was feeling at that moment . . . I knew
that I was ready to have sex with Dray. I could remember how excited I was, yet thinking, *If this Negro's sex
game is wack, our friendship is going to be so over!*)

*"Boy, are you crazy?" I asked him with a half-con-
fused/half-amused look on my face. "What the hell are
you trying to do?"*

*Dray stood there with this horn dog look on his
face. "Just go on and use the damn toilet, girl," he
said, waving me off, with a smirk on his face. "I'm not
bothering you."*

*"Yeah, okay," I said, rolling my eyes at him. Dray's
actions had me totally thrown off. "Just know that
you're tripping right now, homie."*

I shook my head at him and stepped into the stall. I took a quick pee, flushed the toilet, and got myself together before I opened the door.

When I walked toward the sink to wash my hands, I got a surprise—a really big one. There was Dray, standing near the sink, all six feet two inches of his fine self. His uniform pants were at his ankles and he was holding his rock-hard, nine-inch penis in his hand. Dray's uniform shirt was off, showing off those fabulous biceps of his. The fitted tank top he was wearing was enough to give me a visual of a six-pack that would put any P90X or Insanity workout fool to shame.

"Wash your hands," Dray ordered while he held on to his erect penis. I did as I told. "Now come over here to me, baby," he said. I did that too.

Most women would have been turned off by Dray's straightforwardness, but for me, fine men and a rock-hard dick had always been my Kryptonite. I felt my knees getting weak, as the song "Your Body's Callin'" by R. Kelly kept playing over and over in my head.

I slowly walked up to Dray. He wrapped his strong, calloused hands around the back of my neck and began kissing me. Then he massaged my ample breasts with one hand, while opening the buttons of my white MTA uniform shirt with the other. Things began getting hot and heavy so I took my boots off. I unbuttoned my uniform pants and kicked them bad boys to the side.

Dray pushed my back against the cold tiled wall. This was when we shared another sweet, passionate kiss while he rubbed his python between my legs. My clitoris was on fire from the friction and the more he dick-teased me, the more I wanted him to take me.

Then I felt myself being lifted off my feet. Slightly up in the air, I wrapped my legs around Dray's thirty-four-inch waist. (I was an avid condom user but I wasn't going to lie, Dray entered me raw dog and I didn't object to it one bit. Of course, I didn't know what I was thinking but, shoot, nothing else mattered but having Dray's oversized man meat inside of me.)

When Dray first entered me, we started off by grinding slowly. But that slow grind didn't last but so long. After a few minutes, we were caught up in the heat of the moment and our encounter intensified with every stroke, every moan and groan. Dray was pummeling and punishing my pussy; he was teaching me a lesson that I had never been taught. As for me, there were these strange sounds coming from my mouth. Not only did Dray's sex arouse the animal in me but it was so good that he almost made tears come to my eyes.

"Oh, Dray, baby, what are you doing to me?" I said, whispering in his ear.

"I'm claiming this pussy, baby," he replied, while long-stroking me into oblivion. "This is my pussy, right? I want this pussy to be mine and only mine."

"Make it yours, baby, make all of this yours," I replied between humps.

And claim it Dray did. Shit, the sex was more than what I had ever imagined. (I was still trying to remember how, but we ended up laid out on that bathroom floor—a bathroom that was the property of New York City Metropolitan Transit Authority. It was super gross. But when you're in the heat of the moment, all of that was irrelevant.)

Meanwhile, Dray still hadn't cum. He had me squirming with pleasure as his rock-hard rod hit every nerve ending of my sugar walls. Five minutes later, he sent me into multi-orgasmic fits, as the excitement of getting caught by somebody made our liaison even more risqué.

In the meantime, my orgasms didn't stop me from returning the favor. I tightened my box around Dray's rock-hard dick and he began pumping faster. Times like these made Kegel exercises worth every minute.

Dray's eyes began to roll in the back of his head. "Oh, damn, baby! Oh, you got me . . . you got me . . ." he began stuttering.

"Got you what?" I asked, taking the liberty of talking as dirty as I wanted to. "Tell me, motherfucker! Tell me what I got you doing!"

"You got me about to cuuuuum inside this pussy, baby," Dray replied in a barely audible voice.

Dray called out my name and, man, was he loud! I wouldn't have been surprised if the commuters heard his yelling over the damn trains. Suddenly, his body began to quiver, letting every drop of his warm semen shoot inside of me and I had yet another orgasm.

So there we were, laid out on the cold floor for a few minutes, trying to digest what just happened. We looked around the drab bathroom and at the peeling grey paint on the walls. The realization of where we were immediately bought us back to our senses. We quickly hopped up from the floor and began cracking up. Dray pulled up his uniform pants, not even bothering to wash my lady scent off him. He picked up his gun holster from the floor and put it back around his waist. I grabbed a few brown paper towels from the dispenser to try to wash myself off. I wouldn't have wanted to spend the remaining three hours of my shift sitting in that booth with a sticky punany and smelling like straight sex.

When Dray finished dressing, he just stood there and watched me while I got myself together. He leaned over and kissed me on the forehead.

"You all right, girl?" he asked while rubbing my face.

I put my pants back on and buttoned my shirt. "Oh, yes, I'm real good now," I replied. "I'm not going to lie, Dray—I didn't expect to get all of that."

A smug expression came over Dray's face. He waited until I was fully dressed to speak.

"So what are we going to do, Ebony?" he asked, with a serious look on his face.

"Okay, give me a minute," I replied, thinking that he was referring to our lunch date. "I'm coming right now. I just have to fix my hair before we walk out of here."

Dray waved me off. "Nah, girl, I'm not talking about that. I've been thinking that I want us to be more than just friends."

I was looking in the mirror, putting a fresh coat of Bobbi Brown gloss on my lips. But when Dray said that to me, I had to stop and give him the side eye. If I wasn't mistaken, it sounded like Dray was talking about getting serious with me.

I was flattered but I didn't want to jump to conclusions. "Is that what you want from me—something serious?"

Dray gave me a tender kiss and I wiped the gloss off his lips with my thumb.

"Yes, I do," he replied, looking into my eyes. "It's obvious that we're more than friends now—we just had sex with each other. But I don't want us to be just friends with benefits. I want us to work on having a committed relationship."

The words coming out of Dray's mouth sounded like music to my ears. Shoot, even I had to admit that over time, I had developed some very strong feelings for the man. I had suppressed these feelings only because I was afraid that Dray didn't want to get serious with me or anyone else for that matter.

"Are you sure, Dray? Because I really don't want this to ruin our friendship." I didn't know why I asked that, but a part of me needed to see if Dray was real about what he was saying to me.

Dray shook his head. "Ruin our friendship? Damn, Ebony. We just fucked each other right on this bathroom floor! And don't get it twisted; it's more than just lust for me. I'm feeling you—I have always been feeling you. Aren't you feeling me?"

I sighed. "Of course I am."

Dray held me in his arms and we shared yet another intimate kiss. And that was our defining moment. I felt so safe being in his arms. After doing the single life for the past five years, I knew then that it was time for me to love again.

"So what are we waiting for?" Dray asked. I smiled. "It's official! From now on, you're my woman and I'm your man."

And that was all she wrote.

Yep, that day in September was the day that Dray and I established that we were going to pursue a relationship with each other. Now all of that barely mattered anymore. I couldn't keep my mind off Dray, our effed-up situation, and how he was possibly playing me. Now I was waiting for late-ass Shah to pick up his son. All of this had me in a shitty mood.

Aside from all of these negative feelings floating around, I had to thank my sweet Baby Jesus that Kare wasn't adding to my aggravation. My sweet little angel was as quiet as a church mouse, playing games on my laptop and watching television in my bedroom. And I was even more thankful that he hadn't noticed that his father was running late. I was glad that he was being a good boy, because I wasn't in the mood for anything else but good behavior. But it would have been unfair of me to take out my frustrations on my child. He didn't have a damn thing to do with his wayward father or my man problems. It's just that I didn't have the patience to deal.

It was already 6:30 P.M. when Mister Shah decided to call me back. This was later than usual for him. I answered the call, hoping that he would have a good excuse. I didn't want to have to cuss his ass out.

"Where are you, Shah?" I asked impatiently as soon as I answered the phone.

"Hello to you too, baby mother," Shah greeted me, with this annoying chuckle.

Shah and I had broken up five years ago when Kare was only three years old. At one time, we didn't get along with each other for shit. This time around, we were trying to work on having a civilized relationship with each other for the sake of our son. We had a long way to go because, unfortunately, I still had to act like a bitch every now and again. This was one of those times.

"What the hell?" I yelled into the phone. "Will you please come and get your son? Where are you anyway? I've been calling you for the last hour and a half!"

I knew that Shah was bothered by my questioning. "I'm on my way now. And don't worry about where I was," he replied, with a hint of sarcasm in his voice. "You're acting like Kare is asking for me or something! Is the boy crying? Is he upset that I'm not there yet?"

"No, he's not! But that's not the point."

"So what is the point?" asked the frustrated Shah. "We go through this same shit every other weekend. You always get upset with me when I don't be there at the time you want me to be there."

I walked into the kitchen and poured me a glass of Sweet Bitch, my favorite wine. I took a big gulp. I needed to calm my nerves.

"Listen, Shah, the only thing that I told you to do was be here at five o'clock! It's an hour and a half later! All I'm saying is get on your job."

Shah groaned. "Whatever," he mumbled, knowing that he was no match for my wrath. "Anyway, is Kare ready to go or what?"

"Um, yeah! What do you think? He's been ready to go."

"And you're gonna stop talking to me any which-a-way," Shah added. "Just be happy that Kare has an active father who's involved in his life. Its so many trifling dudes out there who don't see or even acknowledge their got-damn kids. I make it my business to see mine and do what I have to do for him."

I wasn't trying to hear anything that Shah said. I just wanted him to make it his business to pick up Kare at the time he was supposed to.

"Okay, don't start that up again. I know what kind of father you are. Woopity-do-dah."

Shah ignored my smart remark and moved on to another topic. "Now that we got that out the way, I have to go to Pennsylvania on Sunday night, early Monday morning. I'm going to take Kare to the UniverSoul Circus that Sunday afternoon. Then I'm going to have to drop him off at my mother's house on Sunday evening. Mom Dukes is off from work on Monday and she said with your permission, she'll take him to school that morning. You can pick him up from her house when you get off work Monday evening."

The mention of my former "mother-in-law" put a smile on my face. "Sure, she can," I said. "I wouldn't mind seeing Ms. Banks. I haven't seen her in a minute. How is she doing?"

"She's doing pretty well. She still calls you her 'daughter,' you know."

"That's the fuck right!" I exclaimed, adding some extra cuss words in order to drive my point home. "And she's always gonna be my second mother. You better let your bitches know that, too!"

Shah couldn't stand it when I cussed and I knew that. "What's with all the profanity? Damn!" I envisioned him shaking his head at me. "Some things just don't change." He cleared his throat. "Anyway, I'll be at your house in like, ten minutes, man. I'm on Rockaway Parkway and Linden Boulevard right now."

"Yeah, a'ight," I said, disconnecting the phone call. I exhaled. My baby boy was about to be out of there. Once he left, I could drink the rest of my Sweet Bitch and work on getting my mind right.

Exactly one minute after I hung up the phone from Shah, who exits the bedroom like clockwork? It was none other than the man of the hour, Master Kare Banks himself. He appeared in the living room, dragging his personalized duffel bag with him. It was packed with his clothes and he had his jacket and hat in the other hand. It looked like Kare was just as much ready to go as I was for him to leave.

I shook my head at the sight of my Kare Bear. I was his mother so it was only right if I thought that he was the cutest kid ever. My baby had the most beautiful sun-kissed brown skin and head full of curly hair. And he was the spitting image of that damn Shah.

Kare walked over to where I was sitting on the couch. He wrapped his skinny arms around my neck and gave me a big, tight hug and a kiss.

"I can't wait to see my daddy, Mommy," he said.

"Aww! I know that you can't wait, Kare Bear," I said, kissing him on the cheek. "You love you some Daddy, don't you?"

"Of course I do!" he replied, looking at me as if I was off my rocker for asking him such a dumb question. "And I have to tell him what I want for Christmas, too."

My eyes widened. "For Christmas?" I asked. "It's the middle of April, Kare!"

"I know, Mommy, but I'm doing my Christmas list early so that everybody will have time to get my things. And I don't want a lot of stuff, either," Kare replied, while playing with my ear. That was something that he had been doing ever since he was a baby.

"Okay," I said, thinking that making an early Christmas list made a lot of sense. I was definitely curious to see what was on it. "What do you mean that you 'don't want a lot of stuff'?"

Kare smiled, revealing his two front rabbit teeth. They had just grown back after falling out six months before his eighth birthday. "I want Daddy to get me a laptop, not a notebook—that's for babies."

"Oh, okay, you want a big boy laptop—"

Kare cut me off. "Yes! And, Mommy, you can get me an iPhone."

A look of surprise came over my face. *Whatever happened to the times when kids just wanted G.I. Joes and Barbies?*

"But you just turned eight years old, Kare!" I replied. "Don't you think that you're a little too young to have a cell phone, let alone an iPhone?" I asked, with a look of concern. I thought about all of the thieving bastards out there who would be trying to kill my baby for that contraption.

"Nope! This boy in my class named Jaylen has an iPhone and he's eight too!"

"All righty then . . ."

"And Auntie Phoenix can get me a Nintendo DS, my grandmothers could get me some games for my DS, and Auntie Joi could get me some Jordans."

"But, Kare—"

He continued talking. "And Auntie Tedra could get me some games for my PlayStation—"

I cut him off right there. Tedra was my older sister and she was cheap as hell. That was the wrong somebody to be asking for a Christmas present.

"Okay, okay, chill out, Tonto!" I said, holding my hand up. "How do you know that people have money for this kind of stuff?"

Kare had the nerve to hold his head as if he were in pain. I attempted to stifle my laughter. He then proceeded to give me the rundown on everyone's financial background.

"Mommy, you have money because you have a good job in the train station and Daddy has money because he drives trucks. Auntie Tedra has a big house and Auntie Phoenix has a BMW. That means that they're rich!"

I couldn't contain my amusement. *Like, where does this little boy get this stuff from?* I laughed so hard that I almost peed on myself. "Boy! Why are you counting what's in other people's pockets?" I asked.

"But, Mommy, you always say that other people's money spends much better than your own!" he replied, with a look on his face that was as serious as cancer.

I was completely floored by that statement. Not only had Kare been listening to my every damn word, he was repeating them to me, verbatim. I knew that my son was just too smart for his own good. His comments only made me think about how dumb I must have been when I was his age. I would have never thought to say anything like that to my parents at eight years old, or any other age for that matter. I realized that I had to be very careful about what I said in front of Kare. He was like a human sponge.

The doorbell rang and Kare hopped out of my lap to run to the door. I looked out the window and saw Shah standing there, looking clean cut and dapper, as usual. As soon as I opened the door, Kare started whooping and hollering. He was always more than excited to see his father. They went through this whole scenario every time Shah came to pick him up.

Shah walked in the house, leaving the scent of his expensive cologne wavering behind him. He said, "What's up" to me, then swept Kare off his feet and into his muscular arms. Looking at the both of them was like looking at a pair of Doublemint twins. I shook my head. Old Shah still had that same killer smile, too. It was the smile that made so many women swoon over the years, including me. It was also the same smile that made me fall madly in and out of love with his sneaky ass.

"Hey, hey, hey, Kare Bear!" he yelled, kissing Kare on his cheeks. I covered my ears with my hands. They were so loud when they got together. "Are you ready to be up and out, Twin?"

Shah put Kare down and he began running around like a madman. "Yeah, Daddy! Yeah, Daddy! Let me get my stuff!" Kare ran to get his bag and almost fell on his face.

"Kare, calm down before you hurt yourself!" I sighed. "That boy gets so hyper when he sees you!"

"He's supposed to get hyper! He loves his dad." Shah looked at me and gave me a head nod. I could tell that he was trying to read my mood. "So what's up with you, miss?" he asked, nudging my arm.

"Ain't much, Shah. Just waiting for you and your son to bounce up outta here," I replied. "Mama gotta do her thang this weekend," I added, referring to myself.

While I spoke, I noticed that Shah was covering every inch of my body. He always had that way of undressing you with his eyes.

"Hmmph," he said. "Yeah, I know you do. Your boy is gonna be gone 'til Monday evening. Do your thang, Shorty."

I shrugged one shoulder. "It is what it is."

"So, what's up with your lame-ass boyfriend?" he asked, referring to Dray. Shah didn't care for him but it wasn't like what he thought made much of a difference.

"He's a'ight. What's up with your brothel of hoes?" I asked, with a smug expression on my face.

Shah smirked. "My hoes? Oh, yeah, my hoes are fine. And they still got love for their daddy," he replied, patting himself on the chest.

I chuckled. "Tuh! I hear that, Daddy!" I replied, putting emphasis on the "daddy."

"You know that I don't have to front about nothing that I do. I have a few female friends but I ain't sweating none of them. I'm happily single. You're the one around here stressing that lame boyfriend of yours," Shah said.

He was such a hater when it came to my relationship with Dray, yet when he was with me, he couldn't do right.

"What do you mean, I'm stressing? I'm not stressing nobody or nothing, not even you, babe!"

Shah put his arm around my shoulder. I gave him a dirty look and he immediately took his arm off me.

"I can tell when you're stressed out. You used to be my girl, remember? You're letting homeboy stress you out. How do I know? Because you're giving me a hard time and the only time you do that is when you and Dray are going through it."

First of all, I didn't need to be reminded that I used to be Shah's girlfriend. Those days of being with him were some very trying times for me. My self-esteem was super low, my confidence was almost nonexistent and my self-respect? Well, let's just say that I played myself on many occasions. Those days were also the times that I contemplated the murder of Shah Born Banks.

"Pfff," I said, giving him the hand to the face. "Whatever, Shah!" I bent down to kiss Kare, who had come back from retrieving the rest of his things. "Be a good boy and have fun with your Daddy and Nana, okay?"

Kare hugged me tightly. "Okay, Mommy. Have a nice weekend without me!" He grabbed his father's hand and began pulling him out of the house. "Come on, Daddy! Let's go!"

When they walked out that door, I wanted to do freaking cartwheels and somersaults! The peacefulness in my house was like music to my ears.

I watched from the front window as they climbed into Shah's Denali truck and pulled off. Then I grabbed the rest of my Sweet Bitch and went to lie down on my couch. While I sipped my wine, I turned on the television, hoping to catch up on some of the shows that I had taped on my DVR. It wasn't like I had anything else to do.

Before I knew it, an hour had passed by. As I watched television, I thought about what Shah said to me about being stressed out. As much as I hated to admit it, he was so right. Dray had been avoiding me and I needed to know what was going on with us. It was time for me to finally face the truth.

Chapter 2

Real Love

Phoenix

It was a Friday evening, around seven o'clock. I was sitting in the living room of my two-bedroom cooperative apartment in Fresh Meadows, Queens, waiting for my blind date, Stuart Childs. He was coming to pick me up for a night out on the town. Stu and I had been talking over the phone to each other for the last two weeks and now we were finally going to meet in person. I was so nervous, yet excited at the same time.

Although I was not very fond of hooking up with guys that I had never laid my eyes on, I was so looking forward to this date with Stuart. I thought, *what do I have to lose?* It wasn't as if the guy wouldn't like me. I was an extremely attractive thirty-two-year-old woman, if I must say so myself. I was single, with no children. I had a pretty decent career as a legal secretary with a prominent law firm. I had been with this firm ever since I graduated from Clark Atlanta University ten years ago. I was raking in almost six figures but it didn't stop there. My father, Jonas, and I, along with my younger brother, Chase, were the owners of Henry Trucking Company. Our family business was doing pretty well and the money was coming in from there as well. So the dough, the looks, and the career were definitely not a problem for Miss Phoenix Janay Henry.

Seriously speaking, the real problem was that I didn't know the first thing about maintaining a loving connection with a man. Yes, I could have sex with them; I could definitely spend their money, too. But the idea of having a full-blown relationship with one guy always sent me into a spiral of confusion. I decided that I was going to try to work on this issue, starting with this date.

Speaking of my blind date, I had already done my homework on this Stu character. He seemed as if he was cool enough to be blessed with my presence. Aside from the fact that Stu was supposed to be this hotshot Harlem promoter, I hoped that he had all of the other essential components to keep me interested, or else this date was going to be a total bust.

And in this new age of technology, I still didn't know how this man looked. That shit really bothered me. I asked him to send some pics of himself to my phone and Stu insisted that we try something different. He suggested that we not send any pictures of ourselves to each other—that we should wait to see each other in person instead. I'm a visual person and of course, I wasn't too pleased with that idea. But surprisingly, the anticipation and surprise factor had me going, making me even more anxious to meet this Stu.

This whole blind date thing came into fruition while I was visiting with two of my closest friends, Capri and Shanell. These two lovely ladies were first cousins to each other and business partners, as well. We had been friends for twenty-plus years and, honestly, these wonderful *chicas* were more like family members to me. Anyway, I always looked forward to our meetings. We were brutally honest with each other and I loved that. I wouldn't have had it any other way.

So there we were, sitting in Shanell and Capri's store, Casha Boutique. It was after hours and we were sipping on some Bartenura Moscato. We were talking the shit that girls talk when the subject of how picky I was just happened to come up. All of sudden, our girly pow-wow instantly turned into a therapy session/roast for Phoenix.

"Girl, aren't you tired of being by yourself?" asked Capri, who was a lighter version of Kelly Rowland from the group Destiny's Child. She was a very pretty woman with a bubbly personality. Everyone who came into her path absolutely loved her.

I swung my eighteen inches of Remy Indian hair weave around my shoulders and fluttered my M•A•C falsies. "Hell no!" I announced, sipping Moscato from my champagne flute. "But, then again, I just haven't found that right somebody yet, that's all."

Shanell rolled her eyes at me. At a size sixteen, my girl Shanell was the thicker one of us girls. I personally thought that she was a little overweight, but Shanell was comfortable with her body. Her face was abso-lutely adorable, though. Even with the extra pounds, she was definitely well put together and this plus-sized diva was happily married for eight years to her long-time love, Majesty. Capri and I wore like a size four and didn't even have boyfriends! I guessed size really doesn't matter.

Capri and I lovingly called Shanell "the Queen Bee" because, at thirty-six years old, she was a little older than we were and was like a big sister to us. She played that big sister role to the hilt. She was always more than willing to find a solution to our dilemmas. On that day, it was my turn. Shanell had chosen to make my single, lonely, miserable existence—her words, not mine—her personal project.

The Queen Bee put her glass on the round center table and stood up, as if she was about to make an announcement. "Okay, you know what? I'm just so sick of this," Shanell said. She ran her hands through her choppy bob hairdo. "Looky here, Miss Phoenix Janay Henry," she began, imitating my voice when she said that. "You're one bad-ass broad and I don't think that anyone has to tell you this. For Christ's sake, you can have any man you want! Notice that I said any man you want. But the real question is, why don't you have no man?"

Capri almost spit out her drink. She grabbed a napkin to wipe her mouth. "Wait, hold up, Shanell," Capri said, with a giggle. She held up her hand to stop her cousin from going any further, and then looked at me.

I was slightly annoyed but tried not to show it. "Maybe I don't want or need a man, Shanell!" I said, instantly getting on the defensive.

"Phoenix, there is nothing wrong with needing a man," Capri explained. "Most of us women 'need' a nice, long, hard one every now and again!" On that note, we all gave each other high fives. "Shit, we can't fuck ourselves! I mean, we can use BOB to fuck ourselves," she said matter-of-factly. BOB was the name that we had for our dildos. B-O-B stood for "battery-operated boyfriend."

Capri continued, "Even though BOB is cool sometimes, I'm sure that you are in need of the real thing every now and again. So my point is that it's nothing wrong with 'needing' a man, even if it's just for the d-i-c-k alone."

I poured some more Moscato into Capri's glass. She was definitely giving the "tea" on a woman's wants and needs. But this whole conversation was being done at my expense so I felt the need to stand up for my beliefs.

"Girl, bye!" I said, rolling my eyes at Capri and Shanell. "Of course I need and want a man, but at what cost? I shouldn't have to settle for the first man who has a big, hard cock and a cute face but no money and no job. Let's face it, the Dick ain't funding my lifestyle—my money is. And I don't need anybody trying to jump on my bandwagon," I added.

Shanell shook her head at me. "I hear what you're saying, girlfriend, but you are so ready to be by your damn self for the rest of your years! Trust me, baby girl; the Queen knows what you need. You need yourself a husband and a baby. Them old-ass eggs of yours needs to be fertilized—and fast! Do you want to be a fifty-year-old, menopausal, private-summer-having, decrepit old maid? Is that what you want, Phoenix?"

We all laughed hysterically. Then I looked at Capri and glanced back at Shanell. "Now why I gotta be all that, Shanell? And how in the hell did we go from talking about men and dick to having babies and getting married?" I asked.

"Having a man, getting married, getting some dick and a baby goes hand in hand!" Shanell said, holding out her two hands.

"And did you really have to say that I was going to be a decrepit old maid? Like really? I'm only thirty-two years old, you know," I said, with my face all screwed up like I smelled something stank.

"Yes, I did! I can give you a description of what your life will resort to if you don't stop acting like you're too good for these men out here. I don't know who the hell you're waiting for but whoever he is, he is not coming, girlfriend—time to stop living on Phoenix's Fantasy Island, Boo!"

We burst out laughing again.

Shanell put one hand on her ample hips and pointed at me with the other. "You know what, Phoenix? I'm

*tired of playing this game with your lonely ass!"
She ruffled through her Marc Jacobs bag and pulled
out her cell. "Sick of your old, dried-up box . . ." she
mumbled.*

*"Oh, so now you're referring to my coochie as an
old, dried-up box?" I said.*

*Capri and I were keeling over with laughter as the
visibly annoyed, slightly serious-faced Shanell dialed
some numbers on her phone.*

*Thinking that she was calling her husband, I spoke
up. One rule that we had during girls' night was not to
take any phone calls unless it was an emergency.*

*"Hold up! I know you ain't calling no Majesty in the
middle of our girls' night," I said.*

*"Oh, no, Missy Poo! I'm not calling Majesty," she
said, putting the phone to her ear. "But I'm about to
rectify this bullshit right here and now! Rowwww!"
Shanell said, throwing her claws up at me. I laughed
again.*

*Suddenly, Shanell's face lit up. "Hey, man, what's
good with you, bruh?" she asked the person on the
other end of the phone. She began laughing and slapping one knee. I was on the other side of the couch,
frowning at this entire spectacle.*

*She continued to talk to this mystery guy. "Yeah,
boy, you know I got you on that party next weekend!
Yep, me and the hubby are going to be there with bells
on! Anyway, I was calling because I wanted to know
if you were still single, Boo?" Shanell paused and began chuckling at the person on the phone. "No, no, the
reason I asked is because there is someone I would like
for you to meet. She's a very dear friend of mine. I'm
surprised you guys didn't meet each other years ago!
She was in my wedding and everything."*

I frantically waved my hands at Shanell. Of course, she ignored me.

"Noooo, man, she ain't no buster—she's a very pretty girl," Shanell continued, taking a quick glance at me. "She is hot!" Then she paused. It was obvious that this person was talking shit because her eyes opened wide. "Does she have a fat what?" There was more laughter. "I don't know, Negro! You're going to have check that one out for yourself!" she replied, forcing me to stand up so that she could take a look at my butt. "Look, I'll give you her phone number so that you can talk to her yourself." Shanell recited my number while I sat right there looking at her in amazement. "Okay, see you later, Mr. Childs."

"That was Stu?" asked Capri. Shanell nodded her head.

"How do you give out somebody's number without their—" I didn't have a chance to finish my sentence before my phone started ringing.

"Answer the damn phone, girl!" she ordered through clenched teeth.

"He better be cute, too." I rolled my eyes at Shanell and reluctantly picked up the call. "Hello?" I said slowly.

"What's up, miss? How are you?" Stu's voice was this very soothing, sexual baritone that tickled my eardrums. I hoped that he looked as good as he sounded.

I got up from the couch and walked a short distance away from the girls. Even though my back was turned, I knew that they were watching me like two hawks.

"I'm fine. Yourself?" I asked, letting out a slight yawn.

"I'm better now," said Stu.

I rolled my eyes again. "Um, I didn't catch your name, buddy," I said, with an attitude.

He chuckled. "Oh, that's my bad. The name is Stuart Childs, babe, but everyone just calls me Stu. And your name is?"

"Phoenix. Phoenix Henry."

"Oh, wow. Nice name. Very different," said Stu.

"Yeah, thanks, Stu."

There was a slight pause in our conversation. I didn't know what else to say to this stranger.

I walked back over to the couch to retrieve my drink. Capri and Shanell were sitting in front of me, looking down my throat. They were hanging on to my every word.

Finally, Stu broke our brief silence. "Well, anyway, Phoenix, I have to go now but I'm going to lock your number in my phone and you do the same. I'm looking forward to talking to you real soon."

"Likewise." It was getting hard to contain my laughter with the two cackling hens sitting in front of me.

"Later, babe," Stu said. He disconnected the call.

"Babe?" I said looking at my phone with my lip turned up. I put the phone away and stared at the chuckling Capri and Shanell, who thought that my reaction to the call was funny as hell.

"What the hell are y'all drunken whores laughing at me for? Do you find me amusing?"

"Your facial expressions are priceless!" Capri said, pointing at me. "You should have seen your face when that phone rang."

"So who the hell is this Stu Childs character?" I asked, with a clueless look on my face. "And how are you just gonna put me on the spot like that, Shanell?"

Shanell cleared her throat. "Stu is Majesty's first cousin on his mama's side—that's Majesty's aunt's son. He's the same age as you, he's from Harlem, and he has no children. He's a promoter and I'm not talking about just local promotion—he's internationally known. He does industry parties, too—I've been to a few of them and they are very nice—dude definitely makes that bread. Have you ever heard of Stu Childs Entertainment?" I shook my head. "Well, you're about to find out about that. Stu is about his business. He knows how to get that moolah. Just like you."

I raised one eyebrow when Shanell said the word "moolah." On that note, Stu did sound like he was a fascinating young man and, more importantly, my type of dude.

"Okay, so how does this Stu fellow look, Capri?"

Capri and I had identical taste in men so I knew that I could rely on her to be completely honest about Stu's physical characteristics. Shanell liked big, burly guys like her fluffy husband, Majesty.

"I'm telling you, Phoenix, this Stu cat is foine, girl!" she exclaimed. "He's a brown-skinned complexion, about six foot three inches and has a very nice frame. And he's a great dresser—Cavalli, Ferragamo, Cartier, you name it; he sports all the designer stuff. So with all of that being said, are you interested in meeting him or what?"

"If he's so fine, why didn't you holler at him?" I asked, with a suspicious look on my face.

Capri's face turned sour. "Are you crazy, girl? Stu is like my family!"

Everything that I was hearing about Stu had me changing my tune about the whole blind date thing. I decided that it really wouldn't hurt to give it a try, now would it?

"Okay! Now, tell me. What kind of car does he drive?" I asked. A man with a hooptie or no car at all was definitely a deal breaker for me.

Shanell stopped Capri from saying anything else about Stu. "No, Capri! Don't tell this heifer a damn thing." She looked at me. "You're going to have to find that out on your own, missy! And stop being so got-damn superficial! It shouldn't matter what kind of car he drives or what kind of designers he wears on his ass! You're trying to see if this guy is someone you wouldn't mind being with!"

I sucked my teeth and crossed my arms in defiance. "Well, I don't know about you but the kind of car that a man drives really matters to me!"

Shanell grabbed me by the arms and shook me. "Forget all that! Hold a decent conversation with the man first. Damn! You just might like the guy."

I didn't see the problem in knowing if I was wasting my time.

"Can you please stop saying that I'm superficial?" I said. "Just because I happen to like quality shit doesn't make me superficial!"

Shanell sucked her teeth. "Please, child!" she said, brushing off my statement and disregarding every-thing I said. "Anyway, girlfriend, you're going to meet Stu and for some reason, I think that you're going to like this man. I'm so sure of that."

I sipped some more of the Moscato. I was beginning to feel the effects of it.

"What the hell am I to you—a charity case? This ain't no What Chilli Wants," I said, referring to the former TLC group member's reality show. "And you damn sure ain't her matchmaker, Tionna!"

We all started laughing again.

"You're not Chilli but you damn sure acting like the bitch with all of your . . . your standards and your list of bullshit expectations!" Shanell shot back.

I pointed at myself. "My expectations are bullshit? You know what? I will talk to this Stu guy on one condition."

"Oh, boy! What is it now?"

I pointed at this dazzling pair of earrings with Swarovski crystals that were hanging on a wall in the boutique. Shanell looked at the earrings then looked at me.

"Oh, hell no! Those earrings are like eighty dollars a pair, girl! I cannot give those to you!"

"Don't you want me to look good for Stu?" I asked her, with one eyebrow raised.

Capri walked over to the wall and reached for the earrings. She put them right in my hand. "Yes, we both," she began, giving Shanell a wink, "want you to look good for Stu, girl. Enjoy."

I stuck my tongue out at Shanell. Then we poured more Moscato in our glasses and continued to chat the night away.

Back at my co-op, my ringing cell phone interrupted these thoughts. I looked at the caller ID. It was Stu. My heart began pounding immediately.

"Hey, Phoenix," he said. "I'm downstairs."

"I'll be right there," I said. Man, was I nervous.

I hung up the phone and threw it inside of my black patent leather Louis Vuitton bag. Then I checked myself in the mirror. My Remy Indian hung loosely down my back and my Bobbi Brown makeup was on point. Meanwhile, the colorful, lightweight Missoni dress that I was wearing hugged my slender frame. My pricey Louboutin platform shoes made me look like a million bucks. And the earrings, courtesy of Casha Boutique, went perfect with my attire.

After making sure that I was looking picture perfect, I threw on a butter-soft Via Spiga leather blazer and walked out the door, locking it behind me.

When I arrived downstairs, Stu was standing at the curb on the passenger side of a black four-door Maserati. He held the car door open for me.

As I got closer, I was more than pleased with Stu. He planted a soft kiss on my cheek. When I was getting in the car, I could feel him staring at my fatty, too. I slowly slid into the passenger seat, purposely revealing a little butterscotch-colored thigh.

"Okay," he said, with a look of satisfaction on his face. "Looking real good there, ma."

I smiled. *Tell me something that I don't know already.* I dared not say that aloud, though.

"You're looking pretty good yourself, Stu," I replied.

He said, "Thank you," and shut the passenger side door.

"There is a God," I whispered under my breath, not able to take my eyes off him.

Stu walked around to the driver's side of his car and got in. When he went to put his hand on the steering wheel, my eyes went straight to the Presidential Rolex on his wrist and I had already peeped the Cartier frames that he was sporting. The spectacles gave him a distinguished look.

"You smell good—what kind of cologne are you wearing?" I asked, trying to break the ice.

"If I tell ya, I'd have to kill ya," Stu replied. We both laughed. "Just kidding, babe. I'm wearing Creed."

That Creed cologne was at least $200 a bottle. The price tag made it smell even better.

"Damn, that smells good. I love it!" I glanced out of the passenger window. "So we finally meet each other in person, huh?"

Stu smiled. "Yeah, finally. You're a very pretty woman, Phoenix. Actually, you're more than what I expected. And you look exceptionally gorgeous tonight. Seems like you're ready to get into some things, too," he added, giving me a seductive look.

"Thanks for the compliment, babe," I replied. "And yes, I'm more than ready for a night out with you, even had to throw on my red bottoms for the occasion," I said, thinking that Stu would be impressed with my equally expensive taste. I didn't want him to think that he was out with a buster.

And from the looks of it, he was impressed. "You must have some serious cash if you're buying red bottoms," Stu said.

I waved him off. "Please! I have a few pairs of Louboutins. I don't do cheap, just chic, honey," I added, throwing that little ditty in for good measure.

Stu shook his head. "But what if you didn't have the Louboutin shoes or Louis Vuitton money? Would you still be the same old Phoenix? Material things can't be that important to you, can they?" he asked, getting all technical with it. Old Stu was obviously trying to use some reverse psychology on a sister.

"I cannot imagine not having all of these things. These are the rewards of my success. And the Phoenix that I am is a go-getter and I can't see me being nothing else but that."

"Okay," Stu replied, shrugging his shoulders.

Stu sort of threw me off with the one-word reply. Now it was my turn to find out what he really was about before our date went any further.

I turned around in my seat to look at him. "So what about you, Stu? I mean, look at you. You're wearing a Rolex and driving this fancy car and all that. Looks like you're just as much into material things as I am."

Stu glanced at me. "What if I told you that I rented this watch and this car, and that these clothes are borrowed—would you still like me then?" he asked, with a smirk on his face.

I must have blinked about fifty times in less than thirty seconds. "Excuse me? Are you serious?" I so hoped that for Stu's sake he was just playing with me, because if he wasn't, he was going to be dating himself that night.

Stu began cracking up. "Damn, girl! You should see the look on your face right now!"

I didn't dare crack a smile. All I wanted to hear is that this Negro wasn't serious.

"Okay, okay," Stu began, seeing that I didn't find his little "jokey-joke" amusing. "I'm just playing, girl, calm down!" He stopped at the light and gave me eye contact. "Look, let's get something straight. I'm not into misleading nobody. If I don't have it, I just don't have it, Stu don't do no fronting. Everything I wear, drive, or have in my pocket and my bank accounts is all mine and no one else's. But I am a modest guy, as well. Usually, I drive a Volkswagen Touareg but Shanell told me that you're supposed to be this fancy, high-end dame so I pulled Midnight out of the garage just for you."

"Who is Midnight?" I asked, completely clueless as to what he was talking about.

"Midnight is this here Maserati I'm driving, babe. It's black on black which is why I nicknamed it Midnight."

That one had gone over my head. "Oh, okay. How cute." I was able to relax a little and even managed to let out a slight chuckle. "For a minute there, you had my nerves on edge when you said that none of this was yours."

Stu gave me this strange look. "Like, would you really be turned off if I didn't have all of these material things?" he asked, with a frown on his face.

I slapped my thigh. "Turned off is an understatement! I mean, I don't want you to take this the wrong way but I have to deal with someone who's on my level, if you know what I mean. Like minds think alike—am I right or wrong?"

I wasn't sure about how Stu felt when I told him that I needed a man to be on my "level." But when Stu's answer didn't come, I decided to keep my trap shut. I didn't want to run the risk of turning the man off with all of my yapping.

To break the awkward silence, Stu turned to a Sirius satellite radio station.

As we continued to cruise the Cross Island Parkway, I leaned back in the passenger seat. I closed my eyes, taking in the sounds of Trey Songz's seductive voice coming through Midnight's Bose speakers. Meanwhile, Stu rested his right hand on my bare thigh. I smiled to myself and didn't object to the gesture, not one bit.

Chapter 3

She Said It's Your Child

Joi

I arose from bed early that Friday morning, dreading going to work. Even with the comfortable Tempur-Pedic mattress that I had purchased a few months back, I was still suffering from insomnia and lack of rest. This sluggishness also had me feeling grumpy as hell. I guess that's why when I arrived at work for 8:00 A.M., I was ready to snap at damn near every person who crossed my path.

This attitude of mine was brought on by Tate, my boyfriend of four years. I hadn't heard from him in the past twenty-four hours, which was a definite no-no for me. I didn't play that. I guessed I could have played the good girlfriend and be worried about him but I was too angry to sympathize with Tate. All I knew was that when he did get around to calling me, the mother-fucker had better have a real good excuse for his disappearing act.

Trust me; I wasn't trying to be the bitchy girlfriend. I had valid reasons for being the way that I was with Tate. After having been through so much with this man, I felt that I was at my breaking point. There was always some type of drama, and 95 percent of the time, the drama was always concerning his daughter's mother, Dara.

Aside from everything else that was going on, I managed to make it through the workday. When I arrived home, I almost expected for Tate to be there, waiting for me. I just knew that he would be sitting on my couch, with the sincerest of apologies, maybe a dozen of roses, a bottle of wine. But I could only dare to dream. There was no sign of Tate. I checked my house phone and there still were no messages on my answering machine from him. Not one.

Sounds pretty aggravating, right? It was. Now my rage was on 105.

At 6:00 P.M., after having been home for almost an hour and a half, I was still lying around. I managed to get up off my ass and draw me up a relaxing bubble bath. I lit a few of my scented candles from Carol's Daughter and turned on some elevator music. Then I put my cordless phone and my cell phone right by the tub, just in case Tate called me back.

As I swished around in the tub of bubbles, I got two phone calls. One was from my mother, Renee, and the other was from my girlfriend Ebony. As much as I wasn't in the mood for idle conversation, I forced myself talk to somebody before I lost my mind. So I called Ebony back. I saved my mother's phone call for another time because I knew that she would only work my nerves. I would have to call her when I was in a much better frame of mind.

"What's up, girl?" I asked as soon as Ebony answered the phone.

"Nothing much," Ebony replied, sounding as blah as I felt. I could hear her voice cracking, which only meant one thing. I didn't want to be fucked up or anything but I wasn't trying to hear no one else's bullshit that day. I had a very serious situation of my own that I was working on.

Ebony must have caught herself. Instead of talking about her man, Dray, like I expected her to, she began talking about something totally different. "What am I saying? It's Friday night, Kare is with his father, and I just got paid. I was wondering if you wanted to hang out with me tonight, girl. Drinks are on me."

I sighed. She knew good and damn well that I didn't hang out like that. I would have much rather been in my own house, chilling with my man. I instantly shut her down. "Sorry, girlfriend. I appreciate the offer but I don't feel like going out anywhere tonight. Tate done got on my last nerve so I just want to take this bath and relax."

It was pretty quiet on the other end. By Ebony not responding to me right away, I knew that she had a 'tude. I know that my friends were probably tired of me and Tate and our issues—we had been going through so much for so long. But if Ebony was supposed to be my friend, she should have understood, even if it was the same damn scenario over and over again.

"Well, don't you think that Dray and I are going through it too, Joi? I mean, damn! I kind of figured that just this once, this one time that you would come and hang out with me and listen to my fucking man problems! But I guess I was wrong. Anyway, I'll talk to you later. I got some other calls to make."

I couldn't have cared less about Ebony's snide remarks or her attitude. I was too focused on my own shit and Tate's whereabouts to care what people were going through with their relationships. Sometimes I was selfish like that.

"Ebony, I'm sorry, hon, but you know that I don't hang out like that."

"Mmm hmm, whatever," she replied, sounding extremely annoyed. Then she hung up on me.

"Oh, well," I said. I put my phone down, then picked up my remote and turned up my music. I was damn near asleep in the tub when, suddenly, my house phone rang. Finally, Tate had decided to call.

I stood up in the middle of the tub. Bubbles dripped down my wet body. "Oh, so you're just now remembering that you have a motherfucking girlfriend, right?" I screamed into the cordless phone. "I don't appreciate you not calling me back or answering my phone calls, Tate! Where the hell have you been?" I yelled.

Instantly, Tate got on some defensive shit with me, just like guilty people do. "Look, Joi, calm your ass down, okay? Sorry I didn't call you back or answer your calls but Chasity was really sick, okay? She had a mild asthma attack last night," Tate said. "Me and Dara were sitting in that damn Brooklyn Hospital emergency room all night long and most of this morning."

Everything that Tate said about his daughter went into one ear and out of the other. All I freaking heard was, "Me and Dara were sitting in the emergency room all night long," which meant that he and his baby mother were together—all night long! My blood was boiling at the mere mention of Dara's name.

I stepped out of the tub and began patting my body dry. "You mean to tell me that you was with that dirty skank all night and day? Is that why you couldn't pick up the phone to call or text me?" Tate didn't say a word, which to me was an admission of guilt. "Oh, hell no! You and this ho gotta be fucking each other! I am not stupid, Tate!" I yelled.

"What in the hell are you talking about?" Tate yelled back at me. "Did you not just hear me say that my daughter was in the motherfucking emergency room all night long because she had a mild asthma attack? I wasn't thinking about an ounce of pussy last night, not even yours! What is wrong with you?"

I ignored that last potshot. "Yeah, I heard all of that but I also heard that Dara was there with you—all night long!"

Tate let out a frustrated groan. "Dara was there because she's Chasity's mother, stupid ass!"

"I know that Dara is Chasity's mother, jackass! What I'm trying to understand is why didn't you call me while you were with her? The fact that you didn't call makes me think that you have something to hide!"

"Why should I have called you? Give me one reason why should I tell you, of all people, about anything concerning my daughter? It's not like you give a hell about her anyway! And it wasn't about you or Dara last night! I was only worried about the number one lady in my life and her name is Chasity!"

Those words cut me like a knife. To hear that Chasity was the number one lady in Tate's life had me on serious hater mode. I knew that there was so much truth to that statement. But I didn't care if Chasity was his daughter; deep down inside, I wanted to be Tate's number one and his only one.

As far as Chasity was concerned, Tate wasn't lying about me not giving two shits about the little girl. This was because I just couldn't face the fact that Tate had had a baby with someone else and that someone wasn't me. Not to mention, the disdain that I had for Chasity's mother was so real that it was too hard for me to separate my feelings and embrace the little girl.

"What makes you say that? I'm just asking you about Dara! Chasity don't have nothing to do with—"

Tate cut me off. "I ain't got time for this bullshit," he mumbled.

"I don't give a . . . Tate? Tate!" Before I had a chance to finish my sentence, the phone went dead. "Oh, so he's just gonna hang up on me now?"

I wrapped my robe around my nude body and dialed Tate's number back. My calls went straight to voice-mail. I couldn't believe that Tate had hung up on me and turned his phone off, too.

I plopped down on my couch. "This bastard!" I said. I was livid but, dammit, I so loved that man.

It was January, 2007 when Tate and I met. The both of us were attending the party of a mutual friend. What I first noticed about Tate was that he had this rugged handsomeness and I was definitely attracted to him. Little did I know that Tate had already inquired about the lady in the royal blue dress, which was what I was wearing. So at Tate's request, I was formally intro-duced to him. From that day on, we were inseparable.

It was amazing how Tate and I instantly clicked with each other. We spent hours on the phone; we took long, romantic walks on the promenade, and before I knew it, I had fallen in love with Tate.

So six months into our union, we ended up taking things a step further than just dating. But the elation I felt was short-lived. Tate had neglected to tell me one important thing—he had a girlfriend named Dara. Came to find out, he had been with this chick for two years. One can only imagine how upset I was when I found out about this.

When I confronted Tate, he told me that their rela-tionship had been over for quite some time and that Dara just couldn't get that through her head. I only believed a small part of that. But, being the woman I was, I wanted who I wanted and I wasn't going down without a fight.

The bottom line was I was caught up with Tate and couldn't let him go. Whether Dara was his girlfriend really didn't matter to me at the time. I had my sights on Tate, and Dara's feelings were a non-factor. Realistically speaking, if the shoe were on the other foot, I knew that Dara wouldn't give a fuck about my feelings if Tate was my man.

Anyway, Tate and I carried on with our "affair" for almost a year before Dara found out about me. When she did find out about us, Tate and I had a bond that couldn't be broken. One day, Dara got into his phone and saw numerous text messages that we sent to each other. There was some sexting as well and, of course, she didn't like the content one bit. Tate and I were carrying on as if she didn't even exist. Instead of being a real woman and stepping off from Tate with her dignity intact, Dara took it upon herself to call me up. I could remember that conversation like it was yesterday.

I had been getting these strange private calls every day for about three weeks and I was so damn annoyed! When I finally answered the phone, it was exactly who I thought it was from the beginning. It was Dara.

"Is this Jay?" Dara asked. At first, I was unsure of who she was talking about. Then I remembered that Tate had me listed in his phone under the letter "J."

I chuckled, ready to give the bitch a serious talking to for calling me with the elementary bullshit. As far as I was concerned, her man was already taken and there was absolutely nothing for us to talk about.

"Yep, that's me, honey. By the way, Joi's the real name."

"Hmmph," Dara said. "So Joi's your name, huh? I saw that Tate has you listed as 'Jay' in his phone. That boyfriend of mine is a real fucking slickster, I tell you. He uses men's names for all of his side bitches! How

clever!" She laughed at her own joke. Then continued with her inquiry. "So, um, Joi, how long have you been fucking my man?"

"Oh, you don't need to worry about how long we've been fucking, Boo. That's not the issue. You need to be worried about me continuing to fuck him, which is what I'm doing now. And not for nothing, you stand to be corrected on a few things. Me and Tate are together and guess who's been demoted to the position of side piece?" I replied, voice dripping with sarcasm. "You, Boo Boo!"

"Oh, no, no! I'm no side piece, bitch! You're a fucking home wrecker!" Dara yelled into the phone.

Bingo! I struck that nerve. That definitely put a smile on my face.

I laughed at Dara. She was trying to talk over me but I wouldn't let her get a word in edgewise. "You're not Tate's wife, so please with the home wrecker shit! You didn't have a home to wreck, okay? And after this telephone call, I'm pretty sure that you're going to be fired anyway! So why don't you save yourself the embarrassment and kick rocks? Because I'm not going nowhere! Do you hear me, Dara? Nowhere!" I was really getting excited about pushing Dara's buttons and loved every minute of it.

"You bitch! All you are and will ever be is Tate's fucking jump off!" she screamed. "I've been with Tate all of this time and I ain't going no damn where, neither, do you hear me? You just wait and see! I'm not going anywhere, bitch!"

Because I was at my place of employment, I couldn't really get up in Dara's ass the way I wanted to. Plus, my switchboard was lighting up just as I was about to have some fun with the girl. As a 911 operator, each and every phone call was imperative and I had to an-

swer them. Not wanting Dara to have the last word, I was still determined to hang up the phone with a bang.

"Whatever, Dara," I said nonchalantly, rubbing my nails across my chest and blowing on my fingers. I knew that I was champion of this fight. "Like I said, Boo, I'm Tate's woman now and no matter how long or hard you stay clinging on to his balls, you dumb bitch, he's going to be with me! That is all!" Then I hung the phone up on her.

After that day, it became an all-out competition between me and Dara. And I'll be goddamned if that bitch wasn't in my way. Tate was the prize and we both wanted to win.

By then, Tate and I had been seeing each other for almost two years when I said enough was enough. I gave him an ultimatum: it was going to be either me or Dara. Apparently Tate made the very wise decision to work on our budding relationship. I was sure he didn't want to lose a good thing. I even insisted that Tate call Dara right in front of me to tell her that he couldn't be with her anymore, and he did exactly as he was told.

Naturally, Little Miss Slutshine was none too happy about this. And she harassed me for a while because of it, leaving nasty messages on my voice mail, even wishing death on me. She eventually stopped calling me but that wasn't the last of her.

It was about four months later after their breakup when Tate got a phone call from Dara. She said she had something important to tell him. That was when she dropped the bomb. She told Tate that she was five months pregnant and that he was the father! Now, this was definitely news to me, considering that Tate wasn't supposed to have been sleeping with the delusional Dara at that time. With her coming up pregnant, it was painfully obvious that they had been sleeping with each other and that the joke was on me.

Tate told Dara that a baby wasn't going to get them back together and she told him that she didn't care about that. She said that she was going to keep that baby and that he was going to take care of it. From then, I knew that she going to use this baby as leverage over my relationship with Tate.

As for me, I had no say. I tried to convince Tate to talk Dara into getting an abortion but he was having none of that. If I wasn't mistaken, it seemed as if Tate was secretly excited about having this baby—it was his first child! And I couldn't believe that he and that floozy of a woman agreed to bring an illegitimate child into the world when they weren't even together anymore. All of the trouble that I had gone through to get Tate and now a baby was on the way. A baby that wasn't mine. Dara's threats kept replaying in my mind: "I ain't going nowhere!" she'd told me. "You just wait and see!"

I guessed Dara showed me, didn't she?

When I first laid eyes on his daughter, Chasity, my jealousy got the best of me. I was hurt. During one of our arguments, which we began to have a lot of, I flat-out told Tate that I didn't think that Chasity was his biological daughter. Tate didn't talk to me for a week or two behind that comment.

I started out by saying these horrible things out of bitterness and contempt—I felt betrayed. But then I really took a long, hard look at Chasity. I couldn't help but wonder where that light skin of hers came from. Tate was the color of milk chocolate and Dara had a light brown complexion. She had these beautiful light brown eyes with a head of long, thick hair. I got this nagging feeling that something wasn't right with this baby. I wouldn't have been surprised if Dara got pregnant by another man.

My ringing phone interrupted my thoughts. I jumped to answer it without looking at the caller ID.

"Why did you hang the damn phone up on me, Tate?" I yelled into the phone. Only it wasn't Tate. The phone call just happened to be from my older brother, Payne.

"Woo!" he screamed back. "Ooh, child, who got your Vicky's Secrets all in a bunch? Because, baaaabyyy, that type of language isn't good for the diva's health, you know!" he added.

I was so mad that he referred to himself as a diva. This was another issue that I was struggling with—my openly gay brother. I understood that he was homosexual but why did he have to have the flamboyant, over-the-top personality to go along with it? Why couldn't he just be gay but act like a regular guy?

I groaned when I heard his annoying nasally voice. "What do you want, Mr. Payne in My Ass?" I asked with an attitude.

"Oh, honey! You so don't mean that! Anyway, my darling baby sister, I'm calling to let you know that our wonderful matriarch, Miss Renee Campbell, is requesting your homely presence at her house on Sunday evening. She's making this big, fabulous dinner for Auntie Gina and her new man, who, by the way, is coming to visit for the weekend from New Jerz. As a matter of fact, they're at her house right now." I was silent. "So, um, are you going or not?"

Payne knew that I couldn't stand family get-togethers, let alone my family. He was always ragging on me, my mother treated him like he was her only "daughter," and I was always getting asked when I was going to get married and have a baby. My mother even went so far as to say, "Damn, even Payne has a child and he's gay!" Like what the hell was that supposed to mean?

I sighed. "I really don't know if I'm coming. I'll think about it, Payne."

Payne began to get impatient with me. "Look, bitch, what is there to think about? Damn! Sunday is two days from now so I need to know right now, little girl!"

My eye started to twitch. "Didn't I tell your homo ass to stop calling me a bitch, Payne? You truly got some nerve when you're more of a bitch than I could ever be!"

I didn't know about other people, but having a gay brother who I didn't get along with was emotionally exhausting. Every time he called me out my name, I resisted the urge to use derogatory names like "faggot" or "batty bwoy," all for my mother's sake. And that was entirely too much pressure for a person with a big-ass mouth like mine. Thankfully, I would always catch myself before I got too disrespectful.

Payne was unmoved by my comments. "So angry you are!" he announced.

I rolled my eyes and quickly changed the subject. "Anyway, is my niece going to be there?" I asked, referring to his daughter, Rayni.

My seventeen-year-old niece, Rayni Simone Campbell, was the product of the last heterosexual relationship that my brother had with a woman. Rayni's mother was Juanita, Payne's high school sweetheart—I just knew that she was going to be the woman he married. Unfortunately, the relationship never panned out. During his college years, Payne came out of the closet. Juanita said she always suspected that about my brother, but there were no hard feelings between them. She had been married for the last ten years and had a young son by her husband. Even more importantly, she and Payne had a great relationship.

"Yes, my sweet Rayni is going to be there," he replied in a sing-song voice. "She's spending the weekend with her dear old dad." Then Payne cleared his throat. "Now back to the subject at hand, are you coming to Mommy's house or not, Miss Not So Joi-ful?"

I groaned. "Okay, okay, I'm coming. Tell Mommy to make me an extra sweet potato pie to go."

"Well, I'll be damned! You're finally going to emerge from the crack of Tate's ass! Yippeeee!"

Payne began laughing hysterically at his own wack joke. I was so quiet that you could have heard crickets on my end of the phone. I was not in the least bit amused.

When Payne noticed that I didn't share his humor, he stopped laughing. "Anyway, Miss-ser-ree, I will see you on Sunday. And please, please, please put on your happy face for the sake of our mother and Auntie Gina, okay, babe? Toodles!"

I shook my head, hung up the call. I threw my cell phone on the couch.

When my phone rang yet again, I was almost afraid to look at it; for fear that it was Payne or my mother calling me back. I was wrong. It was the call I had been waiting for.

"What do you want, Tate?" I asked, with a mixture of annoyance and relief in my voice. Truth was, I was always happy to hear his voice. But I wasn't going to let him know that. Instead, I prepared to give a verbal attack.

"Joi!" he screamed into the phone. "I didn't hang up on you! My battery was low—that's why the phone went dead!" he volunteered. "And why were you blowing me up like a maniac?"

That set me off. "You know what, Tate? I don't have to . . ."

And then we began our arguing all over again.

I knew that I could have easily walked away from Tate, Dara, and all of the drama. And yes, maybe it would have been in both of our best interests to go our separate ways. But my belief was when you truly love someone, letting them go was sometimes the hardest thing to do. In other words, I wasn't ready to know what life without Tate or the drama was like. I just wasn't ready.

Chapter 4

I'm Not Gon' Cry,
I'm Not Gon' Shed No Tears

Ebony

It was nine o'clock on a Friday night. So far, hanging out with my friends seemed like it wasn't going to happen. Yet, I was still half hoping that somebody, anybody would call me at that point with something to do. Stressing over Dray had me feeling as if I didn't know my ass from my elbow and I didn't want to be home alone.

I had tried to recruit Phoenix, to see if she wanted to hang out with me. She texted me back something about how she was out on a blind date with some guy named Stu. Then I got desperate enough to call my other girlfriend, Joi. As usual, Joi and her man, Tate, were going at it for the millionth time. I don't even know why I wasted my free mobile-to-mobile minutes on that hussy. Joi was never in the mood to do anything but be up under her man and she wasn't trying to hear about anyone else's man problems.

Then, last but not least, I called my young girl, Saadia. That twat hadn't even bothered to answer her phone or call me back. I figured that she was probably running around with the rest of her twenty-something year old friends, having a great time, as she should have been.

What I really was trying to do was not call Dray—it was definitely some avoidant behavior on my part. I

was wondering why I was still unsure of where I stood
with this man, even after being with him for the last
three years. I also knew that I would probably never
be able to get the answers that I needed from him, if I
didn't call him.

I held back my tears. After searching aimlessly through
my list of contacts, I finally decided to bite the bullet and
dial Dray's number. I decided that whatever was going to
be with us was just going to be. I was going to have to face
the music.

After the first ring, I wanted to hang up. Just as I was
about to do that, Dray answered the phone.

"What's up, Eb?" Dray said, acting like he had just
spoken to me yesterday.

I was completely thrown off by his casual attitude
but I didn't let that deter me. I took a deep breath, trying to find the right words to say to him. "So, um, what
have you been up to, Dray? I haven't heard from you in
a minute."

"I know, I know, babe," he began.

I knew he was about to come with a lame excuse.

"I'm so sorry that I haven't called you back for the
past few days—"

I cut him off. "You mean, the past week."

"Yeah, the past week. I have this new patrol sergeant
who has been on our asses to meet these quotas and
whatnot. I had to do some major overtime behind
that shit, too. So you know when I get to the crib, I'm
sacked! As a matter of fact, I'm working right now."

I raised one eyebrow. "Oh, really? It sounds kind of
quiet in the background."

"It's quiet because I'm at the base, babe, sitting here
in the lounge area. Came back here for my break, you
know. I don't get off until eleven o'clock."

Dray was pissing me off with lie after lie. I had to get
to the bottom of this.

"Right," I replied, so not believing a word he said. I got straight to the point. "Okay, so when are we going to get together?" I asked. "We need to talk."

Dray groaned. "Damn, babe, I know that you've been feeling neglected lately and I'm so sorry about that. As far as us having this talk, I'm going to have to find the time to do that. I've just been so busy lately, man. I don't know."

Things may have gone over my head sometimes but my mother didn't raise no got damn fool! I knew that Dray wasn't keeping it official with me and I needed for him to stop sugar-coating the fucking inevitable. *Why are men such cowards when it comes to breaking up with us?*

"Hell, yeah, I've been feeling fucking neglected lately! And why does it seem like you're trying to avoid me? Is there something you need to tell me?"

Of course, Dray had the gall to get upset with me for being upset with him. *What a narcissistic jerk.*

"Oh, boy, here we go!" Dray said. "We could be having a good conversation and here you come with your all accusations and insecurities and shit! Nobody is fucking avoiding you, Ebony. I mean, damn! I didn't have to tell you nothing, you know! I'm just mad busy— that's it!"

"Busy, huh? So you're too fucking busy to pick up the phone and call your woman?" I listened to Dray hem and haw. "What's the deal with you, man? I mean, why don't you just keep it real? Are you seeing somebody else? Do you want this relationship or not?"

Dray was still on the defensive. "That's the problem with you, Ebony! You don't ever believe anything I say!"

"Oh, my God, Dray!" I yelled. "Is this relationship over or what? Tell me now!"

"What the hell, Ebony? A dude can't have a few days to himself without you thinking the worst! Damn, you're so fucking needy, man, I swear!" Dray was getting real cocky and hitting below the belt.

"Needy?" I chuckled. "I'm needy because I don't believe shit that's coming out of your disrespectful, lying-ass mouth? What I'm trying to understand is why do you keep playing mind games with me, Dray? If you don't want me, stop being a stinking coward and just say it! And to think that I was holding on, ready to work on our relationship. But if you're not, step off and let the next man do what he gotta do for me!"

"So go ahead and mess with other dudes, if that's what you want to do! I don't have time for this stupid shit! Like I said, I'm at work! Good-bye, Ebony!"

Then he hung up on me.

Instead of calling him back, I decided to do something else. I put on a sweat suit and some Nike Air Max; then I grabbed the keys to my Nissan Altima. It was time for me to go on a much-needed excursion to Dray's house.

When I got into my car, I threw on my Jazmine Sullivan CD. One of my favorite tracks, "Bust Your Windows," came blaring through the speakers. *Fuck that.* I needed some inspiration. I had a mind to do just what Jazmine did—bust the windows out of Dray's car. I could only imagine how pissed Dray would be if he found a broken windshield and a big-ass brick sitting on the front seat of his beloved BMW.

I rolled down the driver's side window and let the spring air hit my sweaty face. I needed to calm myself down before I made my way over to Dray's Flatbush residence. It was a trip that normally took about twenty minutes. But I was driving so damn fast, I got over there in like ten.

When I arrived on Dray's block, I found it very strange that his BMW 525i and the hooptie that he drove to work every day were parked near the front of his building. As I suspected, that asshole had straight-up lied to me, and I was so mad I wanted to draw blood.

Fortunately for me, I got lucky and found a parking spot a few feet away from the entrance of his building. Then I waited for a few moments to get up the nerve to get out of my car. I took a deep breath. This was the first time I had done anything like this and I was nervous as hell.

Five minutes later, I was standing inside of the small foyer of Dray's building. Normally, there was a lot of traffic coming in and out but for some reason, not one single soul walked out of that locked door while I was standing there. I hadn't banked on ringing the intercom.

I pressed apartment 7A. There wasn't any answer so I pressed it again. No luck. I pressed the bell for the third time and when there wasn't an answer, I almost believed that he was really at work. Then the unthinkable happened. Just as I was about to turn around and leave the foyer, a female voice came booming through the intercom.

"Hello?" she said. "Hello?" I was in shock and quieter than a church mouse. "Dray, is that you, babe? Why are you ringing the bell? Did you forget the key, daddy?"

I just stood there with a stunned expression on my face. Another woman was answering the intercom for 7A? Another woman was in my man's apartment? What the hell was going on?

"Hello? Hello?" she repeated.

No words came out of my mouth. I was unable to speak from the initial hurt and disappointment of hearing another woman's voice. Not only had I not heard from him in the past week but I truly didn't

think that Dray could be that disrespectful to have
another woman in his house and answering his damn
bell like she lived there. I paced back and forth and told
myself not to jump the gun. I wanted the woman who
answered the intercom to have been anybody else, a female family member, maybe—just maybe? But I knew
she was none of those. She had called him "daddy" and
Dray didn't have any daughters. I chuckled to myself.
For all I knew, this bitch could be his real girlfriend and
I was the goddamn side piece.

The beads of sweat began forming on my forehead.
The butterflies in my stomach fluttered just thinking
about what I was about to do. I stood in the small foyer
area of Dray's building, trying to figure out my next
move. That's when I told myself to not to go any damn
where. I was going to wait for someone to open that
downstairs door, no matter how long it took.

Lucky for me, a man walking his dog opened the
downstairs door and held it opened for me. I said,
"Thank you," and quickly walked to the elevator. Before I even had a chance to think about how crazy I was
acting, I was inside of the elevator, pressing the button
for the seventh floor.

"Fuck that. I'm gonna whoop somebody's ass tonight," I whispered to myself.

Before I beat the hell out of somebody, I had to ask
myself, was this bastard really worth me getting ar-
rested, losing my job, and humiliating myself over?
And how pathetic was I? It was quite obvious that Dray
had made his choice and it wasn't me. But I was about
to go out with a bang. I was tired of getting played by
these sorry-ass men.

As the elevator made its way upstairs, I geared myself up for what was about to happen. I began cracking
my knuckles. I was about to do a Rock-A-Bye Baby

on this mystery skank. This ho was not about to play
Ebony Mahogany Harris and get away with it.

I walked out of the elevator and stood in front of
apartment 7A. I didn't hesitate, or even have time to be
nervous anymore—I was too angry for all of that petri-
fied shit. Okay, I wasn't thinking rationally and I was
behaving like a freaking teenager but hey, so was Dray.
I knew that he had to be bat-shit crazy to have another
woman all up in his apartment when I was supposed to
be his woman.

I put my hand over the peephole and knocked on the
door. As soon as she opened it up, I punched her dead
in the mouth! Girlfriend didn't have a chance. Her
head jerked back from the force of my power-packed
punch and her lip began bleeding. Next thing I knew, I
was all up and through Dray's apartment, beating this
broad up, throwing her around, and knocking over all
of his shit. At one point, the woman tried to run away
from me but I wrapped my hand around her weave and
pulled her ass right back to me. The poor thing did her
damndest to defend herself—bless her heart. Unfortunately, she was no match for my polished fighting
skills.

After I got several hits off, the hussy managed to
break away from my grasp. She ended up cowering in
the corner of Dray's living room between the couch and
the window.

"Who are you and why are you here?" she screamed,
with her eyes bugging out of her big head and her hand
on her busted lip. "You're crazy!"

I tried to catch my breath. "No, bitch, the question
is, who the fuck are you? And why are you in my man's
house?" I screamed back at her.

Suddenly, I heard the keys in the door. Dray walked
in and froze in his tracks. Of course, he hadn't expected
me to be standing in his living room so he was more

than surprised. He dropped the bag that he was carrying and looked at me in disbelief. Then he glanced at the helpless woman trembling in the corner.

"You said that you didn't have a girlfriend, Dray!" she screamed from the side of the couch, still afraid to move.

I swung my head around like I was Linda Blair in *The Exorcist*. I felt the color rush out of my face.

"Is that what you told this bitch?" I yelled at Dray.

Dray put his hands up, as if he was trying to keep me from hitting him. "Ebony, let me explain—"

"Yeah, I'm gonna need you to do that! You have a whole lot of fucking explaining to do!" I yelled. I angrily pointed my finger at the female, who was now making her way from behind the couch. "Who is this bitch?" I asked.

When she saw my finger, she hesitated before taking a step further. She must have caught a flashback of that ass-whooping I just gave her.

"I asked you a question, Negro!" Dray wouldn't even look me in the eye. "Who the hell is this tramp and why is she here? Is this the bitch you've been cheating on me with?" I asked, tapping my foot on the hardwood floor. Even though I had my arms crossed, I was ready to pounce into action again.

Suddenly, the female sprinted past me and went to hide behind Dray. I hopped over his shoulder and ended up punching her in the head. Dray tried to protect her by pushing me backward with his shoulder. I almost fell but I caught my balance. That was when I hauled off and punched him in his face too. Dray held his cheek and then slapped the hell out of me. The slap knocked me down.

While I was on the floor, Dray stood over me but didn't volunteer to help me up.

"Go into the bedroom and lock the door behind you, Anisa," he ordered the female. Anisa ran her petite, scary little ass right into the bedroom, too. That only proved one thing: Anisa was the girlfriend. From what it looked like, I was the one about to be kicked out of Dray's house and straight to the curb. I couldn't believe that all of this was happening to me.

After a few seconds had passed, I managed to get up from the floor. I was holding the left side of my face but the sting of the slap was nothing compared to the emotional pain I felt. "This is what it comes down to?" I asked Dray. "You're protecting that bitch and you're supposed to be my fucking man?"

"Who told you to come over here, Ebony?" Dray asked, totally disregarding my question. "What the fuck are you doing in my apartment without my permission?"

I just stared at him. It was like I was looking at a complete stranger. "No, the question is what the hell is this woman doing here? Is she the person you've been avoiding me for?"

Dray looked up at the ceiling. "Look, Ebony, Anisa lives here now," he said. He looked down at the floor. "I'm sorry."

Frustrated, I raised my clenched fist in the air. Dray flinched like he thought I was going to hit him again.

"I do not believe this shit!" I exclaimed. "You . . . you got this woman living here now? You actually moved this ho into your apartment? Oh, God!"

Dray hunched up his shoulders. "I didn't know how to tell you! And yes, that's why I haven't been calling you. Our relationship . . . our relationship had run its course and I'm just not in love with you anymore."

I held my head back and closed my eyes. *Damn, that shit hurt!* It was like I actually felt several pointy jabs to my heart. Instead of going off again and causing myself any further embarrassment, I walked toward the door. The least I could do was leave Dray's apartment and our relationship with what little dignity I had left.

Dray stopped me and held me by my arms. "I never meant for you to get hurt."

I looked at Dray and scowled. I wanted to kill that n-word with my bare hands. Instead, I spat in his face. I happily watched him wipe the disgusting glob of phlegm off his right cheek with his shirt sleeve.

"Fuck you, Dray!" I whispered, voice cracking with sadness. "And fuck that bitch, too! Y'all fucking deserve each other!"

I pushed past him and walked out of his apartment. Then I ran down the stairwell and out of the building. I could not for the life of me understand how it was just that easy for another woman to come and take my place in Dray's heart.

My lips began quivering. "I fucking hate you, Dray!" I said aloud to no one in particular.

Two minutes later, I was driving home and crying hysterically. This was definitely not the way I had planned to spend my weekend. But as soon as I turned the corner of Dray's block, I missed having him around. I wanted to turn back the clock and start time all over again. I wanted to go back to the days when Dray and I were the best of friends and we were happy. What happened to us?

There was a part of me that depended on the relationship that Dray and I used to have. In my mind, he had taken the time to make me an honest woman. With my track record, I didn't think that it was possible for me to fall in love or for a man to love me the way I thought he did. Now I was alone again. What was I supposed to do now?

Chapter 5

Feel Like a Woman

Phoenix

It was almost 9:00 P.M. when Stu and I arrived in Manhattan. The traffic on the Cross Island Parkway had been horrible due to some major accident. Thank God, we got through it and our date was unaffected by it. Plus, Stu and I managed to exchange some great dialogue while we were in traffic. We were definitely getting to know each other better.

Stu pulled into a parking garage near Broadway on the Upper West Side of Manhattan, instructing the attendant to be careful with Midnight. He got out of the driver's side, then came around to the passenger side and opened the door for me. He was such a gentleman. I was impressed with his chivalry. He even held my hand as we walked toward the restaurant.

"So where are we going tonight?" I asked.

Stu looked at me. "Damn, girl! You don't like surprises, do you?" he asked.

I laughed. "Of course I do."

"Well, let me do this. I know that you have your business and you're used to taking charge and all but I'm gonna take the lead tonight, okay, champ?"

"Hmmph. Excuse me, Mr. Childs, do your thing!"

We walked around the corner to Carmine's Italian Restaurant. It just happened to be my favorite eatery. I was quite pleased with Stu's choice.

"Carmine's! I totally love this place," I said, smiling from ear to ear.

"I know. I remember you telling me that from one of our phone conversations. That's why I decided to bring you here tonight."

"How thoughtful, Stu," I said, walking through the door as he held it for me.

When we approached the maître d', Stu told him that he had reservations for two. The man looked it up and smiled at us. He picked up two menus and led us to a booth in the back of the restaurant. It was a nice setting, with dimmed lights and very private, away from the hubbub in the front of the restaurant. Right away, Stu ordered us a bottle of Merlot.

"You're taking charge for real!" I said, smoothing out the cloth napkin on my lap.

"Yep, that's what I do," he replied. "Some women don't like for men to do that. Let me find out you're that type."

I shook my head. "No, I'm not that type of woman. I like for a man to take charge but that's only if the man has his shit together."

The chilled bottle of Merlot came. The waiter opened the bottle for us and poured it into our glasses. Then he put the bottle on ice and asked if we were ready to order. We decided to skip the appetizers. Stu ordered the veal parmesan and I ordered the chicken Marsala. The waiter took our orders and left the table.

Stu and I made a quick toast. "So a man has to have his shit together in order to take charge, huh?"

I took a sip of the wine. "Yes, he does. Is there something wrong with that?"

"Sounds like you have some real control issues, girl."

"How do you figure that?"

"At the end of the day, a man is a man. He's supposed to protect and provide for his woman, within reason, of course."

"What's within reason?"

"I mean, as a man, you should give your lady what she wants, but I'm not with the all the extras. If we're trying to build with each other, we should focus on what's priority, and the other things come second."

I chuckled. "Well, I like nice things, Stu. That's why I work hard to maintain a certain lifestyle for myself—I had a co-op by the time I was twenty-five years old, I drive a 2011 BMW convertible, got my own money in the bank—"

Stu interrupted me. "And you still don't have a man," he said while shaking his head.

I was speechless. *Did he just try to come for me with that statement?* "Excuse me?" I asked, giving him the squinty eye.

Stu smirked. "You heard me. I didn't stutter."

"You don't know me well enough to say something like that!"

"But am I lying?"

"No, but that's not the point," I replied.

"So what is your point?"

I was beyond insulted. I couldn't believe what Stu said. At that moment, I should have got up from that table and left his fine ass sitting right there in Carmine's.

"Let's just eat and drink this Merlot," I said, with an icy attitude.

Stu looked at me and gave me this devilish smile. I wished I knew what he was thinking. Seeing that he struck a nerve, Stu changed the subject.

"Look, I have to stop by one of my venues to see how's everything going—would you mind rolling with me?" he asked.

I wanted to tell Stu to go to hell but I decided to be a good sport. It was hard to stay mad at a dude who looked like him. I relented. "Nah, I don't mind, babe. I'm with you tonight."

He held my hand. "Cool." Stu took a sip of his wine. "I apologize for what I said to you a few minutes ago. Sometimes I can be a little too blunt."

"I see," I said, with a smirk. "But I'm a big girl. I can take a whole lot."

"A whole lot of what?" he asked, flirting with me.

"Stop being fresh with me, Stu," I replied, blushing like crazy.

"And if I don't?"

Stu was quite the character. And even more importantly, he was giving me a run for my money. Most men were intimidated by me but he wasn't. I couldn't do anything but respect him for that. "I don't know what it is but I'm starting to kinda like you, Stu."

"Oh, you're only starting to kinda like me?"

"Okay, I like you already."

"Ditto, babe, ditto," he replied. That Stu was just too cool for his damn self.

Twenty minutes later, our food came and we devoured it. We couldn't eat it all—Carmine's gives you so much food—so we decided to take home the doggie bags, too. We didn't walk out of Carmine's until eleven-thirty that night. We then made our way uptown to the Cherry Lounge to check out Stu's event.

Cherry Lounge was located on 128th Street. Harlem was Stu's hood so when we walked into that place, it was like I was with a celebrity. Of course, I got some side-eye glances from a few nasty-looking chicks with their cheap-ass outfits on. They even felt the need to get real extra by giving him hugs and kisses right in front of me. They obviously wanted to put on a show for me, I guessed. But I wasn't worried about any of them Forever 21 outfit–wearing freaks. I was the one with Stu. He let them know that when he took my hand and led me away from them.

The music was off the hook, courtesy of DJ Clue. While the patrons were rocking to the sounds of Drake and Nicki Minaj, Stu walked me over to the bar. He said something to the shapely bartender chick. She gave me the thumbs-up and I smiled back. I assumed that meant that she was going to take care of me. I loved to drink so that was right up my alley.

While I nodded my head to the music and people-watched from my stool at the bar, Stu leaned over and whispered in my ear.

"Order anything you want, babe. The young lady behind the bar—her name's Mitzi—she got you. I'm gonna be at the front door, talking to my team, okay?"

I nodded my head. "No problem."

Stu kissed me on the cheek and walked away, leaving me alone at the bar. There were a few guys sitting near me who were waiting for an opportunity to spring into action. But I rolled my eyes at them and commenced to ordering one of my favorite drinks: coconut Cîroc with pineapple juice—Coco Loso, as it was called. It was definitely going to be my drink of choice for the night.

It was about an hour and a half later and I was nursing my fourth CocoLoso. Mitzi, the bartender chick, had me buzzed. And Stu had come over to check on me once or twice within the hour but by that time, I was feeling no pain. As a matter of fact, I was partying like a rock star. I even danced with a few of the fellas there and they kindly offered to buy me whatever I wanted at the bar. But shit, I was already tipsy. The combination of Merlot and the Coco Loso was doing a number on me.

Before the end of my night, I was getting my rump shaker on. That was when Stu came over and wrapped his arms around my waist from behind. But it wasn't because he was trying to dance with me—he was pulling me off the dance floor.

"Time to go, babe," he said. "I think you had enough."

Only the party wasn't over for me. I was truly having a blast. "Wait, Stu! Why are we leaving? I'm having a good time!"

We walked past the bouncers who were standing by the front, and went straight out the door. Once we were outside, Stu lifted me off my feet and carried me. I was too blitzed to even enjoy being in his arms. Stu put me in the passenger seat of his car and peeled out of the parking spot.

He looked at me and shook his head. "Babe, you are so wasted right now. Did you want to come to my house or do you wanna go home?"

I didn't know what was on Stu's mind. All I knew is that I wanted out of Midnight and into my bed.

"I wanna go home," I moaned, feeling like crap.

I must have passed out right there in Midnight's passenger seat because about thirty minutes later, we were parked in front of my building. I felt Stu's hand going up and down my exposed thigh.

"Wake up, ma. You're home."

"I'm home?" I asked, looking around with this bewildered expression on my face. "Shit, that was quick."

Stu sighed. "Yeah, I know. I was trying to get your ass home before you threw up in Midnight."

It was funny he mentioned that. It sounded like something I would have said.

"No, no, no. I feel much better now. I don't have to throw up. I just have to pee."

Stu opened the driver's side door and got out. "Come on. I'm gonna walk you upstairs, girl."

"Thanks, Stu," I said, grateful that I finally met a dude with some manners. Some men would have dropped my drunken ass off at the curb, said deuces, and peeled off.

When we arrived upstairs, I unlocked my door and almost stumbled into the hallway of my apartment. I dropped my bag to the floor and kicked off my shoes. Then I ran straight to the bathroom, not even bothering to close the door while I used the toilet.

After Stu finished using the bathroom, I heard the toilet flush and him washing his hands. Then he walked into the living room. And surprise! There I was lying on my couch, as naked as the day I was born. I had sobered up a little but white liquor always made me horny as hell. Not to mention, it had been almost nine months of me not having sex and I wanted to take advantage of the available dick. I figured that Stu would be more than happy to get a free crack at some pussy that night.

Stu looked at me and licked his lips. "Got-damn," he whispered, rubbing his chin. He had that glare in his eye that had me convinced that he wanted me.

I wanted him too. "I want you so bad, Stu," I replied along with a seductive stare. I slowly trailed my finger down to my clitoris and began playing with myself right in front of him.

"I can see that," Stu said, grabbing his dick through his pants. From that gesture alone, I just knew that old Stu was ready to jump my bones and tear something up. "But too bad I can't stay, babe."

I could hear the DJ scratch the record playing in my head.

"What?" I asked, with a surprised look on my face. I stood up and walked toward him. My titties were out, my clean-shaven veejay was exposed, and my ass was bouncing everywhere. I got up in his face. "Oh, so you don't wanna fuck me, Stu? What the fuck is up with that?" I slurred.

"Because you're drunk, Phoenix. I'm sorry but I just don't do sloppy, drunken-ass buns."

"But this is my drunken-ass buns!" I yelled at him. "And sloppy?" I propped my leg on my armchair to give Stu a slight visual of my punany. "See? This twat ain't nowhere near sloppy, motherfucker!"

Stu shook his head in disgust. "That's the problem right there! I know about your type too damn well!"

Stu walked out of the living room and I followed him toward the front door, still in beef mode. Then I stood in front of him, blocking him from opening the door. He shook his head again and kindly pushed me to the side.

"I'll call to check on you tomorrow, Phoenix. Thanks for hanging out with me tonight," Stu said. He gave me a peck on the cheek. "Later, babe."

Then he opened the door and walked right out of my house. When the door slammed, it knocked me out of my trance. I couldn't believe that I was standing there, stark naked and in shock because some dude had the nerve to walk out my door without fucking me. *Shit like this just does not happen to Phoenix Janay Henry.*

A few minutes later, I had on my pajamas and was preparing for bed. I had the only attitude. I popped two Advils and made a mental note to call Shanell as soon as I opened my eyes. I was going to cuss her out for hooking me up with Stu's bitch ass.

Chapter 6

Hurt Again

Ebony

After leaving Dray's apartment, I was inconsolable. I mean, as soon as I walked through the door of my house, I practically ripped that sweat suit off my body. Then I went into my bedroom and climbed into bed, balling up into the fetal position under my goose down comforter. From the looks of things, that was probably the only comfort that I was going to get.

For a brief second, I thought about calling some of my friends, just to vent. But who wants to listen to a bitch whine and moan about how her man did her dirty, especially on a Friday night? I knew I wouldn't want to hear it. Shit, they were probably out somewhere enjoying themselves, something that I should have been doing. But instead I was in my bed whooping and hollering over Dray's punk ass. Even Joi, who was like the epitome of misery sometimes, was probably having a blast screaming on Tate. And I couldn't even be mad at her for that. At least she still had a man.

So there I was, feeling sorry for myself, wishing that I could be anywhere else but with my thoughts about Dray. It was so hard to stop thinking about what happened that night. I was still reeling over the fact that our three-year relationship had gone down the drain just like that.

I must have fallen into a deep sleep because it was like twelve in the morning when I was awakened by my vibrating phone.

"Hello?" I answered groggily.

"Hey, girl! Do not tell me that you're sleeping in on a Friday night! Isn't Kare with Shah this weekend?"

It was my young girl, Saadia, on the other end.

"Get up, girl!" she yelled into the phone. The music in her car was super loud in the background. "It's a party tonight!"

"Yeah, Saadia, yeah," I replied, sounding sleepy and unhappy as fuck.

She turned the music down. "You sound like you have a sack of marbles in your mouth! What's the matter with you?"

"I just woke up."

"Nuh uh. The way you're sounding isn't from sleepiness. I know you too well, Ebony. What's the problem?"

I began crying out of nowhere. "Dray fucking dumped me! He had the nerve to fucking dump me!"

"What did you say?" she asked.

I didn't tell her about the fight or that Dray had moved another woman into his apartment. I wanted to act like that never happened.

"You heard me! I said that Dray dumped me! He told me that he was seeing someone else and that he didn't want to be with me anymore."

Saadia sighed loudly. "You mean to tell me that you actually *let* that zero, Dray, dump *you*?" she asked.

"I didn't 'let' Dray do a damn thing, okay? He did that shit all on his own."

Saadia, who was twenty-seven years old, and six years my junior, was so disconnected from serious relationships. She had that free-spirit mentality and always claimed that before she got locked down with a man, she was going to live the single life to the fullest. And she was doing just that. Not that I could say I blamed her for thinking that way.

"Don't you remember that I told you to get rid of that asshole right after I saw him with that other female last year?"

It was about six months ago when Saadia called me and told me that she spotted Dray hugged up with some woman near Broadway in SoHo. When I approached Dray about this, he told me that the girl he was with that day was his son's aunt, the sister of his baby's mother. I'd met his son's mother before but I had never laid eyes on the woman's sister. I didn't believe him but there was no evidence—just some he said, she said.

Honestly, at that time, I wasn't prepared to leave Dray just yet, especially over some hearsay. Now that everything was crystal clear, I wondered if the woman Saadia had seen him with that day was Anisa. Now I was annoyed that Saadia made me relive that day, as if I wasn't feeling bad enough already.

"Dray told me that the girl was D.J.'s aunt. . . ." I replied, getting choked up at the thought, yet trying to save face at the same time. "Plus, you just can't tell somebody to break up with their man over something that you saw with no real proof. Breaking up is a—"

Saadia stopped me from speaking any further. "Come on now, Ebony!" she said. "Do you hear yourself? That wasn't no son's aunt or baby mother's cousin's sister and them—hell no! Unless he's fucking his son's auntie—I'm telling you now like I told you before, Dray was all over that woman. And yes, I could tell you to let him go if I want to because, in my opinion, you deserve better. I'm looking out for your best interest, not his!"

I wasn't up for hearing about Dray's past exploits and listening to Saadia tell me that she told me so. "I

really don't wanna hear about all that right now. I'm
fucking over it."

She sucked her teeth and gladly moved on to the next
subject. "Anyway, I was calling for you to hang out with
me tonight—my family is having this welcome home
party for my cousin, Casper. He just came home from
the military. I'm on my way over there to get you so
throw on one of your cute little dresses and come out
with me."

"I don't feel like going anywhere—"

Saadia ignored me. "Where's Kare Bear?" she asked.

"With his father."

"Exactly. That's why you're going out with me tonight. I'm not going to allow this trick, Drayton Jackson," she began, putting exaggerated emphasis on
Dray's full name, "to fuck up my friend's weekend!
Shah has Kare so why do you have to stay home and
be miserable? And, besides, you're a very beautiful
woman! You're stressing this fool when it's so many
other men waiting in line to take his place!"

"Oh, my God! I know this but . . ." Knowing Saadia
like I did, she wasn't about to leave me alone with my
broken heart. The heifer wouldn't take my no for an
answer.

"Girl, I'll be there in ten minutes. So start getting
ready." Then she hung up on me.

I looked at my phone and dropped my head back
onto the pillow. *That's what I get for being so desperate to hang out with someone.* And to me, hanging out
after a bad breakup was kind of premature. I didn't
even have a chance to grieve my loss.

But as much I hated to admit it, Saadia was dead-on
about lying around in my bed all weekend. Here I was
acting like Dray quitting me was the end of the fucking
world. All I would have been thinking about was him
and Anisa, who were probably having the time of their

lives now that I was completely out of the picture. Shit, I might have been a little lovesick but I wasn't dead. So, in the words of the young girl, Saadia, why was I stressing this fool again?

My body was aching from depression and sadness but I managed to crawl out of my comfortable bed. I walked a few steps to my closet to look for something to wear to this event that Saadia had me going to. Thanks to American Express and my Visa credit cards, I definitely had plenty to choose from.

I picked out a tight-fitting black and silver minidress with some Aldo platform pumps. I grabbed a leather clutch purse and some matching costume jewelry from my bag of accessories. Once I got everything together, I hurried to the shower, expecting Saadia to ring my doorbell at any moment.

And, just like clockwork, as soon as I got out of the shower, the bell rang. I wrapped the towel tightly around my wet, nude body and ran to answer the door. Saadia walked in looking absolutely fabulous with a simple black dress with sequins and some multicolored pumps. Every follicle of her short hair was curled neatly into place. Her ruby-red lips looked great against her French vanilla–colored skin and her body was built like a Coke bottle. Yep, the young girl Saadia was a certified banger.

She gave me a tight hug and I refused to let my tears flow.

"Oh, Eb," she began, still holding me tightly. "I know how you feel, girl. Remember when I broke up with Johnny two years ago?"

I nodded my head. Saadia was a hot mess after that breakup.

She continued, "I thought I was going to die! But that was only because I had immersed myself into the relationship, severing ties with my friends, male and female, even some of my family. I lost myself and so did you."

I couldn't do anything but agree with her. Dray had become my world. Then Saadia pulled me away from her and stared me dead in the face.

"You're going to be okay, girlfriend. You can go back to that bitch-ass crying after we come home from this party. I just want you to come out with me tonight and try to have yourself a good time. By the way, feel free to hook up with any one of my cutie cousins."

I couldn't do anything but laugh at her. "Now where in the hell did that come from? Do you think that I really need to mess with anyone else in the condition that I'm in?"

She waved me off. "Now, come on, Ebony! How long have you and I been friends? Since I was twelve years old, right? I used to look up to you and your crew. Shit, I wanted to be just like y'all. So stop acting like you ain't had your share of men. You can dismiss one and another one will be walking through your door!" I giggled. "That's right, Miss Thang, you was a certified, bona fide hottie! That's why I can't understand how in the hell you got caught up with Drayton's cheating ass and stayed faithful to him all of this time."

I sighed. "I don't know, Saadia. Being faithful to Dray wasn't about him, it was about me. After Shah, I didn't think that I could ever be faithful to any man again and I did it. I had to prove it to myself. And I'm not going to lie, right now I'm asking myself, what was it all for?" We both shook our heads. "I don't know. I think the hardest part for me is accepting the fact that I became a better woman for a man I thought was so worth it. But I was wrong. I don't like being wrong."

Saadia followed me into the bedroom so that I could finish getting dressed. She sat in the leather armchair near my bed. I loved Saadia but her advice was a little harsh and unwarranted sometimes. And it was always the truth. I also had to remember that Saadia was twenty-seven years old and I was thirty-three. That six-year age difference between us had a lot to do with our different views on life, relationships, and men.

"Pfff! Please! You're a single-ass woman and I so believe that you're single until you get married. And if these men aren't talking about having a solid future with you, then it's no need for you to take them fucking serious. That's just my take on it."

I put lotion on my nude body then slid into my dress without putting any panties on. I decided that I was going to go commando that night and air that thing out. "You're right. I mean, Dray never talked about marrying me or even us taking things to the next level. He was just going with the flow and now that I think about it, so was I."

Saadia slapped her thigh. "See? Now do you get it? Dray wasn't as committed as you thought he was. Then again, neither were you. Just look at it like this—it just wasn't meant to be, Eb, so don't be feeling too bad about it. God allows people into our lives for a season and a reason, *chica*."

I sighed as I slid my feet into my five-inch heels. "Girl, you make so much sense. And you know what? I feel a lot better now. Our relationship ran its course," I said, using Dray's exact words, "and maybe it is somebody better out there for me."

Saadia agreed. "I *know* that there's somebody out there better for you—a man who can take care of you and your son. Someone who will be there for you in your time of need and you can do the same for them without feeling like you're wasting your time."

After I finished getting dressed, I applied my makeup and pinned my long hair in an upsweep. I put on some dazzling earrings and bangle bracelets, adding the finishing touch to my look.

If Saadia hadn't invited me out, I would have had my ass cooped up in the house, feeling like shit. But there was no need to mope around when I had so much going on. I happily sprayed on some of my Juicy Couture perfume and grabbed my clutch bag from the dresser.

"Let's go, girl," I said to Saadia, shaking my booty. "I'm ready to par-tay!"

Saadia pumped her fist in the air. "Hey! Party over here!"

When we arrived at the Vulcan Hall in Crown Heights, I was happy that I made the effort to come to Saadia's event. The Cassells were a close-knit family with Panamanian roots. I grew up with these people and I loved them like they were my own. I knew the guest of honor, Saadia's cousin Casper, very well. He had a very sexy younger brother, who was about my age, by the name of Mateo, who I'd met at a family function years ago. Mateo was this former bad boy who hailed from South Jamaica, Queens. I hadn't seen him in a while because he'd done like two or three bids in jail. I was looking forward to laying my eyes on him again.

While Saadia greeted some of her extended family members, I walked over to her parents. The Cassells were an attractive older couple who had been married for almost thirty-five years. I used to spend more time at their house than I did my own. I personally never knew what it felt like to live in a two-parent home until I stayed with them. Saadia and her siblings were lucky to have that. My mother and father always had a very toxic relationship so both of them were always in and out of the household. Even though Saadia's parents were married for three decades, I always admired how they remained in love with each other. When I looked at them, I knew that what they had was something that I wanted for myself.

Mrs. Cassell saw me first. She walked right over to me and gave a warm, motherly hug. Man, she didn't know how much I needed that.

"Oh, Ebony! *Besos!*" she said, kissing me on the cheek. "My second daughter! How are you, beautiful girl?" she asked, with her strong Panamanian accent.

"I'm well, Mrs. Cassell," I replied. "How are you?"

"Oh, I'm fine, baby, just fine! I'm here to support my nephew and his accomplishments, you know, I'm so proud of him! How is your adorable son and your family?"

"Everybody is fine and Kare is eight years old now. He's getting smarter and smarter every day!"

"Oh, my!" she announced, putting her hands on her cheeks. "Good God! It seems like you were just pregnant! God bless him. I know you teach him well, Ebony, you're a smart girl!" She gave me another one of those great hugs.

"Thank you, Mrs. Cassell," I said, hugging her just as tightly. "Where's my Mr. Cassell?"

Mrs. Cassell glanced over at the refreshment table. "Mr. Cassell is over there at the punch bowl, probably spiking it with liquor," she said, looking in her husband's direction. We both shared a laugh. "You enjoy yourself, *mi bonita,* I'm going to make my rounds."

I kissed Mrs. Cassell on her cheek. "Okay, I'll see you throughout the night, Mrs. Cassell."

When Saadia's mother walked away, I walked over to her father and gave him a warm hug. He was a short, stocky man with a laidback disposition. Mrs. Cassell was definitely the queen of her castle and he worshiped the very ground she walked on.

"Hey, Mr. Cassell!" I said. "You look great!"

"Oh, thank you, *nina*—you do too! I'm just over here trying to add a little *estallido* to this punch, you know?" I laughed at him as I watched him pour some gin from his flask into a punch bowl filled with red juice. "This juice isn't for the *muchachos* and *muchachas!* Grown folks only, Miss Ebony!"

I laughed and kissed Mr. Cassell on the cheek. Then I went to look for Saadia. I found her in the corner, talking to a few of her female cousins. She introduced me to them, and then grabbed me by the hand, leading me straight to Casper, the guest of honor. Casper was standing next to Mateo, who looked like he had jumped off the cover of a male fitness magazine. That man was just too fine for words.

"Ebony!" Casper said when he saw me. He wrapped his arm around my waist. "I haven't seen you in mad years! You look good!"

"You look good too, Casper. The military has preserved you."

Casper smiled. "Yeah, it did. I'll be thirty-seven years old and I feel like I'm twenty-seven. I can't fall off, know what I'm saying?"

I looked to his right and I noticed that Mateo was biting his bottom lip and staring at me. I tried to keep my eyes on Casper but it was hard to do that with someone as cute as Mateo all up in my grill.

Saadia cut Casper off before he went into some long, drawn-out conversation. She had moments when she was the greatest listener but then she had this very bad habit of interrupting people while they were talking. She even did it to me sometimes.

"Casper, Casper!" she said, brushing him off. "Come on, man! Stop trying to hog the conversation! You done talked to Ebony a million times! I brought her over here to talk to Mateo," she added, rolling her eyes at the smirking Casper.

I blushed. "Hey, Mateo," I greeted him, holding out my hand for a handshake. "Long time, no see, man."

Mateo waved me off. "I don't want to shake your damn hand," he said. "I want a hug! I haven't seen you in a minute!"

He ignored my hand and pulled me to him. Mateo's broad chest pressed against my 34-C-cup breasts. It felt good. When we came up for air, he nudged Casper with his elbow.

"Yo, bruh, who would have thought that our Ebony would grow up to be so gorgeous?" Casper shrugged. "Damn, Ebony," Mateo said.

The sound of my name coming through those sexy lips almost made me cream in my panties. Then I remembered that I wasn't wearing any.

"Damn, Ebony, what?" I asked.

Saadia and Casper had tiptoed away from us, leaving me and Mateo standing there, all alone. That was when I realized that Saadia had set the whole thing up. Mateo and I attempted to have a conversation over the loud Soca music.

"So, Ebony, where have you been all of this time?" Mateo asked.

I smiled. "No, the question is where have you been? Oh, my bad, I know where you've been."

Mateo laughed it off. "Yeah, I did my time in jail. But so what? I'm home now and doing quite well for myself, too. You don't see me because I stay away from a lot of family functions because—well, shit, you know how my family is."

I chuckled, thinking about Saadia's family. They looked down on Mateo and his criminal exploits. "Yeah, I do. But it's definitely a pleasure to see you at this event."

Mateo licked those killer lips of his. "Likewise, *mami.*"

I sighed and looked around the party. Saadia's relatives were definitely in the house. They were so loud that I could actually hear them talking over the music.

"What are you doing after this?" Mateo asked, obviously noticing my discomfort. I was still reeling from the Dray thing.

"Well, I rode with Saadia so I guess she's going to take me home."

"Why don't you let me take you to breakfast? I'll drop you off at home afterward."

I sort of hesitated. I had heard quite a few stories about Mateo's "bad boy" ways. I didn't want to be riding around with him and somebody shoots up his car with me in it.

"Um, well . . ." I looked in Saadia's direction.

Mateo waved his cousin off. She was too busy talking to someone to notice me watching her. "Please, I'm sure that my little cuz won't mind if you hang out with me. And don't worry, I'm a changed man. Been home for the last four years and me and my boys are into flipping houses. I'm legit now."

I sort of relaxed when Mateo told me that. Then I thought, *what the hell? I'm newly single; I might as well start taking offers.*

I shrugged my shoulders. "Taking me home sounds like a good idea, Mateo."

Mateo planted a juicy kiss on my cheek. That kiss made my body tingle all over.

I managed to break away from Mateo and walked over to Saadia. She gave me a tight hug.

"What was that for?" I asked, with a confused look on my face.

"I just wanted you to know that you are going to be okay, girl. You are going to be just fine."

And with that being said, we partied the night away. The sounds of Soca, hip hop, reggae, and R&B could be heard coming from the large speakers that were surrounding the hall's dance floor. We had so much fun that it was almost five in the morning when people began filing out. Saadia and I stood among the party-goers, mingling and cracking jokes, when Mateo suddenly appeared through the throngs of people standing outside. He grabbed my hand and told me to say good night to everyone, prompting Saadia and her female cousins to start giggling at the gesture.

"Good night, y'all," I said, waving to them and feeling slightly inebriated.

"Bye, Ebony! Bye, Mateo!" Saadia and her cousins said in unison.

Mateo and I walked up the block toward his ride, still holding hands.

"Are you ready to eat?" he asked.

Are you? I thought. I was staring into his eyes and having some of the naughtiest thoughts. Amid all of the things that had transpired that night with Dray, it was hard to believe that I had sex on the brain.

"Of course, Mateo," I said, giving him a seductive smile. "You lead the way."

Mateo smiled back. "Hmmph. Trust me, baby girl. Mateo Cassell don't have one problem with leading at all."

With those words, I already knew what was going to happen between Mateo and me.

"Here I go again," I whispered to myself.

Chapter 7

Just Fine

Phoenix

The next morning, I tried to lift my head up from the pillow but to no avail. I was experiencing a serious hangover. I was sort of surprised at the way I acted that night because I didn't normally drink myself into oblivion. I definitely knew my limit. Why I chose to drink like a sailor while I was out on a date with this guy, Stuart, was beyond me. I tried to remember how the night with me and Stu had ended. When I did remember, everything was in 3D, right in my face like it was happening all over again.

What the hell was I thinking? Stu had been more than a perfect gentleman all night and I had ruined everything with my drunken antics. But damn, he could have at least given me some vitamin D! Maybe I wouldn't have felt so bad.

I looked at the iHome clock sitting on my dresser. It was 10:18 A.M., Saturday morning. I instantly picked up my house phone to call Shanell to tell her about my night and her funny-style cousin-in-law. I was sure that she would be at the boutique by this time.

"Casha Boutique, our style is unique—how may I help you?"

"What's up, girl?" I said, voice sounding like a fire-breathing dragon over the phone. My mouth felt like I'd been chomping on some dried-up shit balls.

"Phoenix?" she asked. "What the hell is wrong with your voice?"

"Lord, please, child, not so loud," I said, holding my pounding forehead. "I went out with your boy Stu last night."

"Oh, for real?" She sounded excited. "So how did you like him? Where did y'all go? What did y'all do?"

"Hey, hey! Calm down, Miss Busy Body!" I said. "We went out to eat at Carmine's; then we went to the Cherry Lounge. He was promoting some event there last night."

"That's what's up! Did you have a good time?"

"Yes, I did!" I replied, meaning that literally. "Stu is a cool-ass guy. Now, me? I'm a whole 'nother story. Wretched behavior, girl, just wretched."

"Oh, God!" she exclaimed. "What did you do?"

"Well, where do I start? I had some Merlot at the restaurant, then when I got to the Cherry Lounge, I had three, four more drinks of Cîroc with pineapple juice. That didn't agree with me. Girl, by the end of our night, Stu had to carry me to his car and drive my ass straight home."

"Then what?"

I chuckled. "He walked me upstairs, I opened the door to my apartment, and I stumbled inside. Em-bar-ra-ssing! After he came out of my bathroom and he walked out into the living room, I was lying on my couch, butt-ass naked, with my legs open so wide he could see my damn uterus, girl! It was a mess!" Shanell didn't respond. She was quiet as hell—so quiet, I thought that the phone had cut off. "Hello?" I said.

"I'm still here."

I rolled my eyes up in my head. "Are you about to get all judgmental on me, Shanell? Because if you are, we need to hang up right now."

"What in the hell is wrong with you?" she said. It sounded as if she was about to reprimand me. "I hooked you up with a good guy like Stu because I'm on a mission to help you find a man who's going to take care of you and vice versa. A man who could help raise a family, do nice things with you and for you, build an empire with you, but you're running around acting like a drunken twenty-year-old! You're a grown-ass woman, Phoenix. I mean, come on now!"

I knew that I deserved every bit of Shanell's wrath. She was absolutely right about everything she said. But I didn't feel that any of my actions warranted Stu's standoffish behavior. I was a hot chick—what man wouldn't have wanted me? There I was, practically shoving ass down Stu's throat, and he didn't even give me a second thought. Who the hell did he think he was?

"Look, you're right, you're right, Shanell," I said, somewhat pacifying her. "But damn, what's up with your boy? I was serving him some of this filet mignon on a platter and he didn't even try to taste it. Maybe your boy is gay or something. I don't know."

That really pushed Shanell's buttons. "You know what, Phoenix? You just don't seem to get it! Stu is a good fucking catch, you know! I think that you should have at least waited to get to know him better before you brought sex into the equation. And tell me, what was the rush? Why do you always have to have things your way?"

Now I was getting upset. "Because what other way is it supposed to be but my way, Shanell?" I asked, stressing her name and acting like she had just said the dumbest thing ever.

"Look, if you don't stop with your selfish, self-absorbed ways, you're going to end up losing the best thing that you ever had and I'm not just talking about Stuart.

I'm sick of women like you always expecting for a man to bow down to them and in turn, y'all bitches don't want to give up anything in return!" I was silent, waiting for Shanell to calm down. I was amazed at how she was getting herself all worked up about my love life.

She continued with her rant. "Pussy means absolutely nothing to a man like Stu. He gets it all the time! That's why you were supposed to be different from the rest of the women. But look what happened. You're no different! And to think that it was my best friend who acted like this! Un-fucking-believable!"

I was calm as ever. I didn't think that I did anything wrong. "Yeah, okay. I don't know what school for dummies you went to but if a man wants to get with me, he has to do what I want. I got the career, the money, the sex—"

"For Christ's sake, nobody cares about what you have, Phoenix!" she shouted into the phone. "The bottom line is that you still don't have a man, you don't have a child to share your love with or even a damn dog to give a bone to. You have all of these . . . these material, monetary things and no one to share it with. You're a walking billboard for a woman with all of these high-ass standards and expectations and in the meantime, you feel that Stu should have lowered his own standards and taken advantage of your drunken ass. The man was trying to respect you and now you're upset with him? You sound foolish!"

I couldn't believe that Shanell was laying into my ass about her so-called "cousin-in-law" so early in the morning. Too bad I wasn't trying to hear anything that she was saying. For one, I was not the bitch for constructive criticism—my mother had tried that technique on me for years and it still didn't work well with me.

Getting bored with all the talk about Stu, I yawned loudly in Shanell's ear. I was ready to end this conversation. "Look, Shanell, it seems like you're a little upset about this. Sooo, er, um, I'm gonna, like, call you back when you feel better, okay?" There was no reply on Shanell's end. "Did this bitch just hang up on me?" I asked myself. That was when I heard the dial tone in my ear.

I couldn't stress Shanell's hissy fit—she'd get over it. I just shrugged my shoulders and put the receiver back on the base. Then I went back to sleep.

Later on that afternoon, around one o'clock, I was up, fully showered, and about to walk out of the house to meet my sister, River, and my brother, Chance, at the Planet Fitness in downtown Brooklyn. Even though I lived in Queens and my siblings lived in Brooklyn, we would usually meet up every other Saturday, which was so cool. I looked forward to our brother and sister moments.

Now, my older sister, River, was someone that I definitely admired. She was a thirty-six–year-old veteran English teacher at Samuel J. Tilden High School. She was also the 360-degree opposite of me. River was such a sensible-minded and positive person, not to mention she was a minimalist. She wasn't into all of the material things like I was. She drove a sensible car—a late-model Honda Accord. She was very comfortable with rocking her old leather Coach bags from the early millennium, and still rented a three-bedroom apartment on Greene Avenue in Bedford-Stuyvesant.

She also had a fifteen-year-old son, my nephew, Dallas, who was like one of the coolest teenagers ever—I called him my nephew/son. My Dallas and my Kare

Bear, Ebony's boy, could get anything they wanted from Auntie Phoenix and they knew it. Having any children of my own was so unnecessary when I had them. I could just spoil my nephew and godson and send them right back to their mamas. That was a good deal.

My brother, Chance, was on a whole different spectrum. He was a bachelor, player extraordinaire, or a ho with a heart, as me and River like to call him. All of my friends loved Chance's cute ass and every time I looked around, one of them was trying to hit on him. Chance and my girl Capri used to go out together when they were teenagers. But Chance and my friend Ebony had a brief fuckship a little while after she broke up with her son's father. I didn't know about this until years later. From what I gathered, Ebony really liked Chance but he knew that he didn't have anything good for her so he left her alone.

On this particular Saturday, I desperately needed to talk to River and Chance about a few things. After Shanell managed to dig me a new asshole that morning, she really had me doing some serious brainstorming about what was really good with me and this life of mine. Maybe this time, just this once, the constructive criticism had affected me.

I arrived at Planet Fitness at 1:30 P.M. sharp. There I sat, in my car, looking at my watch and impatiently waiting for Chance and River. River was slow as hell. She was so slow that I swore that grown-ass woman would be late for her own damn funeral, as my mother would always say. Meanwhile, I was laid back and relaxing in my driver's seat. I had my eyes closed while listening to Jill Scott's *The Light of the Sun* album, playing on the iPod that I had plugged in my car. As the soothing sound of Jill's sultry voice came through the speakers, I was taking in all of her seductive words. I wasn't a smoker but at that moment, I wouldn't have minded puffing up on a fat blunt filled with some good old weed. I needed a mental vacation from my fucked-up reality.

"'Why does my body ignore what my mind says?'" I sang along with Jill. I was vibing for like ten whole minutes when the knock on my car window startled me. I opened my eyes and it was River, standing outside of my car.

"Fee," she said, calling me by my childhood nickname. "Don't you know that it's too dangerous to be sleeping in this BMW in a public parking lot in Brooklyn? This isn't Fresh Meadows or Jamaica Estates, babe!"

I opened the door and got out of my car with a huge smile on my face. "What's up, sister?" I said, giving her a warm hug. "Where is freaking Chance?" I asked, with a frown on my face.

She waved me off. "Please!" she said. "You know that Negro is laid up with some pu-pu. He told me tell you that he love you, though," River said, imitating my brother's voice.

We had already missed like two Saturdays of hanging out at the gym together but from what I could see, River was definitely keeping up with her end of the bargain. Her body was looking a whole lot trimmer than what I remembered. And she had this new haircut—a choppy bob with some blond highlights in her light brown hair. I smacked her on her ample hips.

"Where are you getting all of this extra mojo from, River?" I asked while looking at her pretty face. "And you're glowing! You look good!"

Suddenly, River, who was about three shades lighter than my mocha-colored brown-skinned self, turned beet red in the face. "Just taking care of myself a whole lot better than what I was, that's all."

I knew that look all too well. "Okay, you're blushing!" We both giggled. "So come on, give it up! Who is the guy?"

"Oh, my goodness, Fee!" she gushed. "I met this man, a really cool, wonderful man," she said.

I felt a pang of jealousy traveling through my bones. Damn, I wanted to meet someone, too. But I was genuinely happy for my sister.

My eyes widened. "Really? So who is he? Name, physical description, background info," I asked as we walked through the front door of the gym.

"Well, Maurice is this football coach and gym teacher at Erasmus Hall High School. I've known him for quite some time but we never had a real conversation with each other until two months ago. When we did talk, it was fascinating! Then one thing led to another," River said, shrugging her shoulders.

River and I put our jackets in the same locker and walked toward the workout area.

I put my hand over my mouth. "Damn, River! You hot ass! You fucked him already?"

River shushed me and looked around to see who was listening. She was so damn corny and conservative, which was probably one of the reasons why her first husband, Keith, left her. She had to loosen up.

"Why do you always have to be so vulgar?" she asked, with a frown on her face.

"Because I want to know if you screwed him yet," I said, throwing my towel on top of the treadmill that I was about to get on. I set the time and the speed. "You're the one who wants to beat around the bush about it."

River threw her towel across the treadmill too. She set the miles and minutes and began walking. Then she looked at me. "Yes, I screwed him. Is that what you wanted to hear?" she said, rolling her eyes at me.

I laughed and pumped my fist. "Attagirl!"

She laughed too. "But having sex with Maurice is really not all that's important to me. What matters to me is that Maurice wants the same things that I want. He has one child, a twelve-year-old daughter, he's never been married but wants to do so, and he is looking forward to having a future with someone."

"So do you wanna get married again?" I asked, trying to keep my pace on the treadmill.

River shrugged her shoulders. "I don't know. I mean, after going through that divorce with Keith, I thought that getting remarried was something that I wanted and needed. Right now, I'm just looking for a good life partner and if marriage is doable then, hey, you never know."

"But Mommy and Daddy have been married for like, thirty-something years. Don't you want that for yourself—again?"

River sighed. "Yeah, I do, but at what expense? For example, look at all the mess that Mommy has been through with Daddy. I mean, I love Daddy dearly but he did have a ten-year affair with another woman."

I held my head down. I knew about that affair all too well. My mother made sure of that. I was a daddy's girl so anything that my mother could do to discredit my father's name; she was going to make sure that I got wind of it. The relationship that I had with my mother was strained because of this.

"Yeah, yeah, yeah," I said, brushing it off. "I know all about the bitch Daddy had been fucking for like, ten years. Mommy still talks about the crap to this day but I bet you her ass didn't leave Daddy neither. Talking about how she stayed with Daddy for me, you, and Chase's sake," I said. "We were damn near grown when she found out that Daddy had been cheating on her. She should have just left him if she wasn't happy instead of making everybody else miserable."

River shook her head at me. "Dang! You and Mommy, boy! Y'all two still don't get along for nothing."

I instantly got on the defensive. "Because she's always trying to shoot Daddy down, emasculate him, talking all reckless to him and whatnot. That's not cool. Why stay with someone who fucked around on you just so you can punish them for the rest of y'all lives? That's just dumb to me!"

"It's not that easy to leave when you truly love someone. I know how Mommy feels. I did it with Keith. Twelve years of joy, pain, lust, love, all wrapped up into one. But the creeping and sneaking around was just too much for me. Women calling my damn phone, telling me about Keith's exploits—it was only so much I could take before I lost it. And I refuse to allow any man to drive me crazy. That's why I managed to stay away from a relationship for the last three years. I needed to work on myself and find out what it was that I truly wanted and needed from a mate. So I chose to date a few men before I got into anything serious, even though I had offers to commit. Now I feel that I'm ready to get serious with that one special person. It's my time."

"But how did you know when it was time to settle down?"

"You'll want to settle down when you know exactly what you want for yourself and when you finally love you so much that you're unwilling to accept anything less from a partner, from anyone."

"So does this . . . this Maurice character drive a nice car, have some property that he owns? Does he dress nice? Is he nice looking?"

River wiped her sweaty brow with her towel. "What are you talking about, girl?" She put the towel back on the treadmill and gave me a disgusted look. "Damn, you still on that superficial, materialistic bullshit?" She sucked her teeth. "I don't know what your type is but Maurice sure looks good to me. I'm very attracted to him and that's what counts. As far as what kind of car he drives or if he owns any property, what does that matter? He is a well-educated, well-rounded man with a great personality who treats me very well—that's what matters to me."

We continued our treadmill exercises in silence. There was so much that I wanted to ask River but she was too caught up in her newfound love affair to even care about my plight. Instead, we talked about other things as we finished up our workout for the day.

After I left my sister, I was still frustrated and left with no answers as to why I couldn't find a man who suited me. I figured that I would call Ebony later and see what she was up to. Maybe she could give me some insight.

Chapter 8

The Love I Never Had

Joi

It was a Saturday morning and I had to wake up early for work. Of course, I was still aggravated from the night before. Tate and I had never come to any kind of happy medium and, as usual, we were still on the outs. The Dara situation was still weighing heavily on my mind.

In a perfect world, I could have been a little more sensitive to Tate and his daughter. The truth was that I wanted Tate all to myself. Throughout our relationship it was like I never had that, due to Chasity and her mother. I knew that I was being super selfish when it came to Tate, not wanting to share him with anyone. But I was okay with that. It didn't bother me one bit.

I arrived at work about fifteen minutes later than what I should have. When I got to my cubicle, I made sure that my supervisor, an ornery old bat named Miss Calloway, didn't see me sliding into my seat. That woman always seemed to be on my case so I had to be easy. I didn't need any more stress. All I wanted was a quiet workday.

As soon as I put on my headset, my coworker, Mercuri came over and sat next to me. "So what happened with you and Tate?" she asked. "Did you ever call this Dara chick like you said you were going to?"

I sucked my teeth. "Me and Tate ain't get shit re-
solved yet, girl. I'm just so sick of him and that baby
mama of his!"

"I know exactly what you mean! I'm tired of James
and his bullshit, too, girl," she said, chiming in with her
man problems. "James called me at five this morning
to ask me if he could come over and get some. Shoot, I
don't know why he thought that he could ask me anything like that, especially since I had thrown his ass out
of my house."

"So did you let him come over and get some or
what?" I asked, giving Mercuri the side eye. I knew her
like a book.

"Of course I did!" she said loudly. We both laughed.
"James knows good and damn well that he can't resist
all'a this." I cracked up as Mercuri rubbed her hands all
over her full-figured body for the effect. "And I left that
ass sleeping in my bed this morning and Dayshawn
was in his bedroom," she said, referring to her six-year-
old son. "I thought that I would let them have some
father and son time together!"

We gave each other a high five. "That's right!" I
agreed. "I don't give a hell about Dara or her kid. That's
where I'm at right now."

"I second that notion! And besides, James is the
one who fucked up. He was the one who went out and
got some twenty-five-year-old skeezer pregnant with
his baby. But I feel like this, Joi, Dayshawn is his old-
est child, so my baby is supposed to get first dibs on
whatever James has, no matter what. That jump off is
gonna have to wait until my son is taken care of before
her and that little rug rat get a dime of my baby daddy's
money! I know that she hates that James is loyal to
me and my son but that is something she should have
thought about before she opened up her legs to him."

"Pow!" I said. We both laughed. "And I got two words for that tramp, *dumb ass!* Man, I can't stand no dumb-ass broad!"

The computer began lighting up, which meant that an emergency call was coming through. That old bat supervisor of mine, Miss Calloway was walking toward us so Mercuri crept back over to her desk. I couldn't get mad at Miss Crab Tree for being tired of us—Mercuri and I were always pussyfooting around. Now it was time for us to get serious and get back to work. Lunchtime couldn't come soon enough.

That afternoon, Mercuri and I decided to take a stroll downtown near Fulton Street to grab some lunch when I ran into my ex-boyfriend, Brick. Brick and I were together for two years and we went our separate ways right before I met Tate. When I spotted Brick, I wanted to crawl under a car and hide. I looked a hot-ass mess. I had on no makeup and my raccoon eyes were in full effect. I hadn't been in the mood to get dressed that morning so I threw on a Victoria's Secret Pink sweat suit and a pair of Nike sneakers. In other words, I was in no condition to be seeing an ex-boyfriend of mine, looking so un-fabulous.

I nudged Mercuri on the arm. "Wow! I cannot believe this!" I said.

Mercuri looked at me. "What's the matter?" she asked.

"It's my ex-boyfriend, Brick!" I said, pointing in his direction. He was headed straight toward us. "I haven't seen him in like five, six years! He can't see me looking like this!"

Mercuri glanced at him. He was at the corner ahead of us, waiting to cross the street.

"He is definitely a cutie and you don't look bad, girl. Cut it out!"

I swallowed. "Mercuri, you don't understand!" I said, getting all animated. "Lord knows I was like obsessed with this man! Brick had some of the best sex that I had ever experienced in my life! I get goose bumps all over my body thinking about this man's touch and the way that he used that mouth of his," I said. Mercuri laughed. "I would never tell Tate that shit, though. He thinks that he's the first guy I ever fell in love with."

"Is that what you told him?" Mercuri asked.

"Yes!" I replied. We laughed again.

Anyway, Brick and I couldn't get enough of each other. Then one day, it was *bam!* The emotional roller-coaster was over. Brick was the one to break it off with me. Of course, I was devastated. He said that we were too hot for each other; there was too much passion, too much drama—he wasn't lying about all of that. He wasn't able to handle us but I didn't feel the same way. I wanted more from Brick and I wanted to continue with our relationship, not realizing that it was toxic for both of us. I just wasn't ready to let him go.

Unfortunately, Brick had to learn this the hard way.

I tell you, lust mixed with love is one hell of a fucking drug and I was hooked! Before it was all said and done between us, I had slashed all four of Brick's tires and scratched the word "BITCH" on to the hood of his car. After I did this damage, somewhere in the back of my distorted mind I expected for Brick to realize how much of a mistake he made and come running right back into my arms.

Of course, that never happened, and to add insult to injury I never heard from Brick again. The man ended up changing his phone numbers on me and everything, even moved out of his apartment. That was a little more than five years ago.

Funny, I hadn't heard Brick's voice or laid eyes on that man until that moment I spotted him in downtown Brooklyn. I thought that I wasn't ever going to see him again. Now there Brick was, standing before me, looking so mature and as handsome as ever. I was honestly happy to see him. I held my breath, hoping that he felt the same.

Surprisingly, Brick was very receptive. "Hello, sweetheart!" he said, walking toward me with open arms.

I exhaled. "What's up, Brick?" I said, giving him a tight hug.

Brick held me in his arms. "Wow, if it isn't crazy-ass Joi," he replied, with a chuckle.

He took a step back and I playfully slapped him on his arm. "Yep, it's me in the flesh! Long time, no see, Brick!" I exclaimed. "How you doing, man? Where have you been?" I introduced him to Mercuri and he politely shook her hand.

"I'm good, Joi, I'm good," he replied, licking his lips. I saw how he was checking me out. "You're looking good, girl! Long time, no see! Now that I'm seeing you, where is my damn money?" he asked, getting all serious on me.

My heart skipped a beat. I knew that our chance meeting was too good to be true. Brick freaking hated me!

"Money for what?" I asked, disappointed by this sudden change of attitude.

"The money for my got-damn truck, woman! You scratched the word 'bitch' on the hood! Remember that?"

I swallowed hard and glanced at Mercuri. She just shrugged her shoulders, clueless as to what Brick was talking about.

"I apologize! I . . . I know that I was so wrong for that," I stuttered. "I truly felt bad about doing you like that."

Brick began cracking up. "I'm just playing, babe!" Mercuri and I laughed too. "Yeah, you were wrong for that but I forgave you a long time ago. You were just hurt, that's all," he replied, with a look of sincerity on his face. "I didn't mean to hurt you, Joi."

"Don't worry about it. We both survived." I immediately got off that topic. "So what brings you to BK? Do you still live in Hempstead?" I asked.

"Yeah, I'm still in Strong Island," he said, calling Long Island by its nickname. "As a matter of fact, I just bought a home in Elmont, I have my own business—life is good." I gave him a nod of approval. "I'm just down here doing some shopping—it's my mother's sixtieth birthday so I came to pick her up a gift or two. What are you doing today?" he asked.

"Okay, wow. God bless her." Brick thanked me. "As for me, I'm still working at Metro Tech, doing the nine-one-one operator thing."

"Oh, really?" he replied. "That's what's up."

I looked at Mercuri again, worrying that she was going to get impatient with me. After all, we were on our lunch hour. Thankfully, she wasn't paying us any attention. She had wandered a few feet away and was doing some window shopping. I was happy about that because I wanted a few more minutes with Brick.

"So, um, what's your status these days? Do you have a girlfriend?" I asked, getting straight to the point. "Inquiring minds want to know."

Brick smiled. "As a matter of fact, I have more than just some 'girlfriend.' I've been happily married for the past three years and I have two beautiful children: a two-year-old son and a five-month-old daughter," he replied.

For some reason, I hadn't expected all of that. That annoying little green-eyed monster of mine went into overdrive. I wanted to run up and down Fulton Street, screaming. When was I going to be a wife and not a girlfriend, dammit? *Damn, damn, damn!*

"Oh, really?" I said, trying to hide my hurt feelings. I didn't know if I was more upset about me and Tate not being married or if I still had unresolved feelings for Brick. "A wife and two kids, huh? Wow. That's um, great, Brick. She's a very lucky woman," I said, hating like hell.

"Shit, I'm a lucky man!" Brick gushed. "My wife is the best thing that ever happened to me. I appreciate having her in my life."

I glanced back at Mercuri, who was now within earshot of our conversation. She began whistling and looked away.

"Wow, um, Brick, that's what's up," was all I could say.

I thought about how Tate and I were no closer to getting married in our four-year relationship—he had too much on his plate. Now I had to hear that an ex-boyfriend of mine, a man I let slip right through my fingers, was married to someone else. Tate was definitely going to get it now.

"So do you have any kids, Joi? As fine as you are, I know you got a husband, girl," Brick said.

I lifted up my left hand and wiggled it. "No ring on this finger! I just have a boyfriend." There was no point in telling Brick how long Tate and I had been together.

Brick placed his hand under my chin and lifted my face up. "Don't worry, Joi. If he doesn't marry you, there's somebody else out there who will, babe. You're beautiful." Then he briefly hugged me again. "Okay, Joi. A brother gotta be out now. Going to take care of my biz and meet wifey for lunch. She's visiting my mother-in-law in Fort Greene. Anyway, it was nice seeing you, babe. Take care."

Brick waved at Mercuri and I watched as he walked away. "Nice seeing you too," I replied, with a wave. "And thank you for fucking up my whole existence," I mumbled to myself.

The words that Brick said to me were still echoing in my ear: *If he doesn't marry you, someone else will.* Now what in the hell was that supposed to mean? Mercuri had to tug on my arm to snap me back to reality.

"Are you okay, girl?" she asked, with a look of concern on her face.

"Yeah, I'm okay," I replied, as we continued on our journey. "I guess it's kind of hard to see an ex-boyfriend, one I was head over heels for, happily married with kids. Like, what the hell is wrong with me, Mercuri? Why can't I get the ring and have some children of my own with the man I love?"

"Please, child," Mercuri said, waving me off. "I have no answer for that one. I'm still trying to figure some of those things out about my damn self!"

I shook my head at the thought. I was truly upset! Seeing Brick had me wanting to give Tate an ultimatum: *either you put that bitch, Dara in her place and we take our relationship to the next level or leave me alone for good. I can do bad all by my damn self.*

Ten minutes later, Mercuri and I managed to grab some food to go from this buffet spot near the job. On our way back to work, she was still talking about Brick and Tate and her man, James. I was in no mood to talk about anything with a penis attached to it—I was about done and I wanted her to drop the entire subject. Then I remembered that our talks about our dysfunctional relationships were actually what held our friendship together.

"So when do you and Tate plan on having some babies?" My eyes narrowed. "Y'all mofos been together for like four years now," she asked.

I didn't know if Mercuri was trying to be funny or what. All I knew was that that ass was about to get cussed out in 0.5 seconds. She was really reaching with the stupid questions that I had no answer to.

"And why are you asking me this again?"

"I'm asking you this because you need to put some things into action!" I rolled my eyes at her. "That's right! Claim your man, girl!" she said, egging me on. "Joi, I know that you love Tate and I believe that Tate loves you too. But if you don't stop sitting back and just complaining all the time, you're gonna end up losing Tate to that baby mama of his."

Mercuri made a lot of sense. At least to me she did. But after talking with Brick, did I really need to hear that? That's a female friend for you. They were always saying the wrong damn thing at the wrong damn time.

"Oh, the same way you almost lost James to his side piece?"

The claws had come out and I was scratching.

Mercuri stopped walking and put her free hand on her hip. I guessed she had figured out that she was getting on my last nerve.

"Ouch!" she said. "I deserved that with me and my big mouth. But since you put it that way, yeah, you're going to lose Tate to Dara *exactly* the same way that I lost James to that young girl." Suddenly, I felt bad about what I said. I gave her a hug and we shared a laugh. "You're so evil, Joi! I swear you are."

"I can be sometimes, especially to people I care about. I'm sorry, girl." We walked a few feet in silence when I got an idea. "You're so right. I've gotta claim my man and I know just how to do that. I'm going to prove that Chasity is not his daughter."

Mercuri stopped walking. "Now how in the hell are you going to do that, Joi? Even if Tate has his own suspicions about the baby, he might not even want to know the truth. Then you might really lose him."

A sinister smile came over my face. "Well, that's going to be a chance that I take. If I have to swab that little heifer myself, I'm going to find out if this baby is his. Meanwhile, we can work on going half on a baby of our own," I said. Mercuri slapped me five. "I gotta put this whole Dara thing to rest because I'm not trying to share no baby daddy with that grimy bitch if I can help it!"

Mercuri nodded her head in agreement. "That's right, girl. Don't be like me."

Fifteen minutes later, we were back inside of the building and practically sucking down our lunch. Half an hour later, we were back on the phones, doing what we were paid to do. The thought of me being married, having Tate's baby, and knocking Dara out of the box for good made me feel good. And I had a smile on my face for the rest of the day.

Chapter 9

You Don't Have To Worry

Ebony

It was eleven o'clock Saturday morning when I finally opened my eyes. I sat up in my bed and stretched and yawned for about ten minutes straight. I was so exhausted from last night's party. Now what happened after the party? Shit, that was another story.

That morning after Casper's party I found myself struggling to get out of the bed. I didn't even have that much to drink that night. When I finally managed to get it together, I reached for my terry cloth robe and wrapped it around my naked frame. Then I slid my feet into some furry slippers to walk into the kitchen. I was hungrier than a runaway slave.

While I was in the kitchen, preparing breakfast, I was surprised to hear my doorbell ring. I definitely wasn't expecting any visitors and no one pops up at my house without calling—I don't play that.

I stopped in the middle of stirring my Aunt Jemima pancake batter and went to answer the door. I was more than surprised to see who was standing on my stoop, like a stray dog looking for a home. It was nobody else but Dray. I was instantly pissed, wondering what in the hell possessed him to bring his trifling ass over to my house after he had dumped me.

"Why are you over here, Dray?" I asked, really trying not to show any emotion but it wasn't working. The very sight of him made me want to vomit.

"Good morning, Ebony. I just came by to return your key," he said, handing me my house key through the cracked screen door.

I snatched it from his grasp and threw the key into my house, in anger. "Don't you remember that we agreed to give each other only one key to our apartments? That means that you could have shoved that motherfucking key up your ass for all I care!"

Dray was unmoved by my tirade. "Oh, yeah, I forgot about that," was all he could muster up to say.

Now I was truly ticked off. My nasty attitude was not affecting this jerk at all.

"If you came over here to retrieve your key from me, Dray, I don't have it. I flushed it down the toilet last night. So if you want it, it's floating in the East River somewhere with the rest of the shit. Why don't you go jump in?"

Dray shook his head. "Look, Ebony, I know the way that I ended things was on a very fucked-up note. But I was hoping that you and I could still be friends."

I laughed dead in his face. Was this dude effing serious? Why do men always want to be a friend *after* they break up with you? In some cases, it might have been cool. But a friendship was definitely a no-go with Dray and me.

"You must be a fucking fool!" I exclaimed, with the look of disgust on my face. "Let Anisa be your gotdamn friend! Didn't you move that bitch into your apartment?"

"Ebony, listen, I just thought that since we've been friends for the last five years—" I stopped him from going any further. "Correction. We were only friends for two years. The other three? It's obvious that you wasn't no damn friend to me! Fuck you!"

Dray chuckled in disbelief. "So do you mean to tell me that the three years of us being together didn't mean shit to you?"

I laughed again. I knew then that Dray had lost his mind. He was not trying to accept any responsibility for how he did me.

"Didn't mean shit to me? Didn't mean shit to me?" I wanted to choke Dray with my bare hands. "Don't you mean that three years didn't mean shit to you?" I tried to hold back tears. "You don't understand how much you hurt me," I said, in a barely audible voice. "You moved another woman into your apartment. You and I were supposed to be planning a future together, raising our children as brothers—we should have been planning . . . planning marriage. . . ." I drifted off and then I caught myself. This was no time to get emotional over a man who apparently didn't want me anymore. "Why are you worried about what anything means to me? You made your fucking choice, now go be with the bitch!" I yelled.

"See, there you go with all that cussing and carrying on! All I'm saying is that we've been friends for five years! Why should we let the fact that we're not in a relationship anymore end up affecting the friendship that we once had?"

"Wait, wait, wait," I said, holding up my hand. "We were really good friends right up until the moment you asked me to be your woman. Then everything just went downhill from there," I added, giving him a thumbs-down. "I should have kept my legs closed and given my heart to a man who was so much more deserving than you were!"

Dray began flailing his arms. I could tell that he was getting aggravated with me because he wasn't getting his way.

"Why do you keep downplaying what we had with each other, Ebony? Is that all you think about us?" Dray shook his head. "At least I was honest with you about what was going on with me!"

"You were honest, all right! And that's exactly why we ain't together now."

"Oh, boy!" Dray said, frustrated that I wasn't giving him one leg to stand on. "Can you just let me come inside and talk to you?" he asked.

I let out a fake laugh. "You're not ever going to step foot inside of my house again, you bastard! Go home to your new woman!"

Not once did Dray mention that girl, Anisa, or the fact I had whooped her ass. I knew her high-yellow behind probably had some serious bruising behind our altercation. I was really trying to stomp a mud hole in her ass that night.

Dray wasn't about to give up. "Why can't we talk inside? You don't have company . . . or do you have company?" he asked, with a worried look on his face.

I frowned. "Don't worry about me having any company. It's none of your damn business! You're not getting inside of this house!"

Suddenly, a shirtless Mateo appeared in my doorway. He stood directly behind me and wrapped his well-toned arms around my waist. Then he kissed me on the neck. And he did all of this in front of Dray.

Although I hadn't expected for Dray to appear on my doorstep, I damn sure wasn't banking on Mateo doing all of that in front of him, either. I was kind of irritated that he had come out of the bedroom while Dray was there. I would have preferred for my ex to hold on to that bad guy title—alone. Now I looked like a major ho and it seemed as if I was playing games all along. All of this would only make Dray justify his actions.

On the flip side of things, Mateo was definitely looking extra sexy! That chocolate skin of his was beaming in the morning sunlight; those pearly whites of his were gleaming! If I had to choose anyone to make Dray jealous, Mateo would win—hands down. And he was winning because Dray hating like a mug.

"Good morning, babe. Are you all right out here?" Mateo asked me, giving me another kiss on the cheek and giving Dray a quick head nod. "You sounded upset."

"I'm okay, baby," I replied. Mateo had already put me on blast so I figured that I would go all the way with it. "Um, weren't you just leaving, Dray? You're interrupting our romantic morning," I said, with an evil smirk on my face.

Dray stood there with a stunned expression. No words would come out of his mouth. After a few seconds passed, he finally found his voice.

"Okay, Ebony. I see how you are now!" He took another look at Mateo and shook his head. "Take care of yourself."

I waved him off. "And enjoy the rest of your life, Dray, because I will definitely be enjoying mine!"

As Dray walked away, he turned back around and gave me this nasty look. He looked pretty upset but oh, well, I had given him a taste of his own damn medicine. Thanks to Mateo, bad timing and all, I was able to do just that.

After Dray left, I was okay with everything that had transpired between us—at least, for that moment. Once Mateo left, I had no idea how I was going to feel. But one thing I did know. I knew that it was time for me to

move on and I was going to do just that, no matter how
much it hurt.

As soon as I shut the door, Mateo pulled me close to
him. We kissed and then he turned me around so that I
was facing the wall. He dropped his jeans to his ankles,
and put on a Magnum condom. He lifted up my robe
and entered me doggie style. In seconds, his rock hard
dick was inside of me, penetrating my sugar walls. I
loved it! He was grinding that sweet dick inside of me
and pulling my hair from the back until I was literally
spraying pussy juice all over my hardwood floors. I
was getting fucked, just the way I liked and needed to
be fucked. I wasn't about to get it twisted. This was no
lovemaking session.

After a few more strokes, I turned around to face
him. We were kissing so roughly that we were practically choking on each other's tongues. It was one of
those wet, nasty kisses, too, the one with the saliva running down the sides of our mouths.

Then Mateo asked me the one question that men
seemed to always ask a woman, even if they didn't give
a shit about her.

"This is my pussy, right?" he asked, as he was pounding into me.

Of course, I gave him the obvious answer.

"Yes, yes!" I screamed. It was no need for me to kill
the mood with the truth. "Keep fucking me right there!
Right there, baby!"

"You like that dick, don't you, baby?"

Now I was wishing that Mateo would shut the hell
up.

"Loooove it! I love it!" I replied.

At that point, I would say anything to keep him from
asking me another question while I was trying to cum.
He was fucking up my concentration.

We ended up on my damn couch; I couldn't remember how we got there. But I didn't want any pussy or cum stains on my furniture. Normally, another day, another time, I would have been upset by that because my red couch was made of microfiber. Before I knew it, I was on the couch with my leg thrown over the back of it.

Meanwhile, Mateo was putting his large hands around my throat and softly choking me, yet stroking the kitty cat ever so gently. This went on for the next fifteen minutes until I came and of course, I let it rain all over my couch. Thank heavens for Scotchgard protection.

"Oh, oh, I'm cumming, baby!" Mateo said.

"Cum in my mouth," I whispered, feeling extra freaky.

Mateo quickly pulled his dick out of my box, snatched the condom off. Then he came in my mouth and all over my face, too. I swallowed all of his babies, wiping the corners of my mouth after I had drunk him dry.

"You taste so good," I said, as I took my tongue and caught the last drip of cum off his dick.

Surprisingly, after I swallowed, Mateo kissed me dead in the mouth. I hadn't expected for him to do that. I couldn't do anything but respect him for being such a freak.

Mateo rolled off the couch. He was sprawled out on the area rug, butt-ass naked and looking up at the ceiling.

"You got some good-ass pussy. I swear you do," he said, shaking his head.

I got on the floor and lay down beside him. "Glad you liked it, Mateo. Shoot, you aren't so bad yourself."

Mateo rolled over and propped his head on his hand. He was staring at me with a smile on his face.

"Thanks, cutie pie," he replied, playfully squeezing my nose.

We lay there for a few minutes, in complete silence, trying to get it together. Five minutes later, we finally got up from the floor. Mateo's jeans were still wrapped around his ankles. I laughed at the sight. He stood there, with his arms spread out.

"See how you got me, girl?" he said with a chuckle. "I didn't even get a chance to take my pants all the way off."

I threw on my robe and went to get him a washcloth and towel for a shower. While I did this, I began thinking about everything that had transpired that morning.

"Damn, Ebony, you did it again," I said to myself.

It never failed. Every single time I was hurt by some man, I went back to my same old promiscuous ways, out of fear of being alone. Sadly enough, I usually ended up feeling even more alone after the sex.

"So the dude at your door was your ex-man, huh?" Mateo asked, taking his jeans all the way off and throwing them on the armchair in the living room.

I sighed. "Yep, that was him," I said, handing him the towels.

"Come and bring your sexy ass in this shower with me," he suggested.

By this time, I was praying for this whole "date" to be over. But of course, I was always the pleaser and didn't know how to ask Mateo to leave. Instead of telling him that it was time to go, I led him into the bathroom.

I ran the shower for us, dropped my robe, and wrapped my hair into a ponytail. I got into the shower first; then he got in behind me. We got our bodies wet and Mateo lathered up the loofah. He slowly began washing my body. I had to admit, it felt so good to be taken care of by *a* man. But it would have felt even better to be taken care of by *my* own man. Unfortunately, I didn't have that anymore.

"So what happened with you and this Dray dude?" Mateo asked while washing me.

Mateo didn't see me roll my eyes at the question. *These men kill me.* Why was my status with Dray so fucking important to him? Didn't he spend the night? Didn't he have sex with me? In other words, why did he care?

I took the loofah from him and returned the favor. "We just grew apart, I guess," I replied, not wanting to go into the part about how Dray had played me. It was none of Mateo's business.

"He dropped you for somebody else, huh?"

I stopped scrubbing and handed him the loofah. Now I was irritated. "What makes you think that?" I asked. I was sure that old Mateo had probably cut off a ho or two in his lifetime.

"Because that's what us dudes do!" he replied. "I bet money that dude showed up on your doorstep, trying to see if you and him could still be friends! Translation: can we still have sex with each other? Talking about he was bringing back your key—*ha!* That was a good one, homie!"

"Tuh!" I exclaimed. "Personally, I'm done with him. We can't be homies, lovers, or friends!"

Mateo squatted down in my tub and began scrubbing my feet. I adjusted the shower nozzle so the water wouldn't hit him in the face.

"Well, I'm glad that I was here to help you put dude on his tippy-toes. Let him think that I was getting up in that pussy while y'all two was together."

"That's how I feel," I lied. Honestly, I hadn't wanted Dray to think that at all.

Mateo stood up to face me. "You probably still love him, don't you?"

"Please, Mateo," I lied again.

Truthfully, I didn't know how to feel. What I did know was that all the talk about Dray was turning me off. What I wanted for Mateo to do was shut the hell up and just make me feel good. Damn!

He kissed me on the lips. "I'm sorry for all the questions, babe," he said, as if he was reading my mind. "There's no need for me to pry. Let's just continue to enjoy each other this morning."

As Mateo kissed the small of my back, a tear rolled down my cheek. I couldn't wait for him to leave.

Chapter 10

I'm Going Down

Phoenix

After the workout with my sister, River, I was exhausted. But this exhaustion wasn't physical. I had been doing some serious contemplating on the drive home and I was emotionally drained.

Once I arrived home, I hadn't even bothered to take my gym clothes off. I just plopped down on my couch and began thinking some more. While I was feeling damn good about my accomplishments over the years, there was one missing factor. I didn't have anyone that I could call my own.

Is my inability to find a decent man my karma?

What I meant by my karma was that I hadn't always been on my best behavior. Over the years, I had had my share of unavailable men—married men, men with girlfriends, the whole nine.

Where did this behavior come from? Well, my mistrust and unwillingness to commit to a man of my own began when I was a young girl.

I was seventeen years old when my mother found out that my dad had cheated on her. My beloved dad, Jonas Henry, had a ten-year extramarital affair with another woman—some lady named Barbara. Mommy didn't find out about this until two years after Barbara and my father were over and done with. According to

River, Mommy found some letter from the woman in the pocket of one of my father's old coats that she was taking to the Salvation Army.

"What if Phoenix or River started screwing married men, Jonas? Then what?" I overheard my mother asking my father one night, during one of their many arguments. I was supposed to be asleep in my bedroom, which was directly across from theirs but I listened intently as they went back and forth. I had this penchant for eavesdropping back then.

"What if Chase had a wife and three kids? Would you suggest that he sleep with other women?"

"What are you talking about, woman?" my father shot back at her. "What does Phoenix, River, or Chase have to do with any of this?"

"I'm saying that you have to set examples for your children, Jonas! Now all of your dirty little sins are going to fall on these kids! And the way that you cheated on me is the same damn way some trifling-ass man could cheat on your daughters! What are you going to say to them if that happens?"

I could hear my father trying to hush her up; for fear that we would hear every word. It was too late for that. I had heard an earful.

"Lana, will you please stop this bullshit? I made a mistake, one got-damn mistake, okay? I'm not seeing Barbara anymore or any other woman for that matter! Now please, will you shut the hell up before my kids hear you? Always acting so damn crazy!"

My mother really lost it then. "I'm crazy? I'm fucking crazy? Barbara is a home-wrecking bitch but that's okay with you, right? You know what, Jonas? I should have left your ass when I had the chance to!"

By then, my father couldn't take any more of her tongue-lashing. I could remember putting the covers over my head, as he began yelling loudly at my mother, so loud that I thought that he was going to hit her.

"So fucking leave then, Lana! Pack all of your shit and get the fuck out of my house! And while you at it, you can leave that damn car that I bought you in the driveway and leave all three of my got-damn kids right here with me! This is their home, too, and they ain't going nowhere!" my father growled back at her.

Even though their arguing continued, my mother ended up staying with my father. Out of guilt and his love for his family, Daddy suffered through years of her incessant nagging.

Although my mother and I didn't see to eye to eye on a number of things, I wouldn't say that Mommy was a total monster. I guess any news of a husband being unfaithful would send most women over the edge. And Mommy stuck around. To end up in a loveless marriage with a man who cheated was a bit too much for me. I knew that I didn't have that kind of tolerance.

That was why I was convinced that the position of the other woman was so much safer—I just had this desire to be in the know. Seeing how vulnerable and clueless my mother was when it came to my father and his affair, I promised myself that I was going be the one to check my expectations at the door. That was why my independence was everything to me. I didn't want to have to depend on a man for anything, not even love.

My ringing iPhone interrupted my thoughts. It was Stu. There I was thinking that he was finished with little old Phoenix. Obviously, I was very wrong.

I answered the phone. "Hello?" I said, giving him the sexy voice.

"Hello, beautiful," he greeted me. "Just because I didn't accept your offer last night doesn't mean that you had to stop calling me."

I giggled. I was sort of relieved that Stu didn't cut me off. It wasn't like I had available men lined up around the corner, and he seemed like a keeper.

"You are so funny!" I said, blushing from the embarrassment. "Anyway, what's going on with you, Stu?" I asked, hoping that he didn't bring up any more details from our night out.

"Ain't shit, babe. I just called to ask what you were doing right now."

"I just got in from the gym, about to go wash this sweat off my body—"

Stu cut me off midsentence and got straight to the point. "How about coming to Uptown to visit a brother? We can have an early dinner at the crib and just sit by my fireplace and kick it. Is that cool?"

I literally jumped out of my workout clothes. "Yeah, that's cool, Stu. Text me your information and I'm all in."

"That's what's up. Call me when you finish getting yourself together."

I hung up that phone and practically jumped for joy. *Finally,* I thought. Not only was Stu handsome but he was single, childless, and, most importantly, he had his own apartment. I couldn't remember the last time I visited a guy at his place.

About an hour later, I was on my way to Harlem. I called Stu to let him know that I was en route. Once I got to the Queensboro Bridge, I decided to call up my girl, Ebony. I needed her to keep me company during my drive to Uptown.

What I loved about Ebony most was that she was such a free spirit. She made me look like a schoolgirl when it came to men. And no matter how wretched her behavior was, she always found some kind of excuse to justify why she had done it.

"Hey, bitch!" Ebony yelled excitedly into the phone.

"Hey, slut!" I said, yelling right back at her. "What do you know good, girl?"

Ebony began laughing. "Not a damn thing, girl! What are you getting into today, hot stuff?" she asked. "I can hear the mischief in your voice."

"Do you remember the guy I went out with last night?"

"Oh, yes, I remember. I didn't get a chance to hear about him yet."

"Well, I'm about to tell you about him. His name is Stuart Childs, he's a promoter, he's single with no children and . . ." I waited for Ebony to finish whooping and hollering on the other end. I knew that my girl was genuinely happy for me. "And he has a condo in Harlem. That's where I'm going right now! I really didn't expect for him to call my ass back," I said, shaking my head at the memory of our date.

Ebony began laughing. "Oh, God! What did you do?"

I laughed. "Why are you asking me what I did?"

"Because you're always into something, Phoenix! As bougie as you may act in front of other people, I already know how you really get down, you harlot!" Ebony replied, with more laughter.

I gave Ebony a quick recap of the date with Stu. By the end of my story, Ebony was hysterical. At one point, I had to yell into the phone just to get her to stop laughing at me.

"Okay, okay, so let me get this shit straight," Ebony began. "You got pissy drunk, offered this man some sex, and he turned you down?"

"Stu was a complete gentleman, Eb. He didn't lay one hand, finger, or nothing on me and I was the one who acted like a fool. I even called Shanell up to tell her that I thought that man was all kinds of faggots and whatnot just because he didn't sleep with me. Now he wants me to come to his house for some dinner and conversation. Do you think I should give him some sex or let him wait on it?"

"I don't know what that man is trying to do now, Phoenix, but the reason that he probably didn't give you any is because you were drunk out of your mind. Thank God, he didn't take advantage by having sex with you while you were in that condition. That's rape, you know!"

I sucked my teeth at the mere mention of the word "rape." Ebony always took her thoughts to the extreme. And besides, I wasn't that damn drunk—I knew exactly what I wanted. Stu didn't give me what I wanted and I was upset about it. Simple as that.

"Come on with this rape shit, Ebony!" I continued my story. "Anyway, who wouldn't want to lay up with all of this gorgeousness?"

"Please!" Ebony said, dismissing my boasting. "I know you think that you're the bomb and all but it's always that one, that one dude who will make you feel like the bottom of an old, raggedy shoe! Not saying that Stu is like that but I think that these men target attractive women just to break them down and build themselves up—make the woman feel as if she's unworthy of being loved and—"

Ebony was definitely going somewhere else with this topic—maybe she was talking about herself because she damn sure wasn't talking about me.

I immediately cut her off. "Hello? What in the hell are you talking about?" I asked, with a confused look on my face.

"I'm talking about you and Stu, crazy!" she replied.

"Nuh uh! You're not talking about me and Stu! You must be talking about you and Dray, honey bunch!"

I respected everything that Ebony was saying but my intentions for right then were to have sex with Stu. Then I was going to let his fine ass do some chasing before I decided to give him some more of me. I felt that I was worth every bit of the marathon that Stu was about to run.

"I never got that from any of the men I dealt with. I always had dudes who were more than honored to be with a woman of my stature."

Ebony laughed. "Oh, really? So where are these men now? Oh, excuse me, I forgot! Those men are with their wives and girlfriends," she said, sounding like a true hater.

That hurt but I was a good sport and laughed it off. "Go to hell!" I said, with a chuckle.

As I made my way to Stu's house, Ebony and I continued to talk each other's heads off about the things that were going on in our lives. She filled me in on her breakup with Dray, who I always felt was a fucking sleaze bucket. They started off as friends but as usual, Ebony ended up fucking him. She made that Negro her world and he took her for granted. I didn't know how she lasted so long but she was my ace so I had to pretend to empathize with her.

"Are you okay, Ebony?" I asked after she finished telling me about Dray. It sounded like she was crying.

"Yeah, I'm cool." She sniffed. "I had to get over that motherfucker real quick, though. He moved on so I had to move on. Anyway, my company just left, or should I say my overnight company?"

We both giggled.

"Damn, that was quick! Who spent the night with you, you trollop?"

"The young girl Saadia's cousin, this guy named Mateo. Her family had a homecoming party for Mateo's brother last night and I just happened to go with her and Mateo and I couldn't take our eyes off each other! We were supposed to go out to breakfast after the party but there was a change of plans. Our night ended right in my bed, child."

"So does that mean that it's officially over for Mr. Dray? No backsies, right?" I asked, crossing my fingers at the same time.

"Yes, it does." Ebony sighed.

"So do you really like this Mateo guy?"

Ebony sighed again. "That's the thing, girl, I don't. He's a cool guy and everything but he was just too much, too soon! I mean, I was seriously ready for the Negro to take his ass home—he overstayed his welcome! Like, damn . . . why can't these guys just get the booty and then leave when you want them to?"

"Funny thing is if you were really into this Mateo, he would have just fucked you and got the hell up outta your house with the quickness!" We laughed. "These men ain't shit, girl. I'm telling you!"

"You ain't never lie," Ebony agreed.

It was almost forty-five minutes later when I pulled up in front of the address that Stu had given me. Ebony and I hung up so that I could call Stu and let him know that I had arrived safely. I just had to find some parking.

When I finally walked up to Stu's building, I must say that I was impressed. The condos had large windows and nice-sized balconies, too. And the area that Stu lived in was totally gentrified. The Harlem that I remembered was predominantly Black at one time. Now, there were White people everywhere, pushing their little bald-headed Gerber babies in their Maclaren baby strollers and walking dogs of any and every breed you could think of.

Stu buzzed me into the building. I pressed for the sixth floor in the elevator. As I got closer to my destination, I began to get very nervous. When I finally was standing in front of Stu's door, I felt as if I was going to faint.

I rang the bell and in five seconds, Stu opened the door. He kissed me, even gave some tongue, and not surprisingly, he was a hell of kisser.

I wiped my lipstick off his lips. "Hey, Stu!" I said, with a smile. "Looks like someone is really happy to see me."

"Why wouldn't I be happy to see you?" he asked, leading me by my hand into the living room area. I took a quick glance around Stu's condo. To say that it was just fly was an understatement. The exposed brick, the stainless steel kitchen appliances, and the granite countertops were nice touches to the modernized condominium.

"I absolutely love your place," I said. "And that fireplace is amazing," I added.

"Thanks, babe. Wait until the wintertime. We could cuddle up by the artificial fire. You're going to love that."

I looked at Stu with a big smile on my face. "Oh, so what are you saying? Are you saying that I'm going to be around that long?"

"After tonight, you just might be," Stu replied, giving me a flirtatious look.

"Okay, I hear that," I said, nodding my head.

Stu took me by the hand again and led me into the dining area. He had the place settings, some candles, and wine glasses already on the table. He even had a vase full of fresh flowers. It looked like he had really put some thought into our dinner date.

"You like?" he asked, admiring his own effort.

"Like? I love! It's great!" I replied.

Stu pulled out the chair for me to sit down. "I want you to relax while I serve you the meal that I prepared."

I watched as Stu walked into the kitchen and began opening up containers. I could see that he had ordered the food from some restaurant.

"So, um, I can see that you took the time to prepare the food for tonight's dinner," I said, with a laugh, humoring him.

Stu looked around at the food. "Man, listen! I have to keep it real . . . I'm not the best cook in the world. I can fry some chicken, make a hell of a hamburger, and breakfast is my best meal; just don't ask me to make grits," he replied. We shared a laugh about that. "So instead of killing you with my cooking, I decided to go to the Lemon Life and pick up this food for us. I hope you like Japanese food."

"I love Japanese," I gushed, looking at how beautiful everything looked.

"Good." Stu brought the food to the table so that he could serve me. Then he pulled out a chilled bottle of Pinot Grigio and poured some into my wine glass. He put some food on our plates, we said our grace, and one minute later, we were digging in.

"This food is delicious," I said, stuffing a California roll into my mouth. "Delicious."

Stu held up his glass so that we could do a toast. "To good food, great times, and even better company."

I blushed. We tapped the glasses and took some sips.

Stu and I ate our food and had some really great conversation. We discussed business ventures and even shared a stock tip or two. There was nothing more attractive than a man with business and street savvy. *What a catch*. After dinner, we took our glasses of wine to the sofa to continue our talk in front of the fireplace. Stu's dialogue, his looks—his whole swag made my lower regions moist. He was even sexier than what I originally thought he was.

Stu picked up the Bose remote control and turned up the slow jams. While a Donell Jones song played on his docked iPod, Stu put his glass down on the glass center table. He pulled me up from the sofa and began slow dancing with me. As we danced, he lifted up my chin and pulled my face to his. We were both caught up in the moment so we kissed. And we kissed and kissed again. He took the glass out of my hand and put it down next to his. That was when things began getting hotter.

I fell back onto the couch and Stu got on top of me. We began dry humping—I could feel the erection through his pants. So I started massaging it for him. Damn, Stu's dick was nice, too. He was harder than Chinese arithmetic under them sweats of his. That was definitely a plus for me. I opened my legs wider, ready to receive every inch of him. After all, the Negro did owe me a good lay, considering the way he had snubbed me earlier that morning.

But before things got too hot and heavy, I decided to make a trip to the bathroom. I hated holding my pee while having sex. "Wait, wait, Stu," I whispered. The grinding felt so good, I really didn't want him to stop. But nature was calling and I had to answer. "I have to go to the bathroom."

Stu sat back on the couch. His dick was protruding through his pants, looking like the Leaning Tower of Pisa. I didn't realize that he had a crooked rod until that moment.

Looking at his dick had me not wanting to waste any more time. "Where's your bathroom?" I asked.

Stu pointed toward a long foyer leading to the back of his condo. I headed in that direction to the john.

Now one of the things that I did when I was visiting a man's home was inspect his bathroom. The type of items I looked for were anything belonging to another woman, like an extra toothbrush, some women's deodorant, hairpins, tampons, etc. *And you never know what kind of medications a brother may have in his stash so I must look through his medicine cabinet, too.* I didn't want to end up with a nut on some kind of psych medication like Zoloft and Paxil. *You never can be too careful these days.*

I walked into the bathroom and immediately locked the door behind me. Of course, I took a quick pee-pee but I didn't flush the toilet right away. I went right to Stu's medicine cabinet to look inside of it. He had the usual toiletries: some Old Spice deodorant, Crest Pro Health toothpaste, Band-Aids, Bacitracin ointment, and all that. Then there were some prescription bottles in there with his name on them. He had some penicillin, some amoxicillin, and there was another bottle of medication named valaciclovir. I had never in my life heard of that one.

"What the hell is a valaciclovir?" I wondered. I quickly snatched my phone out of my jeans pocket and called Ebony.

"Hello?" she answered.

I looked at the bathroom door and began whispering. I gave Ebony the correct spelling of the medication. "Listen, girl," I began. "I don't have the time to look this up right now and I need to know what it's for. Hit me back as soon as you can. I can't stay in this bathroom too much longer."

Thank God, Ebony already knew the drill. "I got you. I'll look it up for you right now."

"Cool."

I disconnected the phone call and flushed the toilet. I slowly closed the medicine cabinet door and washed my hands. Then I crept out of the bathroom and headed back into the living room.

When I got there, Stu was standing there half-naked in his Burberry drawers. I had to admit, his body was very nice. And as much as I wanted to give him a blow job to die for, I wasn't putting my lips on nothing until I got that text back from Ebony.

Stu kissed me then I reminded him of one important component—a condom.

"I'll be back," Stu said, giving me another peck on the lips. "I have to get a condom from my bedroom," he added.

While Stu was in his bedroom, my phone began vibrating. I snatched it out of my pocket and looked at Ebony's text:

"Girl, get the fuck up out of that man's house!" she wrote. "That medication is used for the herpes virus! Stu got the herps, girl!"

That was all I had to see. I was out of there!

While Stu was still in his bedroom, rummaging around for a condom, I kindly gathered up my things. Then I ran to the front door, unlocked it, and jetted down the stairwell. I made a beeline for my car, got cranked up, and was heading back to Queens all within three minutes. By the time I turned the corner of his block, Stu was blowing up my phone but I kept sending his calls to voicemail.

Chapter 11

Be Happy

Ebony

After Mateo left and the laughter from Phoenix's hilarious escapade had stopped, I was left to face a bitter reality—I was officially a single woman. This was always a title that I had never been proud of. It seemed as if single women were categorized as lonely desperadoes or just plain crazy. That was why she was by herself, people would say. I didn't know about other women but, to me, having a boyfriend or husband was so much more respected.

I hadn't had the time to grieve over the loss of Dray—not that I could say I wanted to. Our breakup was a long time coming. Dray's wrongdoings were brought to the forefront but I still tried to understand where did *I* go wrong in the relationship? I thought that I was doing the right thing by choosing to be exclusive with one man. Unfortunately, Dray made me realize that he was never really worth all the effort. *Just look at the thanks that I got in return.*

When and why Dray decided to move this woman, Anisa, into his apartment was beyond me. We had discussed moving in with each other about a year ago but nothing ever came into fruition. Then this mystery woman came along and—voilà!—she's his girlfriend, they're moving in together, and I was sure that they were making plans for their future. Meanwhile, I didn't have a clue as to where my own love life was headed. I didn't know who or what type of man turned me on anymore. Half of the men I had sex with were not even remotely close to being someone I would have a future with, and I knew this. Then the other half were unavailable or gay.

There were also my control issues. In my mind, I always believed that I could control any man with my vagina. It was a known fact that most men are slaves when it comes to the pussy and I had sung this same tune for most of my adult years. Just like my male counterparts, sex for me had almost become habitual. Having casual sex with someone was so much easier than actually being in love with the person.

Now it was a Saturday night, the day after the Dray saga. There I was sitting in my bedroom, browsing the Internet on my laptop with absolutely nothing to do, no one to call. The emptiness that I felt was beginning to get the best of me.

So at the last minute, I decided to treat myself to a dinner and maybe a glass of wine or two. It wasn't like I had anything else going on. I took a quick shower and then threw on a pair of tight-fitting jeans and my favorite T-shirt. I hopped into my car, not having any idea as to where I was headed. I ended up at this restaurant named Peaches, located in the Bed-Stuy area. There was usually a very eclectic crowd there, which was right up my alley.

When I arrived at Peaches, I discovered that it was a Saturday night hotspot. Most of the tables were occupied with patrons, and the bar was, too. I wanted to get a window seat, which was adorned with fluffy colorful pillows. But from the looks of the crowd, that wasn't going to happen anytime soon. It was a full house.

Fortunately for me, someone left the bar just as I walked in and I was able to get a seat. The bartender came over to me almost immediately and I ordered myself a glass of Moscato. Before I could reach in my bag for money, a tall, dark-skinned gentleman walked over to me. He offered to pay for my drink.

I was grateful for the kind gesture. "Thanks," I said, smiling at him.

The guy smiled back at me. He had the cutest little smile and that was when I noticed his boyish good looks.

"It was not a problem, babe," he replied, accepting his change from the bartender and leaving a tip.

He stood beside my seat at the bar. "I noticed you when you walked in. I said to myself, 'Now there goes a cutie pie!'" I blushed. "But I was also wondering why you were here by yourself? Are you waiting for some-body?" he asked, with a curious look on his face.

I sipped my drink and shook my head. "Nope. I'm here alone," I replied.

The handsome stranger held out his hand for me to shake it. "Well, in that case let me introduce myself. My name is Westin Davis. But all my people call me Wes. What's your name, babe?"

I shook his hand and smiled. "The name is Ebony Harris and it's a pleasure to meet you, Wes," I said.

"The pleasure is all mine," he replied, smiling back at me.

Wes ordered an Absolut with cranberry for himself. Someone sitting next to us excused himself and he was able to sit on the stool beside me.

"So, Wes, who are you here with?" I asked, sipping on my Moscato.

He took a sip of his drink too. "Man, I was in here earlier with two of my boys. We had some food, some drinks, and I was in the process of leaving; that is, until I saw you. So I walked outside with them and acted like I was getting into my truck. When they pulled off, I got out of my vehicle and came back inside just to talk to you. You caught my attention."

I let out a hearty laugh. "You mean to tell me that you ditched your friends for me?" I asked, pointing at myself. If that was the truth, it was extremely flattering.

"Of course, I did! It was no way those cats would have let me have a peaceful moment with you! Trust me, they would have been getting jokes on me! Those cats are embarrassing!"

I shook my head. "Sounds like those friends of yours are a piece of work."

Wes sighed. "Yes, they are."

We continued to have a random chat with each other for the next half hour.

"Are you hungry?" Wes asked.

I patted my stomach. "Yes, I am. I was going to ask for a menu . . ."

Wes called the bartender over. "Um, yes, could I have a menu for this young lady?" he asked, pointing at me. The bartender obliged and handed me a menu from behind the bar. "You could order whatever you want, babe. I got you."

I frowned. "Aren't you sweet? Let me find out that you're trying to—"

Wes cut me off. "Nah! It's not what you're thinking at all! I'm not trying to ask for anything in return except your phone number."

I breathed a sigh of relief. "Oh, okay," I replied, looking over the menu.

I felt Wes looking at me. His stare felt as if it was burning holes on the side of my face.

"Yes? May I help you, Wes?" I asked, without looking up from the menu.

"You are a very beautiful woman, do you know that?"

I appreciated the compliments but I couldn't help but think that Wes had an agenda. I was too afraid to trust any man at that point, especially after the way Dray had done me. I decided that I wasn't going to get my hopes up too high when it came to the opposite sex. Wes and I would probably exchange numbers, go out on a few dates, and I would end up fucking him just like I did with the rest of the men I met. Same old shit. But fucking them and leaving them alone seemed like a much better deal than trying to pretend that it was going to be anything more than that. I was so tired of being hurt.

"Um, thank you, Wes. You're fine too."

He chuckled a little. I assumed he was amused with my nonchalant attitude. I was right.

"No, seriously, Ebony, you're a beautiful woman and I'm not just talking about your looks. Has anyone ever told you that?"

I rolled my eyes. "Yeah, they did—when they wanted something from me. You don't even know me."

Wes shook his head and moved his chair closer to me.

"I know that I don't know you but check this out, I'm a great judge of character. I felt your aura when you walked through that front door. I even ditched my dudes to talk to you. And trust me, I get pussy so it's not about that. That shit means nothing to me. When I saw you I said, now there's a woman I wouldn't mind spending some of my time with—that's why I'm sitting here with you right now."

I felt like crying. Not because I was holding on to every word that came out of Wes's mouth but because

I was thinking about how Dray had never once said those words to me. He would come out with the "I love you's" and the "oh, baby baby's" every now and again. But not once, not once did I remember him saying that I had a beautiful spirit or even that I was gorgeous. Dray just wanted what he wanted out of me. He had a friend in me already so I was the obvious choice at that time.

Then a light bulb went off in my head. There was something about Dray that I didn't recognize until that moment. I thought about his new girlfriend and some of his women from the past. They all had one thing in common: they had lighter skin than I did. Now the demise of my relationship all made sense to me. I realized that I just wasn't a preference of his.

"So you really think that I'm beautiful, do you?" I asked after ordering my food.

"Hell yeah!" Wes exclaimed, not missing a beat. "Honestly, I always had this thing for dark-skinned women and I'm a dark-skinned man. I love the smoothness of your skin and you have some nice features—nice eyes, lips, nose . . ."

My eyes were slanted, my nose was straight, and my full lips were the reason that white women had their lips injected. People always said that I favored that booty model, Kenya Moore.

"So you like dark-skinned women, huh?" I asked, giving him the side eye.

Wes sucked his teeth. "Hell, yeah!" He moved closer to me. "Let me explain something to you, I love my people, babe! I don't do white girls, Spanish chicks love me but I don't love them back. Lighter-skinned women are always trying to make a dude believe that I'm supposed to run after them! Plus, my mother was a beautiful dark-skinned woman. Why wouldn't I love a woman who favors my mother?"

I nodded my head. He did have a good point. In the short time I had known him, I was learning a lot from Wes. He seemed like he was a very wise man and I liked that.

"Wes, I hope you don't mind me asking but how old are you?"

"I'm forty years old. I'm about to be forty-one in July."

Damn! I thought. I could have sworn that we were around the same age. Not saying that forty is old but Wes was considerably older than the men I had dated in the past.

"How old are you, babe?" Wes asked, taking a sip of his drink.

"I'm thirty-three. I'll be thirty-four in December."

"Sagittarius, huh?" I nodded my head. "You're a fire sign! You just might steam this crab!"

I frowned. "What is that supposed to mean?" I asked, thinking that the statement was a sexual innuendo.

Wes put up his hands. "Hey, I didn't mean anything by that. It's just that Cancer the Crab is a water sign and Sagittarius the Archer is a fire sign. And don't you need water to put fires out?"

"Absolutely!"

We shared a laugh but then my mind began to wander. In the midst of me having a nice time with Wes, I was still thinking about Dray. I shook my head at the thought and Wes looked at me strangely.

"Are you okay, babe? Seems like you have a lot on your mind."

"I'll be okay," I said, giving him a fake smile.

About two minutes later, my food came. I immediately began digging in. After a few bites, I wiped the sides of my mouth with the napkin and sat back in the seat. I didn't have much of an appetite, after all.

Wes laid his hand on mine. "I know you will, babe."

The entire time that I was at Peaches, Wes stayed there with me and talked. Throughout our conversation, I found out that Wes had been a firefighter for seventeen years. He also had two teenage sons and had recently divorced from his wife of fifteen years. I didn't know the woman but from what he was saying, she sounded like she was on the verge of losing her mind. But I was sure that her mental instability wasn't all of her fault. I could only imagine what Wes's fine ass had put that poor woman through. By the end of our night, Wes was asking me out on a date.

"So would you like to go out with me this weekend?" he asked while we stood outside of the restaurant. "I really would like to see you again."

I hesitated. "Well . . ." I didn't know what to say.

Honestly, Wes was a little "mature" by my standards. I was in my early thirties and he was in his early forties. I didn't think that we would have anything in common. He'd been married before, he had teenage children, and he was very manly. I wasn't ready for that. I could see myself calling him every now and again but I figured that I would put him on the back burner for now.

Wes stopped me before I went any further. "Look, Ebony, it's no rush. Would you rather we just talk on the phone for a while before we see each other again? My divorce has just been finalized a month ago. We both don't need to rush into anything. I know that you're not ready to see other people and I'm not ready for anything serious."

I smiled. "We can do the phone for a while. I think that that would be more appropriate."

Wes gave me a hug. "No problem, babe. I'm going to respect your wishes. But that doesn't mean that I'm not going to ask you out again. We can take our time. Cool?" he asked, giving me a fist bump.

I chuckled. "That's cool, Wes. And again, thanks for everything. I really enjoyed our night."

Wes flashed that million-dollar smile of his. "I enjoyed *you,* babe. Until we meet again."

I waved at him and got into my driver's seat. I watched as Wes hopped into his Range Rover and pulled off. After he left, I sat there for a while, contemplating my next move and tried to snap myself out of the funk that I was in. Meeting sexy-ass old man Wes just wasn't enough for me to fulfill the void that I felt. Like an addict, I was in desperate need of a sexual fix. I looked through my cell phone to see who I could call to help me out.

Chapter 12

Love Is All We Need

Phoenix

It was a beautiful Sunday morning and I was awakened by the sounds of little birdies chirping in the trees outside of my open window. The clock on my nightstand said 10:05 A.M. Amazingly, I felt very refreshed. I was surprised at how well rested I felt, considering the chain of events that had occurred during the weekend. *Guess I really needed that sleep.*

Once I got myself together, I thought about Stu and scratched my head. I cracked myself up, finding it hard to believe that I had met and lost a dude all in one weekend. It was a damn shame.

"Phoenix, I'm sorry if I did anything to offend you," Stu said, on the very last message that he left on my voicemail. "Please call me back!"

The poor guy sounded so genuine that I picked up that phone and begun dialing his phone number. But after the sixth number, I decided against it. The images of that herpes prescription bottle kept popping into my head and I wasn't the one to be dealing with the nasty shit that homeboy had going on in his pants. *Yuck.*

I sat up in my bed for a brief second. Then I plopped back down onto my fluffy pillows. I thought about the busy week that I had ahead of me. Plus, I was fucking horny! It sure would have been nice if a chick could have got her some disease-free vitamin D over the weekend. Shit, masturbation just wasn't going to cut it. I had been doing that for the past couple of months. My hands were cramped up and my dildos were burnt out. And there was no way I was going to the Pink Pussycat for any new sex toys. I needed some real sex with a real dude to put me on chill mode. And at the rate I was going, that didn't seem like it was going to happen anytime soon.

My growling stomach made me get up out of bed a little faster. While I made myself a hearty Sunday breakfast, I did my usual self-reflection. After the Stu incident, I realized that it was time for me to change. The deep-rooted issues that I had with being in a committed relationship were going to have to be dealt with head on or else I was going to be by my damn self, like Shanell said. After all, I was thirty-two years old and my biological clock was ticking. What the hell was I waiting for?

Now that I had made the decision to think about settling down, I was scared to death. I had this list of demands that was a mile long! This was because I didn't want to settle for something or someone I didn't want.

Thirty minutes later, I had the 'itis after eating some pancakes, turkey bacon, and egg whites. I was heading back to my bedroom for another nappy nap when suddenly my doorbell rang. I wasn't expecting any visitors and I stood in the middle of my living room, wondering if I should pretend that I wasn't home.

"Who is it?" I said with an attitude after I cautiously tiptoed to the front door. I would have had a fit if Stu, the walking STD, was standing out there in the hallway. I looked through the peephole and breathed a sigh of relief when I saw who it was.

"It's me, tramp!" Shanell said from the other side of the door. "Open up! I got some mimosas for us."

At the mere mention of mimosas, in true alcoholic fashion I immediately flung open the door. Shanell walked in with a shopping bag in her hand. As soon as she stepped over the threshold and into the hallway of my apartment, we gave each other a big hug.

"What brings you out here this early in the morning?" I asked, genuinely happy to see her.

I followed Shanell into the kitchen. She began removing articles from the shopping bag. I clapped my hands at the sight of the Moët bottle.

Shanell turned around to face me. "I came over to apologize for hanging up on you yesterday. I am so sorry, girl. I didn't mean to get upset with you about this whole Stu thing. You and I were girls way before his ass came into the picture."

I hugged her again. "It's okay. I should be apologizing to you for playing myself with your boy."

She waved me off and slid onto one of my barstools. "Stu told me that you came by his house last night."

I took a quick sip of my drink. I tried to remain calm, wondering what Stu had told Shanell about me. "Yep, I sure did." *Men talk just as much as women! Sheesh!*

"So what happened?" Shanell said excitedly.

I told Shanell about the dinner at Stu's, how much I enjoyed it, blah, blah, blah. And that's all I told her. I couldn't bring myself to tell her that I had practically run out of that man's house because I suspected that he had some sexually transmitted disease. There was no need to hear that kind of information from me.

"When did you speak to Stu?" I asked, curious to know when this phone call to Shanell had occurred.

"He called my house to speak to Majesty last night. I guess it was shortly after you left his apartment."

Correction—got the fuck up outta dodge! I just nodded my head. "Oh, okay," was all that I said. I wanted
to laugh so badly.

Shanell poured some more Moët and Tropicana orange juice into the flutes. "It doesn't sound like you're
really interested in pursuing anything with Stu. I mis-
takenly thought that you guys were hitting it off considering how quickly you were about to give him some yum
yums the other night," she said, with a slight chuckle.

I smiled. "Nah, Stu is a cool dude but he doesn't
have to be the only man I talk to," I replied, sipping my
drink. "And yes, I like Stu, but the real reason I was going to give him some the other night was not because I
was into him. I was just hornier than a mug! I ain't fuck
a man in nine months!"

Shanell laughed. "You are a head case, girl!" She took
a sip of her drink. "Look, I don't want you to think that
I'm prying into your life or anything. I just want what's
best for you, Phoenix. You're like family to me. Sometimes I feel guilty about being happily married when
my closest friend and my favorite cousin can't even
find a decent man out here. Not to say that Majesty is
an angel but I do know that he loves me and treats me
like a queen. I just want that same thing for you and
Capri. Am I wrong for that?"

I was shocked to hear that Shanell felt like this. After
all, me finding a husband or a man was more of my
worry than hers. It was thoughtful of her to think about
my happiness.

I rubbed her back. "You don't have to feel that way,"
I said, comforting my friend. "I believe that it's a good
man out there for me and Capri, and my girls, Joi and
Ebony too. I'm gonna pray for us all."

"Wow!" Shanell said at the mention of Joi's and Ebony's names. "What's up with those ladies? I haven't seen Miss Ebony in a minute. And that Joi," Shanell said, rolling her eyes. "Is she still going through it with her man and his baby mama?"

I sucked my teeth. "Of course, she is! That broad Dara is bat-shit crazy! My people who know Dara put me on to her. Word on the street is that the little girl is not even Tate's daughter. But I'm not telling Joi no shit like that. You know what people do to the messenger of bad news . . ."

Me and Shanell chimed in at the same time. "Shoot them!" we said in unison.

"Thank you!" I replied. "I'm not telling Joi nothing about Tate. I ain't trying to get cussed out by no woman over her man. If she likes it, I love it!"

"Shit, I always say if any one of my friends hears about Majesty doing something, please, don't hesitate to tell me a thing. I want to know about these rumors so I can do my investigating. But the problem nowadays is that you can't even be an honest friend to these bitches nowadays! Either she thinks that you want her trifling-ass man for yourself, or her dumb ass ends up telling her man the 411 that you gave her about him. Of course, the man is going to get pissed at you because you're looking out for your homegirl! I just can't do it!"

I sighed. "I know, girl, I know. As much as I hate to admit it, Joi is getting back what she dished out. Not to talk about my people but shit, if it was me, I would say the same damn thing about myself. Dara was Tate's girlfriend first, way before Joi came along and rained on her parade. Now Joi is getting the payback for moving in on that woman's relationship. And to think that after four years, Tate ain't marrying either one of them bitches."

"I don't understand some women . . ." Shanell said.

I zoned out, thinking about what I would do in that situation. It wasn't like I hadn't ever rained on another woman's parade before. That's was probably the reason my ass wasn't married or had a man. Karma is a bitch, I tell you.

"There you go with that daydreaming again!" Shanell said, after she had to finger-snap me back to reality. "What in the hell do you be thinking about, girl?"

I gave Shanell a fake smile and quickly changed the subject. Men were something else. But us women? We just made it so much fucking easier for them bastards to do their dirt.

Chapter 13

Family Affair

Joi

The next morning, Tate got up out of bed before me. By the time I opened my eyes, he was already showered and half dressed.

I sat up in the bed and stretched. "What's up, babe?" I asked, rubbing the sleep out of my eyes. "Where are you going?"

Tate slid into his jeans. "I have to leave early. I have these tickets to take Chasity to the UniverSoul Circus today."

"Oh, okay," I said, trying hard to hide my disappointment. I secretly wished that I could join them but that wasn't going to happen. We both knew this.

Tate put on his sweater and leaned over to give me a kiss. I gave him a smooch on the lips and he screwed up his face.

"Make sure you brush your teeth, too . . . Your dragon is on fire!"

I playfully shoved him and covered my mouth with my hand. "You are so silly, Tate!" I replied, with a laugh. I watched as he put on his Timberland boots and a Yankees baseball cap.

"So is Dara going with you and Chasity?" I asked. I just had to know. The curiosity was killing me.

Tate shook his head. I could tell that he was trying not to catch an attitude. He hated when I asked him about Dara.

"Dara is not going with us, okay?" he said slowly, talking to me like I was mentally challenged. "Me and my boys are taking our kids to the circus. Is that okay with you?"

I sucked my teeth. I would have hated to know that Dara was going with my man and her kid to the circus and I wasn't. I didn't give a shit if Chasity was her daughter or not.

"Did you want me to make you something to eat before you go?" I asked, trying to stall him.

Tate threw his jacket on. "No, sweetheart, I'm good. I gotta run home and get these tickets, pick up Chasity, and meet up with my dudes near the entrance of Roy Wilkins Park in Queens at twelve." He kissed me again. "Aren't you going to Miss Renee's house today?"

I fell back onto the bed. "Don't remind me! Payne is gonna be all the way turned up today and my mother is gonna drive me up the wall with all her nagging and talking over everybody."

Tate laughed. He thought that Payne was hilarious and he adored my mother. Truthfully speaking, he probably liked my family more than I did.

"Well, go over there and try to have a good day with Mom Dukes and your family. Tell Miss Renee that I said hello and don't forget to bring me home a plate."

I would have loved for Tate to come with me but I knew that his rug rat came first. Damn, that little girl was such a distraction.

"Anyway, I'm out. It's a little after ten and I have to be on the Belt Parkway before eleven. You know that the Sunday traffic is crazy."

I got up from the bed to see Tate to the door. Before he walked out, we shared yet another kiss. I loved those tender moments between us. I stood by the window and watched as Tate climbed into his truck and pulled off. Once he was gone, my insecurities began kicking in. Every time Tate did something with Chasity, I felt that way.

I still was up in arms as to how I was going to prove that Chasity was not my man's child. I had mentioned it to Mercuri but that was going to be the last time she heard anything like that from me until I found out the truth. No need to continuously make a fool of myself and I wasn't doing shit about it. I had a few ideas in mind as to what and how I was going to do it but I just had to play a different role when it came to Chasity in order to get it done. I was sure that Tate would be more than surprised and happy with my newfound attitude, which was exactly how I needed him to be.

I prepared myself a light breakfast with a cup of coffee. Then I proceeded to get dressed for a day at my mother's. After I took a nice, hot shower and moisturized my body, I squeezed my big butt into a pair of designer jeans, applied a light touch of makeup, and flat-ironed my hair.

It was one o'clock in the afternoon when I began my excursion to my mother's house in Queens from my East New York apartment. I had to say me a prayer as soon as I slid my behind in the driver's seat of my Toyota Camry. Lord knows I needed every ounce of my strength to deal with my dysfunctional family.

My mother still lived in Hollis, Queens, in the very same house that my brother and I had grown up in. It was a quaint home, just big enough for the three people who lived in it. As a little girl, I used to love being in my powder pink–colored bedroom with my canopy bed, all white furniture and vanity mirror, pretending that I was a fairy princess. Even then, I used to dream of some Prince Charming sweeping me off my feet.

Then there were the fond memories of my maternal grandparents. They were both deceased but we used to look forward to them coming to visit and staying with us for weeks at a time. They used to take care of me and Payne while my mother worked her regular job and then her weekend job at a local bar. Those were some of my happiest memories.

While driving on the Belt Parkway, I thought about my old block buddies. The friends I use to play hop-scotch, skelly, and double Dutch with were now grown, married with children, and long gone from the neigh-borhood. It was funny how I had neither. Of course, this bothered me. But my day was coming. At least, I hoped my day was coming.

It was almost 2:30 in the afternoon when I pulled up in front of my mother's house. Cars were already lined up in the driveway, which meant that everyone was there, everyone except me. I rolled my eyes as I walked by my brother's brand-new Porsche Cayenne. I swear he was such a show-off.

I rang the bell and my niece, Rayni, opened the door. She was about an inch taller than my five feet four inches, and was absolutely adorable. She looked like a prettier version of her father.

I hugged her tightly. "Hey, baby!" I greeted her with a smile and almost lifted her off her feet. "You look so cute! I love the hair," I said, admiring her long weave. "A little grownish but it's very nice."

Rayni blushed. "Auntie," she began, leaning her weight on me. "I'm seventeen years old and a senior in high school, you know! This is how most of the girls are wearing their hair now."

I kissed her on the cheek. "Yes, you are a senior and seventeen years old now. You're growing up so fast, I swear."

We both walked into the living room together. All of the people who were supposed to be there were obviously sitting around and waiting for me. Auntie Gina walked over to me first and gave me a wonderful hug. Out of my mother's three brothers and two sisters, Auntie Gina was our favorite aunt. She and my mother were extremely close, too.

"Hey, baby," she said. "You look great! How are you, Niecey?" she asked, calling me by the pet name she had for me.

"I feel good, Auntie," I said. I looked at Auntie Gina from head to toe. "You look like you lost some weight, too."

Auntie Gina blushed and waved me off. "I did lose some weight!" she said, posing for me. "I'm having lots of sex, baby," she whispered. I laughed at her. She took my hand and led me over to the couch where her male friend was sitting. He was a nice-looking man, very handsome and distinguished looking with salt-and-pepper hair. Auntie Gina introduced him to me and he stood up to shake my hand.

"Hello, Joi, I'm Harold," he said. "I've heard so much about you."

"I hope some good things," I said.

We all laughed. "Nothing but!" he replied.

Suddenly, my mother and Payne, her daughter/son and my brother/sister, sashayed into the living room wearing matching aprons. They had just set the table in the dining room. My mother smiled when she saw me. She gave me a kiss on the cheek and Payne just waved at me from afar.

"Oh, Joi, I'm so glad you're here," my mother said. Then she looked at my outfit and stopped in her tracks. "I thought you were going to wear something a little dressier than that, though," she added, giving me a disapproving stare. She was definitely showing off for Auntie Gina's man. "Payne decided to get dressed up for the occasion!"

I grunted. Why was there always the fucking comparison between me and Payne? And what occasion? I had to admit that Payne was looking extra dapper in a pair of tweed slacks, an argyle sweater vest, and a bowtie but that was him. He always overdid it.

"You look wonderful, Niecey. I love what you're wearing!" Auntie Gina said, knowing what time it was. She gave my mother the evil eye. Of course, my mother didn't catch her sister giving her the look.

"Yeah, you look fly, Auntie," Rayni whispered. "Grandma is just hating on you."

My niece and I shared a laugh with each other. "Well, dinner's ready everyone!" my mother announced.

We all scurried to the dining room. Dinner was on the table and everything was looking absolutely scrumptious. My mother prepared a fried turkey, macaroni and cheese, and fresh collard greens with smoked turkey. Then there were her famous candied yams with marshmallows, along with her cornbread stuffing and some gravy on the side, too. Cooking was definitely my mother's specialty.

Now if she could just work on getting and keeping a man.

Everyone took a seat at the large dining table. Rayni and I sat on one side, Auntie Gina and Harold sat on the other. Payne and Mommy, the two queens, were sitting at both ends of the table.

Then, as usual, it was time for the Payne show. He cleared his throat. "Before we bless this food, I just would like to say how happy I am to be around my wonderful family. I want to say *gracias* to my wonderful *madre,* Miss Renee Campbell, for taking the time to prepare this fabulous meal for all of us. And much love to my beautiful baby girl, Madame Rayni Campbell, who is going to be graduating from high school this June and attending Clark-Atlanta University—"

Rayni cut him off. "And don't forget that I want you to style me for my prom, Daddy!"

Everyone laughed at that comment, except me.

Payne's hands fluttered in the air. "Why, of course, my darling," Payne replied, emphasizing the word "darling." "You know that Daddy is going to laaaace his baby girl!"

He continued, "I would definitely like to give thanks to my Auntie Gina, who is the kee kee queen of the family! She is where I get my amazing sense of humor from!" Then Payne looked at my mother. "Sorry, Mother Renee!" he said, suggesting that my mother had no sense of humor at all. That much was true.

Everyone laughed, including me. "I also want to give a shout out to Mister Harold, the man who is responsible for putting that extraordinary smile on my auntie's face!" He looked at Auntie Gina and winked. "You go, girl!"

My aunt waved him off. "You are so crazy, nephew!" Auntie Gina replied.

"And last, but certainly not least, my baby sister, Joi, has come out of her cave today." He yawned and began slowly clapping. "Yippety doo dah." They all began cracking up again. I wanted to laugh but I composed myself. Payne was such a jerk-off.

"Anyway, may we bless the food now?" he said.

I flipped him the finger and Payne stuck out his tongue at me, all while my mother blessed the food. After the grace was done, we said amen and dug in.

While eating dinner, my family and I talked about the old days, like when my grandparents were still alive. Even my niece shared a few fond memories about her childhood. And a day at my mother's house would not be the same without Payne talking about his occupation, what celebrities he met, and what industry parties that he attended. After we finished eating, we all retreated to the living room, with full bellies.

Back in the living room, Payne, Mr. Attention Whore himself put on some old school music and began singing, like he was auditioning for *American Idol*. Surprisingly enough, we didn't have one argument during dinner but now it was just too much for me to bear. Harold looked uncomfortable, Auntie Gina seemed annoyed, and my mother was smiling from ear to ear. Me and Rayni opted to retire upstairs to my old bedroom and let her father have the floor.

Back in my old bedroom, I felt a sense of comfort. I wanted to go back to being Mommy's little girl and my dreams of being married to my Prince Charming. Those dreams were what kept a smile on my face. Now I spent a lot of my time angry and uptight with Tate, Dara, my brother, and my mother—I was letting these people sap all the energy out of me.

I lay across the bed and Rayni lay down next to me. She grabbed a pillow and propped her head on it.

"I know that my dad and Grandma get on your nerves, Auntie," she said.

From the mouth of babes. "And I thought it was just me," I said, shaking my head.

"Nope. It ain't just you. I notice everything. Did you see Mr. Harold's face when Daddy started singing?" We both began laughing. "I don't think he was ready for my dad's dramatics!"

"No, he wasn't! But I blame your grandmother for not telling Payne to sit his butt down. She entertains that stuff. Okay, I understand that you're a gay man but I feel that there is a time and a place for everything. Meeting your favorite aunt's man for the first time is not the time to be acting out. Unfortunately, not everyone is cool with that lifestyle."

"Are you cool with it?" Rayni asked, with an innocent look on her face.

Because Payne was her father, I was unsure of how to answer that question. I didn't have a problem with someone living an alternative lifestyle. It's just that Payne's choices had always put my mother and me in a position to have to defend him. This was a never-ending battle for us because of the rampant homophobia, especially in the African American community. Payne always had effeminate characteristics when he was a boy, and growing up he was teased because of it and so was I. I was also the one who fought his battles, yet my mother always scolded me for fighting. The only thing that I was doing was protecting my brother and his honor—I couldn't win. This was why Payne's homosexuality had always been a major issue in our family, especially to me.

I always felt that I was robbed of a normal childhood and healthy relationship with my mother because she was always so focused on Payne's well-being. This led me to have to fend for myself and this entire situation had made me bitter and resentful.

"Just put it like this, Rayni Poo: I love your daddy. Whatever choices that he made in life, I can't do anything but respect those choices."

Rayni shook her head. "I never told anyone this but it's so hard having an openly gay father."

"I know it is."

"Do you know how many fights I had over this?" she said, sounding as if she was reliving my past. "Do you know how many friends I lost because their parents didn't agree with this gay stuff, and how many boys and girls think that I'm gay or bisexual because of my dad?"

That was the first time my niece told me how she felt about her father. It was painfully obvious that she had these feelings bottled up for a long time.

"I love my father, I really do, but he has to know that not everyone agrees with the way he lives, what he represents, you know what I'm saying? I worry about him, sometimes, especially when you hear about the biased sex crimes being committed against gay men and women and the HIV cases—I don't want to lose my dad."

I put my arm around Rayni. I could tell that my brother's situation had had a serious effect on my niece as well, like I knew it would. I would have loved to talk to Payne about it but talking to him was like beating a dead horse. Besides, Rayni was only my niece. She was his daughter. That was a line that I didn't dare cross.

"Look, Rayni Poo, I know that it's not easy dealing with your dad but there's nothing you or I or even he can do to change it. Why don't you try to talk to him about toning things down?"

"I did!" she replied. "I asked him if he could stop acting so flamboyant when we're out together and he said that no one is going to stop him from being who he is, not even his own daughter. He said that he's the father, I'm the child, and that he's effing gay and everyone just needs to get over him already."

I frowned. "Really? He said that to you?" I asked, getting upset at the thought of Payne brushing his only child's feelings under the table. Not cool. No one was telling him to turn into a straight man; she just wanted him to stop with all the extras.

Rayni sighed. "Yes, my dad said that to me. So now, I don't say a thing about it. I just wonder what my future holds for me and him. Does he even stop to think about how I feel? I love him but what if I get married and my husband says that he doesn't want our children around their grandfather because he is a gay man? I always think about stuff like that."

I kissed Rayni on the cheek. "Honey, you have too much to accomplish in life to worry about your father and his life. As far as some children and a husband are concerned, you will cross that bridge when you get to it. But for now, just do what you have to do for Rayni. Live your own life, stick with the positive, and God will see you through the rest."

Rayni hugged me. "Thank you, Auntie." She looked at me. "You know that I love you, right?" she said.

"Yes, I do and I love you too, Rayni Poo."

Rayni propped her head on one arm. "By the way, when are you getting married and having some kids of your own? Tell Uncle Tate that I need some little cousins to spoil!"

I shrugged my shoulders. I didn't even know the answer to that question.

Suddenly, a knock on the door interrupted our moment.

"Come in," I said.

It was my mother. She walked into the room with a slice of her sweet potato pie in her hand. Damn, I loved that pie.

"Where's my slice, Grandma?" Rayni asked.

My mother pointed to the door. "Downstairs, baby. I need to talk to your auntie for a moment," my mother replied, handing the pie to me. I sat up on the bed and Rayni walked out of the room, closing the door behind her.

"So how are you feeling these days, Joi?" asked my mother as she watched me dig into her delicious pie.

"Fine, Ma. Just fine." My mother and I didn't have much dialogue so I was unsure of how to react to her sudden interest in me.

"I'm so glad that you took the time out to come over today, baby. I really am."

I took a good look at my mother. She was only fifty-five years old but I could see the crow's feet forming around her eyes. Aside from that, she had the body of a thirty-year-old and she was a good-looking woman. What was crazy was that the only men I remember her being with were this man named Paul, who had since moved on, and my father, who I had no contact with. Looking at her made me think that if I didn't get my shit together soon, I was going to end up just like her—manless.

"I just wanted to take this time out to have a heart-to-heart talk with you, Joi. I know that we don't always get along but I wanted to let you know that I love you. I want to make amends with you."

I was taken aback by what my mother was saying. And no, we weren't ever that close to each other because she had always made Payne a bigger priority than me.

Although we had guests, I figured that my mother was most likely seizing the moment to talk to me. I didn't come over that often so I guessed there was never really a right time for us to chat. Now I guessed that it was a better time than any for the both of us to bury the hatchet and iron out the issues that we had with each other.

"Can I ask you something, Ma?" I asked. She nodded her head. "Did you always love Payne more than you loved me?" I blurted out.

My mother shook her head. "That's absolutely ridiculous, Joi! I love you and Payne equally! You and your brother mean the world to me."

"So why does it seem like you and Payne are always ganging up on me?"

My mother sat on the canopy bed beside me and took a deep breath. I could tell that there were things that weighed heavily on her.

"Joi, I know that I haven't made the best decisions when it came to raising you and your brother. But I never said that I'm perfect."

Laughter and loud talking could be heard coming from downstairs. It sounded like one of my uncles had just walked in the house.

"And I'm going to tell you again, I don't love Payne any more than I love you. It's just that I never really had to worry about you. You've always been strong-willed and independent, and a hell of a fighter, too, even from a child. I always felt that you could take care of yourself. Trust me, I'm proud of you for that."

To hear my mother say that to me was like music to my ears but it wasn't enough to put my mind and my heart at ease. The inquisitive side of me had to dig just a little deeper. "Thanks, Ma. I love you too. But why does it always seem like you make such a big deal over Payne? Sometimes I need your undivided attention too, you know."

My mother sighed, as if she was about to bring up something that was very painful. She took my hand into hers and I immediately stopped munching on my pie.

"I never told you this, Joi but when your brother turned eighteen, he made a startling confession to me. He told me that he had been sexually molested by a family friend when he was six years old. He had held on to this secret for twelve years. Then, along with this shocking news, he confessed to me that he was gay, even though I already had an idea that he was." My mother looked up to the ceiling and then into my eyes. Her eyes felt as if they were piercing my soul. "Can you imagine what kind of torment that boy went through holding in these secrets? Not only did I almost lose my mind when he told me about the molestation, I went into protector mode, losing sight of everything! I wanted to kill somebody! Shit, at one point or another, I felt like I wanted to kill myself!"

I listened intently as my mother continued. "I blamed myself for not being there, for working so much and not giving myself enough time to spend with my babies. And when Payne told me that he was gay"—my mother closed her eyes, as if she could still feel the pain from that day—"I knew that my baby was going to have a long, hard road ahead of him. That's why I'm always jumping to his defense. I feel so guilty about what happened to him. I feel like I'm responsible."

I held back my tears. Now I was feeling like a piece of shit. "Damn, Ma, I didn't know about all of this. I'm so sorry that happened to Payne, to you. And you need to let those feelings of guilt go. Please. It wasn't your fault."

My mother wiped a tear from her cheek. "You don't have to apologize for nothing, baby. You didn't do anything wrong. I'm the one who should be apologizing to you. You didn't have your mother and you needed me. I don't want you to continue through life being bitter over the mistakes that I made when it came to you."

I put my hand on her shoulder. "I didn't know that you were going through this, Ma. And here I was, only thinking about myself. Why did you wait so long to tell me all of this?"

There was a distant look in my mother's eyes. "Because I could never find the right words or the time to tell you about this. And for years, I've been too busy doing things to ease my own pain, trying to forget that this ever happened. Now I'm all alone and I don't know how to get back to just being me."

I felt like there was another point to my mother's story. I just didn't know what it was.

She rubbed my face. "I know that I'm going in a whole 'nother direction but the point I'm trying to make is . . . I just want you to be happy, Joi. Please live your best life. Have faith in God and find a partner who is going to love and honor you."

I frowned. "Are you telling me that Tate is no good for me?"

My mother stood up and walked toward the door. She shook her head. "I'm not saying that at all. I'm just saying that you're my only daughter, I love you very much, and I just want the best for you. Do not hesitate to call on me if you need me, you hear?"

A faint smile appeared on my face. "Okay, Ma. I won't."

"That's what family is for and don't you ever forget that."

When my mother walked out of that room, I looked down at the small piece of sweet potato pie that was left on my plate. I had completely lost my appetite for it. My mother's honest, upfront conversation had softened me up. It seemed as things between my mother, Payne, and I were going to be rectified. Meanwhile, I had to work on the other issues, such as the ones I had with Tate. Also, my mother had me contemplating my future with this man. It was obvious that she saw something in me and my situation that I didn't. Now it was up to me to find out what it was, once and for all.

Chapter 14

Seven Days

Ebony

The next morning, I was still thinking about my Saturday night out. What started out as me treating myself to a quiet dinner ended up with me meeting Wes. Wes was a very attractive man and, upon talking to him, I saw that he was intelligent and had a great personality. But his grown-man confidence made me very uncomfortable. Being with someone like Wes would only make my deep-rooted insecurities go into overdrive.

After I left Peaches, I decided to get into other things besides going home to wallow in my own misery. It was a little after 9:00 P.M. and I was feeling horny as hell. Unfortunately, I couldn't think of anyone to call to scratch my itch. I scrolled through my contacts. As I went through my list of booty calls, I realized that there was no one to call. I mean, shit, this one was married, that one had just had a baby with a girlfriend, and another one was recently engaged.

I shook my head at my desperation. But shit, I was feening. All I really needed was a nice, little quickie—I didn't even want a full lovemaking session with anyone. Mateo came into mind. I could have easily called him back over for rounds three and four. His sexual performance deserved a standing ovation and he was certainly nice to look at. But after Dray had suddenly appeared on my doorstep the morning that Mateo was there, I was too embarrassed to see him again. I was sure that my ex showing up at my house unannounced put me at the top of his ho list. Mateo did not need to see all that especially after he had just fucked me for the very first time.

Anyway, after sitting in my vehicle for about ten minutes, I called the one person I knew would come through for me. I thought of him as Old Reliable and he probably thought the same thing of me. I had known him for years and, yes, our fuckship was semi-incestuous because he was like a little brother to me.

I looked at the number and tried very hard to resist the urge to call this guy. But I said, "What the hell." I dialed the phone number anyway and waited. I prayed that the self-proclaimed party animal/ladies' man I was about to call picked up his damn phone for me.

"Aye yeo!" answered Chase, Phoenix's younger brother. "What's up, baby mama?" he asked. "What say you?"

I breathed a sigh of relief when I heard that voice. Chase always managed to put a smile on my face. He was such a character.

"What's up, baby daddy?" I replied, calling him by the pet names we had for each other. "Where in the fuck are you?"

"Ah," Chase began, "I was headed to the crib. Just came in from the gym, getting my late evening workout on. You know I gots to keep this body tight, girl. You know how I do."

I rolled my eyes up in my head. "Boy, bye!" I exclaimed. "You swear you're the flyest thing out here!"

"I am, baby mama! You know it, the hoes know it, and so do I!" We both laughed. "Anyway, where the fuck you at? It sounds like you're out roaming the streets."

I sighed. "Yeah, I am. I just came from Peaches restaurant. I treated myself to a night out and now I'm
horny. So I'm calling to find out if you're going to lace
me with some that good dick of yours."

I listened as Chase unlocked his apartment door and
walked into his house. I could hear him throwing keys
on the glass coffee table in his living room.

"Okay, so let me get this straight. You're horny,
you're tipsy, and you're up the block from me, too? Ah,
shit! Bring your sexy ass over here, baby mama, so I
could put a beating on that pussy for you. You know
how your baby daddy do," Chase boasted.

I laughed. "Whatever! I'm on my way, Negro," I said,
anticipating getting served the way I like to be served.

"That's peace, ma. Let me get in this shower real
quick and wash these balls for you to lick on."

I chuckled. "You ain't said nothing but a word," I
replied.

Chase Henry lived in Clinton Hills, on Washington
and Lafayette Avenue, about ten minutes from Peaches.
It was a great neighborhood, with slightly upscale living
conditions and sort of pricey. Chase was an entrepre-
neur and the Henrys were an upper middle-class family
so he could afford it.

Chase had always been a little "mannish", which
was the reason I was attracted to him in the first place.
He used to flirt with me and because he was my best
friend's little brother, I never paid him no mind. That
is until one day while I was waiting for Phoenix at their
home, one thing led to another and we ended having a
sexual romp in Chase's queen-sized bed.

By the time, Phoenix found out that I was having sex
with her brother, Chase and I had already been fucking
for two years. Naturally, she was pissed with us, especially me. She tried to say that I took advantage of her

little brother but I did nothing of the sort. I was going through a lot with Shah at the time and Chase was my go to guy. Fortunately, Phoenix and I remained friends, of course, but it took Miss Thing about six months to a year to get over our "deception," as she called it. Their older sister, River, thought that that the shit was hilarious. She was impressed and amazed at the fact that her younger brother had enough game to get his older sister's best friend in his bed.

As for Chase and I, there was never any love connection between us, at least, not in a girlfriend/boyfriend type of way. Strangely enough, even after having sex with him, I still considered Chase my family. We didn't have any blood ties to each other so I didn't see one problem with what we had going on.

After I found parking near Chase's apartment building, I called and told him that I was on my way upstairs. When I arrived upstairs to his apartment, Chase opened the door with nothing but a towel wrapped around his waist. He had just gotten out of the shower and his chiseled body was glistening with beads of water. I stepped inside and Chase closed the door behind me.

As soon as I got through the door, I snatched the towel from around Chase's frame to reveal his manhood. His concrete-hard rod was standing at attention and pointing in my direction. I could feel the juices flowing between my legs, as Chase began jerking on it.

He licked his lips. "Take your clothes off, baby mama. Take them off real slow," he said in his sexy-man voice.

I smiled seductively and proceeded to do as I was told. I was going to give Chase a strip tease. First, I kicked my shoes off. Then I turned around with my ass facing him and eased out of my jeans, revealing my lacy thong. I took my shirt off and slowly peeled off my bra and panties. I did all of this while singing my own a cappella rendition of R. Kelly's "Feelin' on Yo' Booty." Thank God, I knew how to sing a little something something. It just made my private cabaret show all the sexier.

As soon as all of my clothes were off, Chase walked over to me and grabbed me by my waist. He pulled me closer to him, so close that I could feel his hardness between my legs. The wetness on my inner thighs was my marinated juices spraying all over the place and he hadn't even put it in yet. The Moscato and Chase's beautifully sculpted frame had me all worked up. I needed that big O and fast.

I pushed Chase onto the couch. Then I got on top of him and began straddling the hell out of his dick. While I was riding him, he held on to my ass cheeks. Chase always told me I had a nice ass. He pulled the cheeks apart, smacked them and rubbed them down.

Judging from the way that I was moaning, it wasn't hard to tell that I was enjoying my fix. Chase's dick to me was like some crack rocks and a pipe to a crackhead. That was because he was one of the few men who knew how to work my pussy the right way. I was glad that he was available when I needed him.

After this went on for like ten minutes, Chase turned me over on my back and spread my legs as wide as they could go. He began stroking this pussy as if his life depended on it. And I loved the way his testicles were slapping against my ass, while he went deeper and deeper into my hairless pit. Chase was definitely getting at that G-spot.

Shortly after, I felt a powerful orgasm coming on. I grabbed Chase's face and made him kiss me in the mouth, while I sprayed on his dick like a water sprinkler. But that didn't stop him. Chase just kept on going.

He was going for orgasm number two and he didn't even cum yet. Such an unselfish lover. He was twisting my body like a pretzel, making sure that he served me the dick on a silver platter. Yes, I was getting the platinum special and I was loving it.

An hour and a half later, we had literally fucked all over Chase's apartment. I experienced another O and I was in heaven. Chase was lying next to me, with his eyes closed, trying to get his equilibrium back. I was looking up at the ceiling with a smile on my face. In all the years that we had been having sex with each other, Chase had never disappointed me.

After our interlude, we were laying side by side but we didn't snuggle up to each other. It wasn't that type of party for us. Instead, we gave each other a pound.

"Woo!" I began. "That was some good sex, boy," I said. "You got me needing a cigarette and I don't even smoke! You never let me down, baby daddy."

He laughed. "Likewise, baby mama. Likewise." There was a silent pause between us. "Yo, Eb. I got some great news," he said with a smile on his face.

I turned around to face him and smiled too. "Really? What is it?"

Chase wrapped the comforter around his naked frame.

"You're the first to know—I didn't even tell my family yet. So keep this to yourself. I want to tell my sisters and my parents myself."

I sat up and gave Chase my full, undivided attention. "Of course, Chase. I got you covered. What's the deal?" I asked.

"I'm going to have a baby!"

A surprised look came over my face. "You? Chase Jamir Henry, the self-proclaimed ladies' man is having a seed? By who?"

"My girlfriend."

I frowned. "Your girlfriend?"

Chase laughed. "Yes! My girlfriend, my woman, my lady! Who else would I be having a baby by?" he asked.

I shrugged my shoulders. "I don't know, Chase. I just didn't know that you were in a relationship, that's all," I said. I felt a tinge of sadness going through my body.

Chase couldn't tell that I was slightly upset by his news so he kept going. "I've been in a relationship with my girl for the past year and a half. You wouldn't have known this because you've been so caught up with that dude Dray for the last few years." He sat up. "Anyway, are you thirsty?" I nodded my head.

As Chase disappeared into the kitchen for something for us to drink, I tried to digest what he told me. Although I didn't have any romantic feelings for the man, how crazy was it for me to be knocked down from his fuck partner to the bottom of the barrel?

Seconds later, Chase appeared in the bedroom doorway with two bottles of water. He handed one to me and I took a giant swig. My throat felt dry as hell.

I swung my legs over the side of the bed. "Couldn't you have told me about this pregnant girlfriend before you fucked me, Chase?" I said, giving him a piercing stare. "I would have saved myself the humiliation." *Bow wow yippee yo yippee yay. What a fucking dog!*

Chase sat next to me and nudged me like I was one of the fellas. "I didn't tell you about it because you know how we do! And besides weren't you the one that called me up tonight and told me that you needed me? Didn't I come through for you?" he asked.

I was visibly annoyed. Apparently, the point I was trying to make to Chase was going over his head.

"Chase, you don't understand. You have a girlfriend. She's pregnant. You didn't need to be fucking with me tonight is what I'm trying to say."

It was Chase's turn to get irritated. "Since when did me having a girlfriend mean anything to you, Ebony? You never asked me if I had a girl so I just figured that you didn't give a fuck!" I shook my head at Chase's statement. He was right. "And why do you care if I'm in a relationship? Don't you have a man?" he asked.

I stood up in front of Chase. "I had a man but not anymore! Dray and I broke up yesterday."

"Damn, girl. I'm sorry to hear that."

I grabbed Chase's robe and threw it on. Then I gathered up my things from the living room floor and went into the bathroom to freshen up. When I walked out of the bathroom, I was fully dressed. Chase was lying in the bed, still naked, most likely waiting for round two.

He sat upright when he saw me in my street clothes. "Where are you going, baby mama? I thought that you were going to chill with me until the morning."

"I can't stay here, Chase. I have to go home." I walked toward the front door. Chase threw on a robe and followed behind me.

"Yo, Eb, I'm so sorry. I should have kept it a hundred with you about my relationship."

I sucked my teeth. "Sorry for what, Chase? You're a grown ass, twenty-eight-year-old man who's about to be a father. Don't apologize for that. And you did keep it a hundred. That's why I'm leaving."

Chase grabbed my arm. "Before you go, let me just tell you this. I had a crush on you ever since I was a little boy. I thought that you were so pretty and sexy and cool—I always wanted a girl just like you. And when we started, well, you know, messing around with each other, I was feeling you even more. Honestly, Ebony, I have the utmost respect for you. But I know how you like to get down. Running around here fucking with random dudes does not make you wife or even girlfriend material. You're more than just somebody's booty call or fuck partner. I wanna see you happy so this is the last time that you and I are going to be doing this. And I'm not just saying all of this because my girlfriend is pregnant. I'm saying this because I love you."

I stood there in awe. To sum everything up, Chase was telling me that no man would take me serious, including him because I was too "loose" of a woman. Then to add insult to injury, he was ending our "fuckship". How did I end up being dumped by a guy that wasn't even my man? Wow. Just wow.

I looked at Chase and shook my head. "Chase, kiss my ass," I said, calm as hell. "It takes a real man to handle what I have to give, okay? And another thing, how can you shoot me down when you've been cheating on every girlfriend you ever had? Give me a fucking break already!"

Chase kissed me on the cheek. "Maybe in another time, another life, we could have got together."

"This isn't about you, Chase. I'm the one who got cheated on by every man that I ever fell in love with. I'm the one that's getting dumped by my best friend's baby brother and we're not even in a relationship with each other. And here I am, doing the very same thing to your girl that a bitch done did to me! So if a man don't wife me then fuck it! Y'all trifling motherfuckers are part of the reason why I'm the way that I am!" I calmed myself down and then sighed. "You know what, Chase? I'm not mad at you, babe. I want to give my sincere congrats to you and your "real" baby mama. Just make sure I get that invite to the baby shower. Deuces."

I unlocked the door and hurriedly left Chase's apartment. Once I was outside, I ran all the way to my car, in tears.

Now I was lying up in my bed on a beautiful Sunday morning, all alone—again. I couldn't understand, why was I good enough to be the side but never a bride? What the hell was a chick doing wrong?

Chapter 15

Take Me As I Am

Phoenix

It was Monday morning. As usual, I woke up at 6:00 A.M. on the nose. I pressed the snooze button on my alarm clock and practically dragged myself out of bed. I so didn't feel like going to work but my boss man, Mr. Samuel Reilly, Esquire, had a shitload of work for me to do and I couldn't let him down. After all, I had to show mad love for the man who signed my healthy bonus checks.

I took a quick shower and had some breakfast. After that, I slid into one of my many suits. On this particular morning, I wore a brown Michael Kors pencil skirt with the fitted blazer to match. Then I threw on a pair of neutral-colored Cynthia Vincent pumps, and did my hair and makeup. I grabbed my Chloe shades and bag from the nightstand near my bed, making it out the door by eight-fifteen. I had to be at my desk by 9:00 A.M. and forty-five minutes was more than enough time to get to my office in Long Island City.

When I walked outside of my building, some sanitation workers were already out there, picking up the garbage. I was always getting harassed by construction workers, cops, and some other blue-collar perverts so I dreaded walking by these mofos. But I had no other choice. I had to get to my car and get my behind to work.

I held my breath as I walked in the direction of the two garbage men. They were in their soiled green uniforms and throwing huge bags of the building's garbage into the back of their sanitation truck. One worker was short and stocky with a full beard, and the other one didn't look half bad. He was much taller with a nice face and great body, too. For a brief second, he had me asking why did a man that good-looking dispose of garbage for a living. How attractive could that be?

Anyway, I promised myself that the first one of those garbage specialists who said something to me was going to get the business. I just couldn't deal that morning. I wasn't in the mood for their shit talking. I even cussed at myself for not parking in my garage spot the night before like I had intended to.

"Good morning, lady," Tall One said as I walked by.

I didn't utter one word.

"I said, good morning," Tall One called out to me again.

I stopped dead in my tracks and turned around to look at him. "Don't you have a job to do?" I asked, with an attitude.

The short guy looked away. I guessed he didn't want to experience my wrath.

Tall One frowned. "Damn! Do you wake up on the wrong side of the bed every day?"

I frowned. "Excuse you?" I answered, putting one hand on my hip.

Tall One stepped a little closer to me and I stepped back. I didn't want any of that disgusting garbage juice spewing off him and onto my $300 suit. He took off the dirty gloves that he was wearing.

Tall One stood in front of me and crossed his arms around his chest. "Every time I see you, miss, you always have this disgusted look on your face. I had to ask

myself, why is this woman always pissed off? I decided
that today I was going to say good morning to you, you
know, try to lift your spirits a little. But even when I'm
trying to be nice to you, you don't even bother to open
up your mouth to say anything back to me. What's up
with that?" he asked, with this serious look on his face.

I instantly went into defensive black woman mode,
with the neck roll and everything.

"First of all, mister, you don't even know me," I said,
narrowing my eyes. "I don't have to speak to no strange
man on the street if I don't want to!" There had to be a
good damn reason why I was entertaining this Negro
but at that moment, I couldn't figure out what it was.

Anyway, Tall One turned around and looked back at
his partner. The shorter guy let out a slight chuckle and
continued to throw the garbage on the truck. The smell
of that shit was enough to make me faint.

"My coworker told me that you were a stuck-up,
bougie-ass broad and I didn't believe him." Then he
yelled out to the short guy. "Yo, shorty," he began, "you
was right, man! She is a stuck-up, bougie ass broad!
I got your fifty dollars right here in my pocket!" Then
he looked back, rolled his eyes at me, and walked back
over to his garbage.

Now I was really pissed. "Who in the fuck are you
calling a stuck-up, bougie ass broad, you garbage-toting
Negro?"

Tall One laughed out loud and Shorty looked surprised. "Whoa! I must have hit a nerve! I gotta call you
a stuck-up, bougie ass broad to get a reaction, huh?"

I threw my hands up. "Why am I even standing here
talking to the likes of you anyway?" I began walking
away from Ren and Stimpy. "Go tend to your trash, Mr.
Garbage Man! I have a real job to go to!"

Shorty began cracking up when I said that. This
time, Tall One wasn't laughing.

I was almost to my car when Tall One started running down the block after me. I tried to get into the driver's side of my car but it was too late. Tall One had already approached me. I immediately went in my bag and reached for my pepper spray.

"You come any closer, I'm gonna spray your monkey ass!" I yelled, holding the canister in my hand.

Tall One held his hands up to his eyes. "Look, miss, it's no need for all that. I apologize for the way I acted back there. It's just that you're a very attractive woman and since I had this route, I've been working up enough nerve to speak to you. I didn't mean to get you upset."

I put away my pepper spray and Tall One uncovered his eyes. "Okay. Apology accepted." I looked at my watch. "Look, I have to get to work . . ."

Tall One held out his hand. "The name is Kevin. Kevin Wright. And yours?"

I looked down at his extended hand, refusing to touch it. I only imagined how much E. coli, salmonella, and other germs were on those rough-looking hands. Kevin must have noticed my hesitation to shake his germ-infested mitt. He looked at his own hand then put it away.

"My name is Phoenix. Phoenix Henry."

Kevin nodded his head. *If only he weren't a garbage specialist, he probably would have some major potential. What a waste.*

He sighed. "Okay, Phoenix. You have a nice day. See you tomorrow."

I gave Kevin a fake-ass smile and slid into my driver's seat. As I was about to pull off, I looked at him through my rearview mirror. He was standing at the curb and waving at me. I put on my Chloe shades and stepped on the gas.

When I finally arrived at work, I said my good mornings to my coworkers and headed straight to my desk. I had to type up some legal documents for Reilly so that I could fax them to him.

As I did my day's work, I thought about Kevin. For some strange reason, I couldn't get that handsome face of his out of my head! Yes, he had me pissed off that morning but I had to give that man an E for effort. It must have taken a lot of balls to approach a woman of my stature the way that he did. And it was funny because the brief interaction with him had made my day. But I'd be damned if I'd let him know that.

The next morning, it was the same scenario all over again. Kevin and Shorty were sitting outside my building. This time, I didn't see them pulling any garbage. I didn't know what was going on but I waved at them anyway and kept walking. Kevin hopped out of the truck and ran behind me.

"Yo, Phoenix!" he called out. I turned around, annoyed that someone in that dreadful green uniform was yelling my government name out in the street.

"Are you serious?" I asked him, with my usual attitude.

Kevin seemed unmoved. "Good morning, sweetheart. I see that you're on your way to work. You look nice."

I sighed loudly. "Look, I don't know what's going on here but shouldn't you be somewhere picking up garbage? Are you stalking me or something?"

He laughed. I noticed that Kevin had the prettiest teeth. *And where did those dimples come from?*

"Nah, I ain't stalking you, girl! I was on my way to my next route when I decided to stop by your building and see you off to work. Is there a problem with that?"

I wanted to smile but I held my composure. "Yes, there's a problem with that, Kevin. You are stalking me. That's not in your garbage man rulebook to be stalking people, is it?"

"Of course it isn't. But I like you and I wanted to make sure that you were all right. A young, single woman like yourself needs to be protected by a real man."

I smirked. "Oh, really?"

Kevin rubbed his chin. "Yeah, really."

I looked at my watch. "Well, um, check this out, I'ma need to keep it moving. Phoenix gots to get to work to make this money to pay these bills, you know what I'm saying? I'm sure that you don't have no bills or rent to pay living with your mama and all—"

"Whoa!" Kevin said, putting up his hand. "Where did you get that idea?" he asked.

I looked back at the sanitation truck that his partner, Shorty, was sitting in. "Because you work for Sanitation! I'm sure that y'all don't make that much money, right?"

Kevin threw his head back and laughed. "What? Are you serious right now, girl?"

I wasn't showing any teeth which meant I was serious. "Yeah," was all that I said.

Kevin shook his head. "You don't have a man, do you?"

"What?"

"You heard me."

"No, I do not."

Kevin gave me this nasty look. "I could see why," he said. Then he walked away.

I stood there for a moment and watched as Kevin got into the driver's seat of the truck and pulled off. I put on my shades and made my way to my vehicle. When I got in my car, I started it up but I didn't pull off right

away. I thought about what Kevin said: he could see
why I didn't have a man. And he wasn't the only guy
who had said that to me. I shrugged my shoulders and
pulled off.

Chapter 16

The Father in You

Joi

After my mother had that heart-to-heart talk with me, it opened my eyes to a few things that were going on in my life. That was when I realized that the only thing that I had going on in my life was Tate and his drama. I barely hung out with my friends anymore and it seemed like I couldn't make a move unless I knew Tate's whereabouts. Even I had to admit that my relationship and getting married had become some sort of obsession for me. Sadly enough, I didn't know how to break the vicious cycle.

Truth be told, I didn't see anything wrong with wanting to get married and have a baby with the man I loved. Either I was going to take my position in that number one spot, or give it up to someone else. This is why about eight months prior, I had stopped getting my Depo-Provera shots, in hopes of getting pregnant by Tate. Of course, he didn't know about this.

I was a stickler when it came to protected sex and I had always used a reliable form of birth control or prophylactic of some kind. After being a self-proclaimed advocate for Planned Parenthood for many years, this was the first time that I had actually wanted to get pregnant. Tate had expressed that he wasn't ready for any more kids until he was married, but shit, this was my body. If he didn't want to marry me without children, I figured that he would marry me with children. At least, I hoped he did.

It was Tuesday night when Tate came over to the house. I was definitely ovulating and ready to go in for the kill. I took the liberty of making a nice dinner for the both of us. I even made sure I had a few of his favorite Blu-rays lined up for us to watch before we retired to the bedroom for the night. My "fuckfit" of choice was a pair of tight-fitting booty shorts with my ass cheeks hanging out of the seat and a wife beater—Tate preferred that over some sexy lingerie.

Lucky for me, he took notice of everything that I was trying to do.

We were sitting in my living room, watching Kevin Hart's *Laugh at My Pain,* when I got up to get us some cold Pepsi's from the fridge. My round derriere in those booty shorts must have caught Tate's attention because he pulled me onto his lap.

"Damn, baby," he said. "You're looking extra tasty tonight. You act like you want me to give you some."

I grinned. "Why you say that, Tatum?" I said, calling him by his full name.

Tate began to nuzzle me on my neck. He knew that I got all hot and bothered when he did that.

"You look good enough to eat, sweetheart. Can I taste some of that?" he asked.

"Do you have to ask?" I replied, giving him a seductive, come-hither look.

Tate swept me off my feet and took me into my bedroom. He laid me across the bed and closed the door behind him. Then he pulled my shorts off and submerged his face into my pussy. While he licked and sucked on my clitoris, I wrapped my right leg around his neck, pulling him into me. My juices, mixed with his saliva, dripped all over my Martha Stewart goose down comforter.

"Tate . . ." I said softly. "Enjoy this pussy, baby."

Tate moaned but didn't let up from his licking. He fucked my vagina with his long tongue. My eyes rolled in the back of my head and I began bucking wildly. It felt like I was about to cum. But I wasn't ready for it to be over.

"Come fuck me," I whispered to my love.

Tate quickly undressed and moved my body to the middle of my queen-sized bed. Then he proceeded to enter me very slowly. I took all of him in, locking him down like I had a vice grip on his dick. The thought of me having Tate's baby only made our sexual interlude even more intense. Tate immediately began calling out my name and I did the same.

"Oh, your pussy is so squishy wet, baby, damn," he said.

I closed my eyes. Damn, I loved me some Tate. He could fuck, eat pussy, he looked good, he was a working man—he had me so open! It was hard to believe that a man could have a woman holding on to him for so long and take him back, even after he had done her wrong. That woman was me. Tate was my addiction, my motivation. . . .

Fifteen minutes later, I was ready. "I'm cumming, baby," I yelled. I grabbed his ass, wanting to feel every inch of his dick inside of me. Then I heard those magic words.

"I'm cumming too, babe, I'm cumming . . . ooooh," he moaned.

We both came within seconds of each other and it felt so good. I took in every drip drop of Tate's semen, imagining his little swimmers inside of my vagina, racing to fertilize that egg. I hoped that the lucky one had made it there. I wanted Tate's baby more than life itself.

We both lay there for a few minutes, staring at the ceiling. We were spent from our erotic episode. Tate leaned over and kissed me on the lips.

"Yo, babe. What are you trying to do to me?" he asked, wiping the sweat from his forehead.

I rested my head on his chest. "Not a damn thing," I replied, while rubbing on his chest.

Tate turned over to look at me. "You did something. That coochie tasted extra good tonight. And it was juicy. It almost felt like some pregnant pussy to me."

I sucked my teeth. "Yeah, you would know what pregnant pussy feels like."

Tate ignored my snide remark. "Anyway, let's go to bed now. I might want some more of that in the middle of the night."

I turned around, with my back facing Tate and he pulled me closer to him. I fell asleep thinking about how fucked up in the head Dara would be once she found out that I was pregnant by Tate. I was working overtime trying to get that woman out of our lives for good.

The next morning, I walked into the office of my OB-GYN doctor, Dr. Moto, for a routine check-up. I knew that I couldn't be pregnant just yet but I made the appointment weeks ago. I just wanted to make sure that everything was all good with me.

I toyed with my phone as I waited patiently for my name to be called. Forty-five minutes later I was in one of the rooms, in a gown and on the examination table. I gave my pee cup to the nurse. When she walked out, my doctor walked in.

Dr. Moto smiled. "Hello, Miss Campbell, how are you?" she asked.

"I'm well, Dr. Moto. How are you?"

"I'm as well, as well can be, can't complain. Are you ready for your check-up?"

I lay back on the table and put my feet in the stirrups. "Yes, I am."

Dr. Moto put on some latex gloves and made sure that she was prepared for my check-up. "Are we still trying to get pregnant?"

I smiled. "Yes, I am! Me and my fiancé, Tatum, are extremely excited!"

"That's wonderful! This must mean that you guys are having lots of sex."

"We just had sex last night," I volunteered.

Dr. Moto laughed. "Great! Were you ovulating?"

"Yes, I was."

"Well, last night would be a little too soon but I'm going to do a pregnancy test on you anyway. Did you get your period last month?"

"Yeah, I did. It stayed on for about three days."

"No heavy bleeding or clotting?"

"No, not at all."

Dr. Moto started her check-up. She put that godforsaken clamp inside of me and I winced.

"Relax, Joi, relax. I just want to get a culture. Make sure that everything is okay with you."

By this time, the nurse walked back in. She stood beside me and helped me relax while Dr. Moto did her thing. A few minutes later, the clamp was removed. I breathed a sigh of relief. Dr. Moto handed the nurse some articles with my name on them. Then she removed the gloves from her hands and told me to get dressed.

"I will be right back, Joi. After you're dressed, I want you to meet me in my office," she said.

I nodded my head and watched her walk out of the room. I quickly put my clothes back on. In the next three minutes, I was sitting in a chair in front of Dr. Moto's desk.

Five minutes later, Dr. Moto walked in with a folder. She had a seat at her desk and took a look at the paperwork inside of it. Then she looked at me.

"Congratulations, Joi. You're going to be a mommy!"

I couldn't believe my ears. "Did you say that I'm going to be a mother? I'm having a baby?"

Dr. Moto smiled. "Yes! You're six weeks pregnant, sweetie!"

I laughed. "Wow! I can't believe it!" I felt like I was on cloud nine.

"I'm going to make an appointment for you to come and . . ."

Everything that Dr. Moto was saying to me was inaudible from that point on. I had heard exactly what I wanted to hear. I could barely contain the joy that I felt. And for the first time in my life, I felt complete. I laid my hand on my stomach and wiped a tear from my cheek.

Chapter 17

No More Drama

Ebony

I didn't even know what to say about my week except that I was back on Mommy duty. I had spoken to Wes a few times in the past couple of days. I told him that I wasn't ready to go out with him. He didn't try to press the issue and I respected him for that. Even Mateo, Saadia's cousin, had called me but I completely ignored his phone call. I didn't feel like being bothered. And in one moment of weakness, I blocked my number and tried to call Dray just to see if he would answer his phone. To my surprise, his bitch-made ass had changed his cell phone number.

Now it was Freaky Friday, all over again. I was stationed at the A train, Jay Street subway station. It was busy as shit and I was ready to unleash the fire on anybody who worked my nerve.

Straphanger after straphanger was asking me the dumbest questions like, "Where's this train, where's that train?" and "What train do I take to here and there?" They asked this when all they had to do was read the goddamn signs and fucking subway maps that were posted all over the place. I issued about 1,001 MetroCards and had like three arguments with one black chick, an older white woman, and some Spanish dude, all before lunch time. My damn pressure was probably higher than a mug and I felt an anxiety attack coming on. I just wanted a break from all the bullshit.

I guzzled on a bottle of Poland Spring water to try to calm myself down. Just when I felt like I didn't want to slap the shit out of somebody, who walked up to my window and asked for a MetroCard? Nobody other than Tate's baby mama, Dara.

Now, I had never met this garden tool personally. Joi had shown me a few pictures of the broad and personally, I thought that Dara was a really cute chick. I could see why Joi was uncomfortable with the relationship that Tate and this girl had with each other. Of course, I would never tell my friend that I thought this. Joi would have chewed my head off and spit it out.

"Can I have an unlimited MetroCard, please?" she asked, with an attitude for no reason. She had some Nicki Minaj powder pink lipstick on them pouty-ass lips of hers and she was poking them out, too.

I smirked. "A monthly unlimited, huh?" I asked. I knew what she was talking about. I just wanted to mess with the skank for putting my girl through all of the unnecessary "rigamarole."

She sighed. "Yes. A monthly unlimited!"

I knew she wanted to cuss me out and I wanted to give her a reason to do it. "Oh, okay, look, hon—you don't have to get loud with me! I can hear you just fine, Boo," I said, with that same smirk on my face.

"Well, it's hard to tell," she said, rolling her eyes at me.

I was smiling to myself as I took her money and put the info into the computer. She was staring at me with a disgusted look on her face.

"Is there a problem?" I asked, with one eyebrow raised. I was a pro at antagonizing a bitch.

"Can I have my unlimited, please? I don't have time for nothing you're talking about right now."

I handed Dara the MetroCard and she snatched it through the slot. As she walked through the turnstile, I put the mic to my mouth and called out to her.

"Oh, yeah, Dara?" She turned around with a frown on her face. "Tell your baby father, Tate that Ebony said hello!" I yelled.

She must have lost all the coloring in her face when I said that but she dared not come back through that turnstile. Instead, she flipped me the bird and ran down the stairs to catch her train. I laughed loudly and took another swig of my water.

"That one was for my girl Joi," I said happily.

Around one o'clock, my relief came so that I could go to lunch. I called Joi, who agreed to meet me at BBQ's on Livingston for a drink and some chicken fingers. I told her to leave Mercuri—that chicken-head coworker/homegirl of hers—at the job. I wasn't in the mood to deal with no loud-talking project chicks that day.

When I saw Joi, I gave her a super tight hug. I noticed that she was a little thicker than usual. Her face was glowing and she seemed happier than what I remembered her being.

We sat at our table and I ordered a Texas-size strawberry daiquiri with an extra shot. Thank God I had a jacket on, hiding my MTA uniform. Somebody would have definitely reported me for drinking while I was on duty. Joi just ordered herself a virgin daiquiri. I looked at her like she was crazy. The whole idea of getting her out to lunch was so that we could sneak some alcohol and talk shit with each other.

I took a sip of my drink and pointed at hers. "What the fuck is that?" I asked. "We know got-damn well we don't do virgin drinks, beyotch!"

Joi chuckled. "Girl, bye!" she replied. "I don't feel like messing with my liver today."

I rolled my eyes at her. "What in the hell are you trying to say? Are you merely suggesting that I'm an alchie?"

She waved me off. "Nah, you're a lush. Phoenix is the alchie of the crew!" We both agreed with that.

"Guess who I saw today, girlfriend? I may forget a name but never a face."

Joi's eyes widened. "Who did you see?"

"Dara."

She almost spit out her drink. "Dara?"

I just knew that she was going to ask for a shot in her daiquiri after I told her that one but that request never came.

"Where did you see her?"

"I saw her at Jay Street. She was buying an unlimited MetroCard."

"How does she look to you?" Joi asked.

"Ah, she ain't all that," I lied. Like I said, I wasn't trying to hurt my girl's feelings.

"I can't stand that chick!"

"I know, Joi, I know. But can I ask you question?"

"Yeah. Shoot."

"Wasn't Tate still with her when y'all started dating?"

Joi nodded her head. "Yeah. So what?"

"So what? You took the girl's man! No wonder she hates you."

"Please, I didn't take nothing that she didn't give away. She wasn't on her job!"

"According to who?" I asked.

"According to her ex-man!"

"And you actually believe that Negro, don't you?"

"Why shouldn't I? He's my man, isn't he?"

I sighed. "I'm not trying to be a downer or any-thing—"

She cut me off. "So don't be."

I ignored the slick statement. "Like I was saying, I'm trying not to be a downer but when a woman takes another woman's man, she always gets them nasty ass leftovers. You don't know what Tate has put that chick through."

"Well, whatever he put her through really didn't matter to Dara because she ended up getting pregnant for him. She was the one that trapped him off!"

"Do you know that for sure? For all you know, Tate could have wanted her to have his baby. Shit, if you ask me, I think that he's playing the both of you ladies."

"I don't know or care what he's doing to Dara. But how in the hell do you feel that he's playing me? Sheesh! Y'all just don't wanna give my man a break!"

"Because he was still sleeping with Dara even after you and him got together! That's how she ended up pregnant," I said.

Joi was so obsessed with that jerk, Tate, that she had made the Negro and everything else in his life her per-sonal project.

"Forget all of that," I said, backing away from the super-sensitive topic."

The waiter came to our table with the food. As we dug in, we started talking about something else.

"Man, I've been feeling so miserable lately," I said.

"What do you have to be miserable about, girl? Is this about Dray?" Joi asked.

"Fuck Dray!" I said, dipping a chicken finger in some honey mustard sauce. "I'm just tired of being just an option for these dudes, you know what I mean? Fuck being girlfriend number two. I'm sick of being the side piece, sick of not being taken seriously. I want a man who is going to love and honor me and make me *numero uno*."

Joi nodded her head. "I agree. You want to be promoted, not demoted."

"Exactly! It seems like every man I meet has some girlfriend, a wife, an ex-wife, a baby mama, their own mama, or some other woman in their lives that's taking time and energy away from me. I need a man who's going to be all in and go all out and I can do the same in return, you know what I'm saying, Joi?"

Joi nodded her head in agreement. "I completely understand. But things can't be all that bad! At least you have Kare Bear to love you."

"I know but the love from a child is not the same. My baby is going to love his mommy regardless. I need someone I could show another kind of love to."

"Wow. Speaking of love from a child, I'm going to find out what that feels like in a couple of months," Joi said, stuffing her face with some French fries. "I'm pregnant."

I continued my rambling. "Yeah, girl . . . *What?*" I exclaimed. "Did you just say that you were pregnant?"

Joi put her fork down. Her face lit up. "Yes! Yes! I'm pregnant," she said, clapping her hands.

I got up and came around the table to hug her. I was so excited for my friend, even though I wasn't too happy with her choice of baby daddy, with his old shady self.

"Oh, my goodness, Joi!" I said as I sat back in my chair with my hand covering my mouth. "I know that you're so happy! How many weeks?"

"I'm six weeks and counting!"

"When did you find out?" I asked, holding back tears.

"I found out Wednesday."

"Did you tell Tate?"

Joi held her head down. "No. Not yet."

A confused look came over my face. "Why not?"

"Because I'm afraid to. I'm scared of what the outcome is going to be. I mean, look at him and Dara. She has a baby by him and they're not even together. I don't want us to end up like that. I want me and Tate to raise our child together."

"You want to get married, don't you?" I asked, with a concerned look on my face.

"Yes, I do. But shit, what in the hell does it take for a woman to get the man she loves to marry her?"

I shook my head. I didn't know the answer to that question—been asking myself that same shit for many years and still hadn't figured it out.

Chapter 18

Talk To Me

Phoenix

It was finally Friday and I was happy that I'd made it through the work week. I had meetings galore, documents that had to be drawn up—it was extremely hectic. I was becoming stressed out over the trivial things—things that would have never bothered me before. What I needed was more than a vacation or some temporary stress reliever. I needed some sex and fast.

I began looking at the sanitation dude, Kevin, like he was a piece of USDA-grades of beef. I passed by him and his partner, Shorty, at least three times that week. Every time I did, it seemed as if he was getting sexier and sexier by the day. I wanted to get his attention but I wanted to do so without making a fool of myself. Shoot, after all, I did tell his ass off.

The first time that I saw Kevin since our last run-in, I waved at him. But the only acknowledgments that I got from him were head nods. Obviously it was no more "good mornings" for Phoenix. Shorty, who had always been the quiet one, was now saying hello and good morning to me. To show my appreciation for his cordiality, I made it my business to speak right back to him. I just couldn't figure out what was up with his partner.

On this particular Friday, I decided to be the one to break the ice with Kevin. I was tired of the silent treatment.

"Good morning, Shorty," I yelled out. Shorty smiled and waved at me. "Good morning, Kevin," I said, giving him a sexy stare. I figured that maybe my womanly wiles would catch his attention.

Kevin did not seem impressed by my effort at all. Instead of speaking back to me, he gave me that damn head nod again.

Now I was getting frustrated with Kevin's attitude. The man wasn't paying me any mind and I didn't like it one bit. I put my hand on my hip and began reading him the riot act.

"What's up with this head nod shit, Kevin?" I asked him, giving it to him straight with no chaser. "Why don't you want to open your mouth to speak to me anymore, man?"

Kevin stopped what he was doing, took off his work gloves, and walked over to me. "Check this out, home-girl: I don't chase no chicks who don't want to be caught. And if you think I'm gonna start chasing you; you must be out your rabbit-ass mind! So I'm just gonna leave you alone and you can start by doing the same thing with me."

I felt like an asshole but was strangely turned on at the same time. "Look, Kevin, I apologize for acting like a bitch to you."

"You're apologizing for that?" He laughed then looked at me and crossed his arms. "Honestly, I don't think that you could help it."

I was only going to be so nice to this motherfucker in ten, nine, eight . . . "Look, Kevin," I said, pointing my French-manicured finger at him.

He held his hand up to stop me from going any further. "Nah, don't 'look, Kevin' me nothing! I got the message the first time and I'm not going to bother you anymore, miss! There ain't nothing we got to say to each other."

Kevin walked away from me and continued doing what he was paid to do.

Not going down without a fight, I called out to him again. I couldn't just let our brief dalliance end like that. Plus, I hated losing.

"Excuse me, Kevin? Can you come over here for a minute? Please?" I asked.

He rolled his eyes and reluctantly walked over to where I was standing. "Aren't you going to be late for work?"

I ignored the 'tude and pulled out my cell phone instead. "Is it okay for me to get your number?" I asked. I couldn't believe that I was actually asking a man for his digits but what the fuck? I had to start somewhere if I wanted to get some dick in my life.

Kevin hesitated for a few seconds. Then he said, "A'ight, fuck it." He willingly gave me the digits and I quickly locked them in my phone.

I smiled at him. "Would you like to hang out tonight? It's my treat."

It didn't look like Kevin had much faith in me. "Yeah, okay," he said, still giving me the brush-off. Only this time, I didn't take it personal. He had given me the number so the challenge was basically over. That only proved that he really did like me.

I walked to my car, thinking about how much I was attracted to Kevin. I mean, shit, the man was acting in a way that I wasn't used to. Being ignored by a man was something that I wasn't accustomed to.

The old me would have thought that I was "lowering" my standards to talk to Kevin. But it wasn't like I had a slew of men of any race, color, or creed knocking on my door.

Now I couldn't wait to get things jumping between the two of us and I was quite pleased with my decision. I headed to work with a big Kool-Aid smile on my face, thinking about how Kevin was going to be my "something new" and it felt damn good.

It was almost 6:00 P.M. and I was more than happy to finally be off from work. As soon as I walked through my front door, I ditched the corporate threads and wrapped myself up in my favorite robe. I had been thinking about that Kevin all day—I couldn't wait to call him. I lay across my bed and hesitantly dialed Kevin's number. I was nervous, anxious, and excited all at the same time. I closed my eyes, silently hoping that he answered my phone call.

"Hello," Kevin said. "Who's this?"

I swear I almost hung up that phone when I heard that. Then I realized that I hadn't given him my number.

I clutched my imaginary pearls. "Um, it's Phoenix. How are you?"

"I'm good. How are you?"

"I'm well. I'm doing just fine. I was wondering if you weren't busy tonight, can I interest you in dinner and drinks?"

"Well, I don't know. My dudes wanted to hang out tonight but I have to see how I feel."

My heart sank. *Oh, God. He's turning me down!* "I wanted to take you out tonight. Remember?"

"Yeah, I remember."

Okay, I couldn't take it anymore! I was going to have to speak up on Kevin's attitude. I got up from the bed and began pacing around my bedroom. It was definitely time for Kevin and me to iron out some shit before we went any further.

"What's up with you, Kevin? I asked if I could take you out and you're still acting like you're angry with me. I already apologized for my behavior so what's up with the funky-ass attitude, man? Come on already!"

"I don't know what you're talking about," he calmly replied. "The only thing that I've done was answer your questions."

This man was going to make me go off on him. "Okay, so you're answering my questions! But it's not that. It's your tone, Kevin. I don't like your tone."

"Why is my tone bothering you? Is it because I'm not doing the 'hey, baby, baby' BS that you're probably so used to?" he said.

I wasn't trying to have the Battle of the Sexes with Kevin. I didn't want to argue, fuss, or fight with him. That wasn't why I asked for his number.

I was losing my patience. "So what do you wanna do, man? Do you wanna roll with me or what?" Then I caught myself. "Wait. Why does it sound like I'm begging you to hang out with me?"

"Because you are begging me to hang with you!" While Kevin laughed at his own joke, I was quiet as shit and embarrassed like hell. As a matter of fact, I felt like a fool for even asking him out. "I'm just playing with you! Of course I'll hang out with you, on one condition."

I slapped my forehead with the palm of my hand. This whole dating thing was super aggravating. No wonder I dated people's husbands and boyfriends.

"And what's that, Kevin?" I asked.

"I will go out with you, only if you'll let *me* pay for everything," he said.

I instantly softened up. "Aw, Kevin! That's so sweet but listen, honey, you don't have to pay for anything tonight. I know that you garbage spe . . . I mean, sanitation workers don't make a lot of money—"

Kevin stopped me from going any further. I had put my foot in my mouth—again. "Come on, babe. Are you kidding me right now? You really don't know what I have in my pockets, let alone how much money I make. So I'm gonna let that shit slide this time but please refrain from taking any potshots when it comes to my job or my salary—that's just not cool." I guessed he told me. I didn't say a word. "I'm coming to pick you up in an hour so start getting ready. Call you when I'm in front of your building."

We said our good-byes and hung up the phone.

I hung up the phone and hurriedly prepared for my first date with Kevin. Exactly an hour later, Kevin's phone number popped up on my iPhone caller ID. I told him that I would be down in five minutes. Of course, I had to do a little more prepping in my full-length mirror before I made my appearance. I wanted to make a good impression. I took one last look at myself and as usual, I looked great. I was ready to go.

Exactly five minutes later, as I made my way to the elevator, I began reciting a Buddhist chant. I needed more than just regular prayer to get me through the date night with Kevin. "*Nam-Myho-Renge-Kyo,*" I whispered to myself. I didn't know what to expect from him.

I kept asking myself if I was crazy for entertaining Kevin. I didn't like his damn job; I started off not liking his ass. But damn, he was so cute and so mysterious—

his aloofness had me wanting to find out what made him tick. And I really wanted to take a walk on the wild side for once. I wanted do something different from what I normally did. Nothing else that I had done thus far seemed to work for me and it was time to switch things up a little.

Then there were my deal breakers. I was worried about those.

I hoped that Kevin didn't have any baby mama drama or child support issues.

I also hoped that Mr. Wright could afford me. I was definitely a high maintenance woman. But if Kevin didn't have the funds to pay for the little things, he might as well lose my number. I was serious about that. Thank God, I had taken my American Express card as a precautionary measure.

When I got downstairs, there were a few cars double-parked in front of my building. I heard Kevin call my name.

"Yo, Phoenix!" he yelled to me. I turned around and saw him flicking the front headlights on an Audi coupe.

I breathed a sigh of relief when I saw Kevin in that vehicle. "Oh, thank you, God," I said to myself.

Kevin got out of the driver's side to open the passenger door for me. I noticed that he had cleaned up real nice, too. He looked like a whole different person without that uniform on. I slid my butt into the passenger seat, Kevin got back into the car and we were on our way.

"So what's up?" Kevin asked, while driving through the streets of my Queens neighborhood, ducking and dodging traffic.

"You're what's up," I said, giving him a look of admiration. "You're looking very dapper tonight."

"Thanks," he replied.

I waited for him to return the compliment. When it didn't come right away, I got annoyed.

I frowned. "Aren't you going to say that I look nice?" I asked, looking at him in amazement.

Kevin took his eyes off the road for a few seconds to look me in the eye. "Do you really need for me to say that you look nice? I'm sure you know what you look like."

"What the hell is so difficult about you giving me a compliment, Kevin?"

"You're hanging out with me, aren't you?"

"Yeah, I am," I replied, having no idea where he was going with that question. "What is that supposed to mean?"

Kevin smirked. "Hanging out with me is a compliment!" he said, with a laugh.

I crossed my arms. "So am I going to go through this for the rest of the night, Kevin?"

"Go through what?"

"Are you gonna continue to act like a pompous jackass?"

He laughed again. "I'm being a pompous jackass?" he asked, with a look of confusion on his face.

"Forget it, man," I said, waving him off and looking out the passenger window, with a slight attitude.

Kevin tapped my arm to get my attention. "Come on, Phoenix," he said. "I'm just kidding around with you, girl! Take the stick out of your ass and live a little! You got to have a sense of humor in order to hang with me."

"For your information, I have a sense of humor, okay?" I said, giving him a dirty look.

"There you go!" he said, with a smile. "That's the Phoenix I like—the feisty, assertive Phoenix. And the answer is yes, you look good—good enough to eat, girl!

I'm sorry I didn't compliment you when you wanted me to." Kevin began pinching my left cheek, as if I were a small child. "You're so cute when you're upset, do you know that?"

I laughed and pushed his hand away. I tried not to laugh. "Whatever, Kevin!"

"Anyway, where are we going tonight?" he asked. "Is it going to be Manhattan? Brooklyn? Staten Island? Or do you want to stay in Queens? The Bronx is out of the question, unless it's City Island, of course."

"Um, maybe we can go to . . . forget it. Then again, you're probably not able to afford that place."

Kevin stopped at a red light and glanced over at me. "Hold up a minute. Now what's all this talk about me not being able to afford shit?" he asked. Now he was the one with an attitude.

I shrugged my shoulders. "I'm just saying . . ." I said, not expecting for him to react that way.

"Just saying what, Phoenix?" The light turned green and he continued driving. "Let me tell you some shit about me before we start this night out on a very fucked-up note," he began. "It's quite obvious that I have to run down my resume to you. I'm a thirty-one-year-old man with no kids. I own a house in Cambria Heights that was left to me by my mother's parents and I live alone. I own two other properties—one in Brooklyn and another building in Queens. Me and one of my cousins own a barber shop called Shavers, located on Merrick Boulevard that makes me a lot of damn money. Plus, I make over a hundred thousand a year just from working Sanitation alone—the job that I've been on for the last ten years. So now do you still think that I can't afford shit?"

While I was quite impressed with Kevin's accomplishments, I felt like a jackass. Just from looking at him in that nasty green uniform, I wouldn't have known that he had all of that going on. Not to mention, he had made more money in the last year than I had made in the last two years. I should have respected Kevin for making an honest living instead of worrying about his job profession and salary.

I apologized to him yet again. "I'm so sorry, Kevin. I didn't mean to offend you."

Kevin ignored my apology. He was dead set on making a valid point. "People should be defined by the way they treat people, the way that they carry themselves. Just because I handle trash for a living don't mean that I'm trash or that I associate myself with trash."

Surprisingly, I was at a loss for words. I couldn't get mad at Kevin for telling me off—he made so much sense. Maybe I was superficial, shallow, and materialistic.

Kevin was the first one to break the silence. "Do you think that the first time I spoke to you was the first time that I ever laid eyes on you?" he asked.

"I don't know." Truth was, I had never noticed Kevin until he worked up the nerve to speak to me.

"The first time that I saw you was about three months ago. I thought you were gorgeous and I wanted to get to know you better. The day that I decided to make a move, my partner, Shorty, bet me fifty dollars that you were going to shoot me down. I told him, 'Nah, not this dame, man. She seems like she has it all together!' Let's just put it like this, I lost fifty dollars that day."

I turned around to face Kevin. "Did I come out tonight for you to get on me? Is this some kind of vendetta date, because I don't understand why you're telling me all of this," I said, not wanting to hear the ugly truth about my lousy disposition.

Like clockwork, Kevin touched on exactly what I was thinking. "Has any man ever taken the time to tell you the truth?" he asked.

I had to think about that for a moment. "What kind of question is that?"

"Answer the question."

"I mean, I don't know! But I can't say that all the men I dealt with lied to me, either."

"In other words, did any one of those cats ever have a sit-down with you and try to get to know Phoenix, the woman, and not Phoenix, the fly girl?"

I thought long and hard about what Kevin was saying to me. I couldn't recall any man I dated who had ever taken the time to figure me out, analyze me, or even pick my brain. Most of the men that I come in contact with over the years were usually just as small-minded and insensitive as I was. They were into imagery and appearances. Then again, so was I. I didn't even know how to handle someone as real and raw as Kevin.

"I don't want to make it seem like I'm being hard on you or anything, Phoenix, because I really do like you."

I liked Kevin too but everything didn't have to be so complicated so soon, either.

I held my hands up. "Well, I like you too, Kevin! Aren't I here with you right now?" I shook my head. "Now can we just try to enjoy each other?"

Kevin sighed. "You're right. That's my bad. Guess I'm just prepping you, that's all."

"Prepping me for what?" I asked, looking at him like he was crazy.

"Prepping you to be my lady," he said, with a wink.

"Ha! I hear that," I replied. I turned to face the passenger window. I couldn't let Kevin see the huge smile on my face.

Chapter 19

Work In Progress

Ebony

It was 10:45 P.M., Friday night and there was absolutely no partying for me. The almighty Prince Kare Bear was at home for the weekend and in his bed sound asleep. I was in my own bedroom, doing some window shopping on my laptop and watching *Martin* reruns on TV One when my phone rang. It was Wes.

I hadn't heard from Wes in a few days so I figured that he had probably grown impatient with me. I didn't agree to go out with him yet and, subconsciously, I was waiting for him to lose interest. I just wasn't up for the challenge.

"What's up, miss?" he said, coming on the phone, sounding quite happy.

"Hey, Wes," I said. "What's going on?"

"Nothing much. I'm about to meet up with a friend of mine so I wanted to give you a call."

I had a feeling that this friend of Wes's was not a guy.

"What friend?" I asked, curious to know who and what Wes was getting into. As soon as I said that, I instantly regretted it. I wasn't like I was giving him any play.

"You wouldn't know them," he said.

I should have left it at that, but for some reason his response had me wanting to pry. "I know that I don't know any of your friends, Wes but is your friend a man or a woman?" I asked.

Wes laughed. "My friend is a woman."

I closed my computer. "Oh! So you're hanging out with a woman tonight, huh?"

"As a matter of fact, I am."

Suddenly, I was feeling very annoyed, maybe even a little jealous.

"So you're actually going to sit here and tell me that you're hanging out with another female, Wes? Really?"

"Wait a minute. Didn't you ask who I was hanging out with? And why can't I keep it real with you? You're not my girl and I'm not your man. We're friends, right? Isn't that what you wanted to be—just friends?"

I groaned. "Yeah, you're right." The problem was is that after Dray, I knew that it was going to be hard for me to be platonic friends with the opposite sex. I just didn't trust them. "Anyway, what are you getting into?"

"Well, I just happened to be in the house for the night. I usually hang out when my son stays at his father's house every other weekend. Thanks for asking me, though," I sarcastically replied.

Wes ignored my sarcasm. "Sounds like you're a great mother," he said, moving on to the next subject. "As for me, I'm going to Atlantic City for the night. Probably gonna hit up the 40/40 Club and the House of Blues while I'm out there, get a suite at the Borgata and chill for the night, you know, nothing special."

Listening to this, I was getting more and more irritated by the minute. "So you're taking this female friend to Atlantic City? She must really be special."

"She's special, but at the end of the day she's just a friend, Ebony. That's all, just a friend."

Why did he keep calling this bitch a friend? If Wes and I were to start dating, was he going to be calling me a friend to the next woman too? Wes was just what I thought he was from the beginning—a damn dog. Just like all the other men I had been with.

"You men fucking kill me!" I blurted out.

"Why are you getting upset with me?" he asked, trying to sound all innocent.

I couldn't explain why I was so pissed with Wes. Then again, maybe it wasn't Wes that I was upset with. . . .

"Listen, love, I would have preferred to take you to Atlantic City but you've been fronting on me. Didn't I show you what type of dude I was from day one? I told you the truth about my divorce and my situation and you haven't even bothered to see me since then. What's up with that?"

"I just broke up with my boyfriend a week ago so I'm not sure if I'm ready to date anyone."

"Ah, damn! You didn't tell me that. How long were you with this guy?"

"Three years."

Wes sucked his teeth. "Three years? Ah, don't worry, babe! You're going through it now but you're going to be just fine without that lame. Try being *married* for fifteen long-ass years and having to start over! Now that shit is crazy! And I already done told you that you're a beautiful woman. It's no need for you to be sitting around the house, feeling sorry for yourself or thinking about some undeserving cat who didn't know what a jewel he had. When I was in the process of getting my divorce, I was a wreck. My ex-wife was trying to take my manhood, my money, she was talking about me to my kids . . . It was a fucking mess! But we had to move on. Now I'm doing what makes me happy."

"Yeah, I see that."

"Yep. And you should do what makes you happy, too, love."

Wes had made a great point, as usual, and I agreed with him. "You're right, Wes. You are so right."

"Well, I'm about to get up outta here. I guess I'll be talking to you when I get back."

"Wes?" I said.

"Yes, babe?"

I decided that I was being too hard on Wes. My baggage was weighing me down. "I'm ready to hang out with you, that is, if you'll have me. As friends, of course."

I could hear Wes snicker. "Let's do that, cutie. Let me know when you're available and I will definitely make the time for you, "friend"."

I smiled. "That's what's up."

After I hung up the call, I kept wondering about the female Wes was hanging out with. I wondered if she looked better than me, if he really liked her, how long had they'd been "friends." I also wondered why Wes and his wife were divorced. Was he having an affair with someone and his wife found out? Did she cheat or did their relationship run its course? And then I thought, why did I give a shit about any of that? I could have been in Atlantic City, staying overnight at the Borgata and popping bottles at the 40/40 Club but, no, I was too busy feeling sorry for myself. I was becoming more and more pathetic.

Ten minutes after hanging up the phone, to my surprise, my doorbell rang. I looked at the time on my cable box. It said 11:00 P.M. I wondered who in the hell could be ringing my bell at that time of night.

I put on my slippers and walked to the front of my apartment, in complete darkness. I looked through the peephole and, shockingly enough, I saw Shah on the other side of my door. I found that to be strange because he almost never came over to my house unless he was coming to pick up Kare. *What could he possibly want?*

I opened the door and Shah was standing there, eyes red as fire. He looked drunk.

"What's up, Ebony? Can I come in?" he asked.

I paused for a moment and then slowly opened the screen door. Shah staggered inside my house. He was reeking of alcohol. Him being drunk was the only excuse that he had for coming to my house at eleven o'clock at night.

"Are you all right?" I asked.

Shah stumbled straight into the living room and plopped down on my couch. I turned on the lamp and sat in the chair across from him.

"Yo, I miss you, girl," he said, slurring a little bit.

I could have sworn Shah said that he missed me. "What did you say to me, Shah Born Banks?"

"I said that I miss you."

I stood up and crossed my arms in a defensive manner. "What are you talking about? And why are you pissy drunk?" Shah couldn't answer that. "Look, Kare is sleeping and, as a matter of fact, I'm about to go to bed too. Your ass can sleep on the couch. I'll get you some covers and a pillow."

As I was about to walk away, Shah stood up and grabbed my arm. "Sit down, Ebony. I'm not trying to cause no problems. I just want to talk to you for a minute. Don't shut me down."

I sat back down next to him, looking like a deer caught in headlights.

"I know that I'm kind of sauced up right now but I've been thinking about this for a while now. Every time I come by to pick up Kare, I always think about what would have happened between me and you. I wondered if we would have gotten married or had another child together. Thinking about this makes me want to see my son every day, Ebony, and you too. I want you and Kare to be a part of my life again—I don't want us to be apart anymore."

People always say that liquor is a truth serum and I was trying to absorb everything that Shah was saying to me. We hadn't been together since Kare was three years old—five years is a long time to be apart from each other. Now drunken Shah was proclaiming that he had all of these alleged unresolved feelings for me.

I covered my eyes with my hands and shook my head. "Can you please, please spare me the drunken rant? We haven't been together in years and my heart can't take any more lies, okay?" I said, with a pleading look on my face.

Suddenly, Shah leaned over and kissed me—with tongue and everything. That's what it was. He wanted some pussy. And I, being as easy as I was when it came to the dick, did exactly what I normally did in these circumstances—I reciprocated.

I felt Shah's hands roaming under my nightshirt. He began rubbing on my clitoris and it was over.

Shah got me so worked up that I slowly began undressing right in the middle of my living room. It didn't take long for him to get naked. Then I got the urge to give Shah something that he always loved—some good old head, some slow neck, a blow job, some brain, were a few of the names that he called it. I squatted down in front of him and took his erect rod into my eager mouth. I sucked and slobbered on his log, damn near choking myself trying to deep throat every inch of it. Shah threw his head back and moaned with pleasure while grabbing my head. He started fucking my mouth like it was some wet pussy and I teased the head of his dick with my tongue; licked his balls, too. While sucking on the Jimmy, I remembered it was the same dick that at one time, I was totally obsessed with. One thing that Shah and I always had was a very passionate, lust-driven relationship and, from the looks of it, we were about to be back to fucking each other all over again.

That blow job must have sobered Shah up because he picked me up and carried me into the dining area. He pulled a chair out from the kitchen table and sat in it. His rock-hard dick looked and felt like a missile; it was thick, long, and hard. I bit my bottom lip and climbed on top of it. As soon as I began riding it like a cowgirl, my pussy began leaking like a broken water faucet. Shah had a grip on my ass and pulled me down on that big old thing of his, making me take in every last inch of him. He placed soft kisses all over my titties while I bounced up and down on the dick. A few minutes of this and then we changed positions.

We began kissing each other again. Shah knew exactly what I liked. His kissing always got me even more excited. We were going at it, too, like it was something that we had been missing for years.

About twenty minutes later, Shah and I were in my bedroom, still going at it. This time we were making slow passionate love to each other. He licked every part of my body, hitting nerve endings that I never knew existed. I came first and then Shah squirted his thick semen all over my naked body.

We collapsed in each other's arms, exhausted from our mini freak show. I intertwined my legs with his, while we lay in my bed together. I still had Shah's dried-up cum on me but I didn't care. For some reason, I just felt like being a nasty girl that night.

Shah tried to catch his breath. "You were always ready to get your fuck on," he said, kissing me on the forehead. "That's one of the things I do remember about you."

"Yeah, you're right," I replied, knowing damn well that I was playing myself by lying in the bed with my ex. "That's a good and a bad thing."

"Ebony," Shah said.

"Yeah," I replied, about to doze off on his talking ass.

"You know that I never stopped loving you, right?"

I held my head up and looked at him like he was stupid. "Don't blow no smoke up my ass, Shah! Please."

"I'm serious! Just say that you'll take me back, Ebony. I need you and Kare in my life. I'll do whatever it takes to be the best man I can be for you and my son."

"Shah, could you please just take your drunken ass to sleep?" I said, scolding him. "We can talk about this shit in the morning."

I fluffed my pillow then stared at the ceiling. Shah knew good and damn well that he and I had some serious trust issues with each other. In other words, us getting back together wasn't happening, Captain. But how could I say otherwise when I had the man lying in my damn bed? I was giving him mixed signals. Thinking about this kept me awake. As I listened to Shah's snoring, I wanted to kick myself. Once again, this twat of mine was about to get me into some serious trouble. I rested my palm on my forehead—I felt a headache and the heartache coming on. Why couldn't I just keep my legs closed?

Chapter 20

What's the 411?

Joi

"I can't believe that I'm pregnant, Ma!" I said excitedly.

It was Friday night. I had headed straight for my mother's house after I got off work that evening to tell her the good news. I was supposed to have stayed for a little while but now it was almost twelve in the morning and I was still there. Being that it was so late, Mommy insisted that I spend the night. That was something that I hadn't done in a while. And since our relationship and the communication between us had drastically improved, I was more than happy to do that.

I sprawled across my mother's king-sized bed, snuggling up against her warm body. She was reading an *Essence* magazine and I was staring into the heavens, feeling wonderfully happy. I had been trying to come up with names for my unborn for the last two hours.

"If it's a boy, I'm just going to name him Tatum Jr.," I said, staring up at the ceiling. "We can call him T.J. If it's a girl, I'm going to name her Tatiana Joi after me and her father. Cute, right, Ma?"

"Beautiful, baby." My mother took her glasses off and put her magazine down. She was staring at me. "Did you tell Tate the good news yet?" she asked.

I looked away from her. "No, I didn't."

"And may I ask why not?"

I began biting my lip. "Because . . ."

"I'm listening," my mother said, not taking her eyes off me.

I sat up. "I don't think that Tate's going to be happy about this pregnancy, Ma."

My mother had a shocked expression on her face. "Why would you say that? Isn't he your boyfriend?"

"I know that he's not going to be happy because of how everything went down with his daughter. And once his daughter's mother finds out about me being pregnant, she's going to try to keep his child away from him! I know she is and he does, too."

Mommy sucked her teeth and waved me off. "You don't know that, Joi."

"Ma, you don't know this crazy woman! She uses her daughter as a pawn every chance she gets."

My mother got real serious then. "So why do you want to have a baby by Tate again?"

"Because he's my man. And I love him, of course."

"Normally, I stay out of your business, but this time my future grandchild is involved. I'm going to be honest, Joi, I don't feel that Tate is a strong enough man to hold you and my grandbaby down."

I looked away from my mother and down at my belly. "Not true! Tate is a very good father."

"To that little girl, yes. You don't know how he's going to be to this one in your belly."

I tried not to get upset with my mother's negative comments. She was pushing my buttons all around the board. I didn't understand why everyone had this vendetta against Tate. But it didn't matter what anyone thought. I was going to have Tate's baby and everything was going to turn out for the best. So instead of going back and forth with my mother, I decided to just retire for the night before I said something that I couldn't take back.

"I'm tired, Ma. I'm going to bed." I got up and kissed her on the cheek.

She put her glasses back on and picked up her magazine. "Good night, baby. Do you need me to get you anything from downstairs?" she asked, trying to lighten the blow.

I rubbed my tummy and yawned. "No, Ma, I'm okay. I'm just exhausted, that's all."

"Okay, baby."

I went into my old bedroom and closed the door behind me. I undressed and put on one of Payne's old T-shirts that I used to sleep in as a teenager. Then I slid into my full-sized bed. After lying there for a few moments, I reached for my cell phone on the nightstand to call Tate. When he answered, I heard Chasity talking in the background.

"Where are you?" I asked, with a frown on my face.

"I'm at home," he replied. "Are you still at your mother's house?"

"Yeah, I'm still here." I paused for a few seconds and listened to Chasity talk. The expectant mother in me thought she sounded so cute. A couple of months ago, the sound of her baby voice would have annoyed the shit out of me. "Look, Tate, I have to tell you something."

"Oh, boy! What is it now, Joi?" he said, sounding slightly irritated. Between Chasity bugging him at those ungodly hours and knowing how I felt about her, he probably expected the worst.

"I'm pregnant."

"You're what?" he yelled into the phone. "Wait, wait, hold on, let me put this little girl back in the bed."

I heard him in the background, putting Chasity in the bed. She was whining a little so I assumed that she wasn't ready to go to sleep. Once Tate got her settled in, he came back to the phone.

"You're pregnant? Really, sweetheart?"

"Yes, I am! Are you happy?" I asked, nervously awaiting his reply.

"Hell, yeah!" Tate exclaimed. "I'm happy as shit! How far along are we?"

That "we" got to me. That's why I loved my man. "I'm six weeks pregnant."

"When did you find this out?" he asked.

"Wednesday."

"It's Friday night, Saturday morning! Why are you just now telling me this?"

"Well, I was kind of nervous about telling you, Tate. I didn't know what your reaction was going to be. I really wanted to tell you in person but you have Chasity this weekend."

"Listen, you don't have to be afraid to tell me anything. I love you and I'm going to do what I have to do for you and this baby, you hear me? I just got some things that I'm trying to work out right now."

I wanted to ask him what those things were but I wasn't going to press issue.

"I love you, Tate."

"I love you too." He yawned in my ear. "Look, I'm about to take it down. I had to work those double shifts at the post office last night and this little girl done wore me out."

We gave each other air kisses and disconnected the call.

After hanging up with Tate, I kept tossing and turning. I didn't know if it was just plain anxiousness or excitement that was keeping me awake. About thirty minutes later, I went into my mother's room. I climbed into bed with her and wrapped my arms around her waist. Then I started to cry.

My mother turned around and held me in her arms. "What's wrong, baby?" she asked, with motherly concern in her voice.

"I'm so scared," I whispered.

"Aw! Don't be scared," my mother said, holding me in her arms. "Everything is going to be fine. Believe me. Everything is going to be just fine. You have your family."

My mother's reassurance and comforting helped me fall into a restful slumber that night. She didn't let me go until I was sound asleep.

The next morning, I was awakened by the smell of turkey bacon, eggs, and French toast. Mommy and I had a mother/daughter breakfast and after that, I made my way back to Brooklyn.

On the drive home, I decided that I was going to call Tate up and invite him and Chasity over to my house for lunch in the early afternoon hours. I knew that I had never been that open to having the little girl around when Tate and I spent time together, but since I was pregnant I decided to take on a different attitude. It was funny how an unborn baby could change a woman's attitude for the better. So I figured that it was time for me to get reacquainted with the rug rat. Not to mention, I had some other plans for little Chasity. I just had to figure out how things were going to play out.

"Hey, babe," I said when Tate answered the phone. "I was wondering if you didn't have anything to do today, why don't you and Chasity come over my house this afternoon? I'm making some mini turkey burgers and swirly fries for lunch."

"Really?" he asked. He was probably surprised that I had asked that. "I'll be there. But I gotta bring Taiwan with me, if you don't mind. Him and my dad are here from New Jersey and, of course, my little dude wanted to hang out with his big brother today."

I smiled. "Oh, yes! That'll be great. How old is Taiwan now?" I asked.

Taiwan was Tate's half brother. After having five kids with Tate's mother, Mr. Marshall's old decrepit behind went and got some woman pregnant. It was sad because Tate's dad was fifty-something years old and Taiwan's mother was in her late thirties with no kids. Like father, like son, was what I always said.

"He's five years old. Chasity can have someone to play with while we're over there."

I was happy that everything was going as planned. "Oh, it's no problem, Tate! My baby brother-in-law is more than welcome here."

"We'll be there around twelve o'clock. Is that cool?"

"That's perfect," I replied, with a sinister look on my face.

I hung up the phone. Everything was going even better than I thought it would. Yep, I had taken it upon myself to purchase a do-it-yourself DNA kit. Call me crazy but I had to know if Chasity was really Tate's child. I was also making a long-term investment into my future.

I ordered the package, having no idea where I was going to get the damn DNA samples from. But now that Taiwan was in the picture, I was catching a break. If I had the chance, I was going to swab Chasity first and then I was going to swab Taiwan too. I didn't know how or when I was going to pull this off but it was something that had to be done. And I was putting everything at stake just to do it.

Once I found out I was pregnant, there was no way that I was going to wait around to find out the truth. It didn't seem like Tate was making an effort to know shit or even cared. But I deserved to know and so did Tate.

It was a little after twelve when Tate and the kids came over. Chasity walked right through the door and wrapped her arms around my legs.

I was surprised by the gesture. "Hi, Chasity," I said, picking her up and hugging her back. She was such an adorable little girl. I almost hated that I was in competition with her for her daddy's attention.

And for a millimeter of a second, I felt badly about what I was about to do, but it was for Chasity's own good. When I put Chasity down Taiwan followed suit and gave me a hug too. Man, that little boy was so funny looking! *God forgive me.* I wasn't trying to give him much eye contact. Lord knows, I didn't want to jinx my unborn child.

I had just finished preparing lunch for all of us so we headed straight for the kitchen. While we sat at the table, Tate and I watched as the kids enjoyed their swirly fries and mini burgers. I even gave them Krazy Straws so that they could have a little fun while drinking their juice.

An hour later, the kids were in my spare bedroom, playing with a few of the toys that Tate had brought to keep them busy. Meanwhile, Tate and I retired to the couch to watch some movies. Like clockwork, it was only a matter of minutes before he was laid out on my sofa and snoring from the 'itis.

I waited about twenty minutes, just to make sure Tate was sound asleep. Taiwan and Chasity were still in the spare room, entertaining each other and watching the Nickelodeon channel on the television. I went into my bedroom to retrieve the package. I already had the directions memorized so it was a go. I casually walked into the room with the swabs in my hand, armed and ready to "play" the DNA game with the beloved little chaps.

I tiptoed into the room ever so gently. "Hi, babies," I said softly. I eased onto the futon and pretended like I was interested in the program on television. "What are you sweeties watching?"

"We watching *SpongeBob,*" said Taiwan, getting more hyper by the second. *Leave it up to the funny-looking kid to start jumping up and down like a wild banshee.*

They both began singing the song from some God-awful kiddie show and, what the hell, I began singing it too. What I did next was open my mouth as wide as I could, pretending that the swab was my microphone. Of course, they imitated me. By this time, I was singing my butt off, leaning my head back for the full effect. They did the same thing. That was when I gestured for Taiwan to come over to me. He did as he was told and opened his mouth. I held his face so that I could swab the inside of his right cheek. To my surprise, he let me do it with no problem. Then Chasity came right over after Taiwan and I did the exact same thing to her. There wasn't any resistance from either child.

I breathed a sigh of relief and deposited the swabs into separate envelopes. I quickly sealed them and walked directly into my bedroom to put them away.

The children continued to sing kiddie songs while I went to check up on Tate. He was still asleep on the couch. If I didn't think that he was going to wake up, I would have swabbed his black ass and I wouldn't have had to go through all that trouble. Truthfully, I wanted to slap the shit out of his behind for putting me through all the trouble. On another note, I was just happy the hard part was over with. Now all I had to do was send the swabs off and wait four days for the results to come back.

I prayed that I was right about Chasity not being Tate's biological daughter. If she was his child, I didn't know how I was going to make it through this pregnancy if Dara and Chasity remained a part of our lives.

Chapter 21

Someone to Love Me

Phoenix

It was Saturday morning and I felt like a brand new woman. The night out with Kevin had been an absolute success. He took me to SriPraPhai Thai Restaurant in Queens and we had a nice, intimate dinner, just an all-around great time. Kevin had shared a lot about himself, which I was grateful for. That was something that I had never experienced before with anyone I dated. Talking to Kevin also made me realize how much I had missed out on when it came to the opposite sex. I guessed men weren't all that bad, after all.

There we were sitting at a table at the far end of the restaurant. The ambiance was very alluring; the dimmed lights made the mood between Kevin and I very romantic, although we weren't trying to be that just yet. But even though we were steadying the pace, I felt myself falling deeper in like with the guy.

"So where's your father?" I asked, while we ate our dinner. "Is he and your mom still together?"

Kevin shook his head. "Nah, they're not together. They got a divorce when I was like twelve years old."

"Really? How did that go?"

Kevin took a sip of his wine. "Not too good. I was wilding out when my parents split up. And I was the only child, too. Shit, as soon as my pops moved out, my bad ass was hitting them streets!"

"Like what did you do out there?" I asked, anxious to know his story.

"What didn't I do? I sold drugs, hung out late, smoked weed, and robbed a few people. This went on until I was around nineteen years old. Then I got my GED and got my life together."

"You only have a GED?" I asked, with a concerned look on my face. Even the married guys that I dated in the past had college degrees. "Do you at least have some college?" When Kevin gave me the side eye, I caught myself. "Well, at least you have your GED," I said, wanting to run out of that restaurant for talking so much.

"Yeah, I do have some college but school just wasn't for me, man. I dropped out after my third semester."

I wiped the sweat from my brow and moved on to the next question. "I know that you don't have any kids but do you want any children?"

"Of course, I would like to have children but with my wife."

My eyes lit up. "I can respect that. I wanted to be married before I have any children."

Truthfully, I hadn't thought about having children or being married until that exact moment. Was this chance meeting with Kevin enough to make me want to settle down and start a family?

"So tell me about you, Phoenix. I don't want to be talking your head off about my life. What's good with you?"

"Well, you know I'm a paralegal at Simon and Foster Law Firm, been there for almost ten years. I have a BA in criminal justice and my minor was business management. Um, I have one older sister, one younger brother, and I am one-third part owner of Henry Trucking Company, along with my dad and my brother."

Kevin seemed impressed. "Okay, okay. You're doing your thing. Now what's up with your love life? Are you seeing anybody?"

I shook my head. "No, I'm not seeing anyone."

Kevin frowned. "Come on! You mean to tell me that no man is trying to lock down a nice-looking, independent, innovative woman like yourself?" he asked.

"Nope! Not one dude." I took a sip of my mango tea. "Can I be honest, Kevin?"

He gave me his undivided attention. "Shoot."

"I always had a certain type of man I was attracted to. But not one of them felt that I was good enough to be a girlfriend or a wife. I had to ask myself the reason why. After you laid into me tonight, I was thinking that maybe it wasn't them—it was me."

Kevin held my hand. "I'm glad to hear you say that, Phoenix. Do you know what my friends and I do with materialistic women who we think are only after us for what we have?" I shook my head. "I hate to sound harsh but we make it our business to just fuck those kinds of chicks and then tell 'em to take a walk. We don't spend no time, no money, or nothing on them— we don't take those chicks seriously. Let's be real, why would we want to be with someone who is no better than an industry groupie or a gold digger?"

I listened intently as Kevin dropped more science on me.

He continued to break it down. "I feel like this. If you weren't with me when I bought this shit, then it ain't yours, period. Now if you're my lady and we're working on *building* together, then what's mine's is yours and what's yours is mine."

"You're right. I feel the same way."

Kevin continued eating. "You did say that you weren't into blue-collar men. Initially, you thought a brother was broker than motherfucker just because I threw garbage bags into the back of that dirty-ass Sanitation truck for a living. And you almost didn't give me a chance with you. Please tell that you're not that type of woman."

"No, I'm not that type of woman," I said, defending myself. I was doing a whole lot of fronting. I was exactly that type of woman that was into the cars, the money, and the career. But at least I was working on trying to change my attitude. I still couldn't resist the urge to ask Kevin about his career choice, though. "Why do you still work for Sanitation if you have all of these properties and businesses?" I asked.

"Medical benefits, stability, a pension, and a 401K plan. Plus, I just like my job."

"Oh, okay. So you like throwing garbage around is what you're saying?"

"No, it's not about that. I've actually met a lot of interesting people since I've been doing this. And you'd be surprised at all of the good stuff I find in people's garbage. I have found envelopes of money, jewelry, and other valuables in some trash."

"So you pick through the garbage, too?" I asked, with a disgusted look on my face.

"Yep," Kevin happily replied. "I'm not ashamed to admit that."

"Yuck!" I exclaimed. "That is gross! I could never."

"Well, I always believed that one man's trash is another one's treasure, don't you think?" he asked, raising one eyebrow. I hoped that wasn't a subliminal. "What about you? Why are you a paralegal and not a lawyer?"

I was stuck on that one. No one had ever asked me that question before.

"Excuse me?" I asked, slightly offended. But I really couldn't think of a decent answer to give him.

"Why didn't you become a law-yer?" Kevin asked, talking to me as if I were slow.

I shrugged my shoulders. "I don't know, I . . . I just never thought about becoming one."

"So how can you judge everyone else and their career choices when you're still a paralegal?"

I looked at Kevin and frowned. "I don't know and can we move on?"

He stuffed some shrimps into his mouth. "Anyway, I have a fight party to go to tomorrow night. Would you like to come through?" he asked, completely changing the subject.

I was more than happy to accept the invitation. "That sounds like a plan," I said, finishing up my meal.

"Okay, take the info right now." I pulled out my phone and Kevin told me the address. "Lock that in your phone. It's in South Jamaica at my boy Duke's house."

"South Jamaica?" I asked, with a worried look on my face.

Kevin gave me a strange look. "Are you all right?" he asked.

Honestly, I didn't step foot in that neighborhood and I damn sure wasn't going there alone. "Could I bring a few of my friends with me?"

"Sure, why not." Kevin put his hand up. "Wait, do they look as good as you?"

I leaned my head to the side, with my lips tooted up. "What do you think?"

"Okay, then you can bring your girls."

We shared a laugh together.

After dinner, we went to a jazz lounge. There we had a few more drinks and did some more of the getting to know each other thing. This time, I didn't overdo it with the liquor, like I had done when I was with Stu.

It was about one in the morning when our date ended. Kevin made sure that I was upstairs in one piece. He walked me to my door, gave me a single peck on the cheek. I was on cloud nine. I stepped inside of my house feeling like a million dollar bill.

That Saturday evening, I arrived at Ebony's house to pick her up for the fight party. She came out of her house, looking absolutely adorable. Her long hair was flowing and she had some tight designer jeans that were hugging every curve of her body. Ebony was all of a size four but she was shapely and had absolutely no stomach, even though she had a baby. When she got in the car, my favorite perfume, Gucci Flora, tickled my nose hairs.

We gave each other a hug. "Hey, cutie!" I said, happy that my girl was coming along for the ride and representing me. "It was kind of last minute but I'm glad that you were able to come hang out with me."

Ebony flipped down the visor mirror to put on her lipstick. "No doubt. Lucky for me, Shah is at my house—he's staying the weekend with me and Kare."

We were on our way to pick up the young girl Saadia and my ace Capri when I stopped the car at the corner of her block.

I turned all the way around in the driver's seat. "Did you just say that Shah was at your house for the weekend?"

Ebony had this blank look on her face. "Mmm hmm. Shah's there."

I chuckled. "When did Shah started staying at your place?"

"Um, since he came over late last night, talking about how he still loved me and that he wanted to be a part of our lives again."

I pulled off. "Did you fuck Shah, Eb?"

She looked at me like I was the stupid one. "What do you think?"

I banged on my steering wheel. "Why did you fuck him?" I screamed. I hated that Ebony was such an easy lay. Shah was not to be trusted and she knew this.

Ebony stopped applying her lipstick and frowned at me. "Why not? He's my son's father!" she yelled back.

"So? All that shit that Shah is talking could be game and you know it!"

Ebony shrugged her shoulders. "Ah, I don't care. I got what I wanted," she said nonchalantly.

I shook my head. "No, you didn't, Ebony. You didn't get what you wanted. You just got fucked, that's it."

She waved me off and switched topics on me. "Did I tell you about this guy named Wes who I met Saturday night?"

I frowned. "Who the hell is this guy?"

"I went to Peaches last weekend—"

I cut Ebony off. "So why didn't you invite me, skee-zer?" I said. "I would have gone with you."

"I know but I needed some alone time. I was feeling down about my breakup with Dray, the drama, and I wanted to get out of the house. I just so happened to meet Wes while I was in Peaches—he even paid for meal and drinks and everything! We ended up exchanging phone numbers and that was the extent of it."

"You mean to tell me you didn't fuck Wes?"

She rolled her eyes at me. "No, I did not! But he's been wanting to take me out and I haven't given him the time of day."

"And why is that?"

"Maybe it's because he's almost forty-one years old. I never dated a guy his age before."

"I mean, does he look good? Is he in shape? Does he have a good job with benefits? Married with children? Or unmarried with no children? I don't see anything wrong with his age. If anything, that should be a plus."

"Wes is forty years old, he has two teenage boys with his ex-wife, he's happily divorced—his words, not mine—and he's been a firefighter for the past seventeen years."

"So what the hell is the problem?" I asked, dodging a huge pothole in the street. "He sounds like a good catch."

"He's so nice and then he's much older than me, more experienced than me—I don't know. I'm so not used to a guy like Wes."

"And that's the problem right there! He has all of the good attributes that you need in a man and you don't like him. What do you have to lose? That's why they call it 'dating.'"

Ebony seemed as if she was pondering what I was saying to her. "You're right."

"I know I'm right," I said, smacking her thigh. "Go out with Wes, girl. He seems like he's different than what you're accustomed to. Look at me. I'm hanging out with a garbage man! Who would have thought that I would be doing that?"

Ebony nodded her head, as if she was contemplating something.

After a few minutes of silence, I spoke up. "Oh yeah, did I tell you that I'm going to be an auntie? Chase's girlfriend is having a baby!"

Ebony tried to look happy but I could tell that she wasn't that excited. It made me wonder if she and my brother were still screwing each other.

"Oh, how nice. Congratulations," she replied, her voice sounding weak as shit.

"I can't wait! Are you going to help me plan the baby shower?" I asked.

Ebony sucked her teeth. "What? Please! I know you are not asking me to plan no baby shower for your brother's girlfriend!"

I laughed at her reaction. "Ah, get over it, girl! Chase was never your got-damn man! All of the dick that you get, you shouldn't be worried about my brother or his girlfriend."

Ebony rolled her eyes at me again. "Do you know how to keep your mouth shut?" she asked.

"I will shut my mouth when you learn how to shut them legs of yours," I said, half joking, half serious. "Guess that's why we're friends!"

As we made our way to pick up the other girls, I was trying to find the right moment to give Ebony "the speech." I had to lay some ground rules before we got to Duke's house. I loved my girl but I also knew that she would fuck a man within minutes of meeting him. I didn't need her to make me look bad.

We pulled up to the young girl Saadia's apartment building in East New York. She was already downstairs waiting for us. Next stop was to pick up Capri. She lived in Queens, not too far from where the party was. I called her and told her that we were on our way.

Once I picked up Capri from her house, I gave her, Ebony, and Saadia, a brief bio on Kevin. When I told Saadia and Capri that he worked for Sanitation, they were shocked that I had even given him the time of the day.

Capri laughed hysterically. "Wait until I tell Shanell about you and the garbage man, Phoenix! Did you fuck him yet?"

I looked at Capri through my rearview mirror. "No, honey, I didn't fuck him! And I'm not trying to—not yet anyway. I'm trying to build a connection with him first. I'm finally ready to settle down with someone and for some reason; I think that Kevin is that person."

"Shit, at least he has money!" Saadia said. "I know that you would have never dated that man if he didn't have any money."

Ebony and Capri gave Saadia a pound for that. They were acting like I was some gold digger.

I shook my head. "First of all, y'all beyotches don't know me like y'all think you know me! For everyone's information, *I* was the one who offered to give Kevin my phone number first and *I* was the one who offered to take *him* out on a date. Then *I* was the one who picked up the phone to call *him* the night that we first went out. I did all of this and I had no idea what kind of money Kevin had. My initial thought was that he was just some broke-ass garbage man and we all know how I feel about blue-collar men. What I'm trying to say is that when I decided to approach Kevin that day, I didn't see anything else but a man—a man that I wanted to get to know better."

I could hear a pin drop in my car. For once, those birds weren't chirping. I had shut them down.

"Wow," said Ebony, giving me a nod of approval. "Not you, going all out to make an impression! You must really like this guy, huh?"

"Yes, I do! And listen up, ladies! I want all of y'all to go in this man's house and act like y'all have some sense, especially you, *Ebony*." We all laughed. "It's about me tonight, not about none of y'all chickenheads. And if you meet anyone, please, please, please, respect yourselves, especially you, *Ebony*."

"You're not going to keep calling my name out like I'm some ho—"

We all cut her off. "*You are a ho!*" we said in unison.

Ebony slouched down in her seat. "Damn, y'all didn't have to say it like that!"

We burst out laughing.

Ten minutes later, I was pulling up in front of Kevin's friend's house. I saw his Audi parked outside and I dialed his cell number. When he answered the phone, there was a lot of noise in the background. I could barely hear him.

"What's up, baby girl? Are you on your way here?" he yelled into the phone.

"I'm outside parking my car," I replied while shushing my giggling friends.

"Okay, I'll come outside and meet you."

I found parking and we walked up the block to the house. I was glad that all of my friends, including me, were looking quite fabulous. I could always count on my girls to represent.

When Kevin walked up to meet us, their mouths dropped. Saadia nudged me on the arm.

"Phoenix," she said, looking at Kevin with a smile on her face. "That man is going to be your husband, girl."

I was already one step ahead of her, with a big smile on my face. "I hope so, Saadia. I hope so."

Chapter 22

Get It Right

Ebony

I had every intention of spending a quiet weekend at home but when Phoenix invited me out, I couldn't pass up on an opportunity to hang out with my girls. I was just glad that Shah was still at my house when she called me.

Speaking of my baby daddy, Shah seemed pretty content during his brief visit with Kare and me. I knew that Kare was happy with the arrangement. That little boy couldn't contain his excitement when he got up and saw his father that morning.

"Daddy!" Kare screamed, jumping into Shah's arms. "What are you doing here? Do you live at my house now?" he asked.

Shah glanced at me. "No, I don't live here, baby boy. I just came to visit you and Mommy," he replied.

Kare hugged his father's neck. "Dang! I want you to live here, Daddy!"

Shah looked at me again but I didn't want to give him any eye contact. I wasn't really sure what Shah was up to but it did feel good having a man around.

It would have been great to have Shah in my son's life on a full-time basis. Kare would have loved that and my son's happiness meant everything to me. So instead of having that much-needed discussion about what was going on between him and me, we spent the early part of that Saturday morning making it all about Kare and nothing else. Whatever we needed to talk about was going to have to wait.

When we walked into Kevin's friend's house, I felt like a kid in a candy store! There was nothing but a bunch of fine-ass "menses," in assorted flavors, looking absolutely delicious. And that Kevin fellow? From the looks of it, my girl Phoenix hit the jackpot with him. She introduced all of us to him. Then he introduced us to his friends, including Duke, who was the host of the fight party. All of the guests, the host, and Kevin seemed cooler than a fan.

Thirty minutes later, there I was standing around with the rest of the guests, rooting for my opponent and waiting for the main event. Instead of mingling like I usually do, I was chilling out and standing off to the side. I just cased the large entertainment room with my eyes.

In one corner, the young girl, Saadia, my protégé, was sucking up every bit of the male attention that she was getting. She was enjoying every minute of it, too— I could tell by her body language that she was feeling flirty. I didn't blame her. And the guys she was entertaining seemed like they were hanging on to her every word.

Attagirl! I said to myself.

On the other side of the room, Capri, who was looking as cute as a button, seemed like she was engaged in some deep conversation with two handsome chocolate-skinned brothers. *Lucky her!*

As for me, I kept my distance from the guys. Phoenix had given me instructions and I, being the devoted and loyal friend that I am, didn't want any problems with Her Majesty. Besides, did I really need to start up another fuckship with yet another guy? I didn't think so. My plate was already too damn full and I had enough sex partners to last me a lifetime.

About an hour later, it was ten o'clock and the main event was about to come on the Pay-Per-View channel. The first round began and all eyes were on the forty-seven-inch LED television. From the way that Kevin and his friends were carrying on, you would have thought that they had bet a shitload of money on Floyd Mayweather. Not one person was rooting for Manny Pacquiao.

I loved boxing probably just as much as I loved men so I was definitely in on the hype. I had even made a small wager with Kevin's friend, Duke. I bet twenty-five dollars that Floyd was going to knock out his opponent in the third round. Duke insisted that it was the fifth round.

"Girl, you're crazy! Manny is a pretty good fighter . . . The third round is impossible! I say that Pretty Boy is probably going to knock Manny out in the fifth round! And I want my twenty-five dollars, too," Duke said, with a smirk on his face.

I stopped mid-cheer to look at him like he was a damn fool. "Man, Pretty Boy is going to knock Manny out in the third round—guaranteed!" I said, talking over the screaming and yelling of the other guests.

Duke threw his head all the way back and laughed at me. "Yeah, okay! You're lucky you're cute or else I would have told you about yourself!"

I felt a flirt coming on but all I kept hearing in the back of my head was Phoenix's annoying ass voice. *Act like y'all got some sense—Ebony! The queen has spoken!* But from the looks of Duke, with his caramel skin, that neatly-lined full beard, and those pretty-ass lips of his, it was going to be hard as hell to be a good girl. Damn that Phoenix! She was such a cock blocker.

Forty-minutes later, we were still watching that television, waiting for a TKO. Floyd and Manny were still fighting. And it was the fifth round, too, much to my dismay. Manny was taking his ass whooping like a champ. Duke continued to talk trash to me and I told him that I wasn't giving up no cash for the bet I had lost.

Now, my conversation with Duke was purely inno-cent, at least I thought so. But of course, when I glanced over at Phoenix, Ms. Killjoy, she was staring at me with the mad face like I was doing something wrong. She made a gesture for me to come over to where she was sitting. I had this funny feeling that Phoenix and I were going to have it out before the night ended.

As I was about to walk over to Phoenix, Duke grabbed my hand.

"Where do you think you're going?' he asked, with a flirtatious look on his face.

I instantly began blushing. "Let go of my hand, Duke! I have to tell my girlfriend something," I said, pointing at Phoenix, who was sitting on Kevin's lap.

I could tell that Phoenix was getting more and more impatient by the minute. She kept trying to get my attention but I purposely wasn't paying her no mind. That Duke was much more interesting.

"You don't have to go over there with them!" Duke said. "Kev Wright is keeping your girl busy. Stay right here and talk to me."

Damn, I was so tempted.

I immediately changed the subject. "You have a re-ally nice house here," I told him, looking around at the décor and ignoring my angry-looking friend.

Duke took a swig of his Heineken and rubbed my arm. "Aw, thank you, babe. Not only are you're very attractive but you have some great taste," he said, licking his lips. "But then again, so do I."

I giggled and playfully slapped his arm. "You are just the cutest!"

Suddenly, from the corner of my eye, I saw Phoenix walking toward me. She told Duke to excuse us for a minute and snatched me by the arm. She pulled me into the empty kitchen area.

"What the hell are you doing out there?" Phoenix asked, with an agitated look on her face.

I shrugged my shoulders, confused by her reaction. "What do you think I'm doing? I'm having a good time at a fight party!"

"I told your ass not to come to this party acting like some fucking ho! Why is it everywhere we go, you have to be up in some man's face, huh?" she asked, talking through clenched teeth.

At first, I thought that Phoenix was joking with me. But from the tone of her voice, the fiery rage in her eyes, I realized that she was dead-ass serious! Now I had a very good sense of humor and had always been a good sport when it came to her slick talking but this Pacquiao/Mayweather fight night was about to be my defining moment. I was going to let this bitch have it! No longer was I going to tolerate Phoenix's wisecracks about how many men I slept with and I damn sure wasn't about to let nobody scold my grown ass like I was a child. I was tired of her putting me down to build herself up especially when she didn't have the best track record when it came to men.

I slammed my cup onto the counter and my drink splashed all over my hand. Phoenix had truly pissed me off.

"Whoa! Wait one got-damn minute, missy! Aren't you the bitch who asked *me* to come to this here little shindig?" I asked, looking at her in amazement. "If I knew that you were going to act like a fool, I would have stayed my ass at home! And I never had any intentions on coming here to meet no fucking man—I have enough guy problems! Like I said, all that I was doing was having a good time! I came here to represent you and now you're acting like this to me?"

Phoenix began pacing around the empty kitchen. I could tell that she was thinking of a valid reason for her actions. But she didn't have a leg to stand on and she knew it.

"Look, Ebony, what I'm trying to say is that I finally met someone that I really like and I want to make a good impression on him! That's why I don't need you to be running around here, flirting with his friends and making a fool of me, or yourself for that matter! I don't want Kevin to think that I associate myself with, with the bullshit!"

I chuckled at the irony of her statement. Phoenix had been nothing but a drama queen and a slut most of her adult life but I never judged the wench—not once. Now she had the nerve to be calling me out on my shit.

I put my hands on my hips. "Ain't this about a bitch? You're worried that Kevin is going to think that you're a ho like me, right?" I was disgusted. "All of this just goes to show what you really think of me. You think that I'm not good enough to be around your precious Kevin and his fucking friends!" I chuckled again. "But it's all good, girlfriend! You can have all of this shit!" I yelled, waving my hands like a madwoman. "I'm getting the fuck outta here! Fuck you, Phoenix!" I said, flipping her the bird for the full effect.

Upset, I burst out of the kitchen. Of course, everyone was staring at me, trying to figure out what was going on.

"Ebony, wait! I didn't . . ." Phoenix shouted out to me. But I wasn't trying to hear anything she said. I was out of there.

By the time I walked outside, I was crying like a baby. I couldn't believe that my best friend, a woman that I trusted with my life, really thought the worst of me.

I walked briskly toward Guy Brewer Boulevard to hail me a cab. Meanwhile, my cell phone was ringing like crazy. It was Phoenix. She must have called me like three times and I pressed ignore on every one of her calls, sending her right into my voicemail. She left me a message every time and I deleted those. The young girl Saadia even tried her hand at calling me. I knew that she was calling me for Phoenix. I sent her ass to voicemail too. I just didn't feel like talking to any of them.

After standing on the corner for ten long minutes, I was able to flag down a livery cab. I got into the back seat and gave him my Brooklyn address.

"That'll be twenty dollars, miss," the cab driver said.

"That's fine," I replied, still wiping tears from my eyes.

I felt like a piece of shit on the ride home. And I couldn't wait to kick that damn Shah out of my house, too. I didn't want him looking in my face and asking me 101 questions. I needed some me time to really think things over.

Chapter 23

Be Without You

Joi

It was Friday, April 29, 2011, six days after I had taken the liberty and swabbed Taiwan and Chasity. It had been a very rough and emotional week for me. I hadn't expected to feel guilty as hell but I did. There I was putting my relationship on the line, for the sake of knocking this tramp Dara out of the box once and for all. I had to be blind, crippled, and crazy to take such a risk but hey, I wasn't blind or crippled. I was just plain crazy—crazy for loving Tate the way I did.

As to be expected, I couldn't stop thinking about the results of the DNA test. What if Chasity was really Tate's daughter? I found myself obsessing over it.

After doing the test on Chasity's five-year-old "uncle," Taiwan, I also worried about the test results being inconclusive. A more precise DNA sample would have had to come from one of Chasity's parents but that would have been freaking impossible for me to get. Thank God, Taiwan was definitely Tate's baby brother—his father had taken care of his own DNA test and it came back positive. So the funny-looking little boy was definitely my saving grace.

Then there was also the empathetic side of me that knew if Tate found out that Chasity was not his real daughter, he would be crushed. After all, he had invested a lot of time in being the perfect father to the little girl.

Now back to the insane, completely fed-the-fuck-up side of me. That part of me said fuck Chasity and her mother, too! If Tate wasn't the girl's real daddy then Dara's whorish ass would have the responsibility of raising an illegitimate child all by herself. And poor, innocent Chasity. She would probably never know who her real dad was but that wasn't Tate's problem. Maybe Dara could go on *The Maury Show* and find out who her daughter's daddy was.

I just prayed that nothing backfired on me.

The day the test arrived, I came home from work and saw the FedEx tag on my door. My heart began beating. The delivery guy had left the package with one of my neighbors, nosey-ass Miss Wanda. I rang Miss Wanda's doorbell and she opened the door with my package in her hand.

"Hey, baby," she said, with a huge smile on her face. Between the gold tooth and the platinum-grey hair pinned up in a bun, she was an odd-looking old thing. I wanted to laugh but I held my composure. "Is everything okay with you?" Miss Wanda asked, with this suspicious look on her face. Her big eyes were wide open and the false eyelashes were fluttering. I figured that she had already read the envelope and was dying to know what was going on with me.

"Thank you for accepting this package for me, Miss Wanda," I said, ignoring her question. "How are you feeling?"

Now why did I ask Miss Wanda that? I had completely forgotten the lonely old woman was a chronic complainer. I didn't want to be rude so I braced myself for her long list of ailments.

"Oh, I'm okay, baby, except for my torn meniscus and my arthritis and the herniated disk in my lower back is bothering me. And I just started taking some vitamin D shots and my knee is killing me—it's gonna rain, isn't it?" I shrugged my shoulders. "But aside from all my ailments, I'm doing fine, baby. Thanks for asking."

I slowly began backing up toward my apartment door. "All righty, Miss Wanda! You take care of yourself and have a nice night," I said, with a smile. "Thanks again."

"Mmm hmm, baby. Anytime," she said, giving me the once-over before closing her door. I waved her off and quickly walked inside of my apartment. Once I was inside of my house, I threw my bags and stuff on the floor. I had prepared myself for the opening of that envelope for the last few days but my hands were shaking terribly.

I said a silent prayer. Then I pulled the paper out of the FedEx envelope. I skimmed through everything else until I saw the numbers that I was looking for. I took a deep breath and the tears began to flow . . . Tate was NOT Chasity's father! I kicked my leg in the air and rubbed on my growing tummy.

"Hallelujah!" I yelled. "I knew it! I fucking knew it!"

Those negative results from the test were bittersweet. I had this urge to call all of my friends, my mother, even my brother to tell them the wonderful news. Then I remembered one very important detail—no else was suppose to know that I took the test. I hadn't even told my friends and my mother, and Payne was a definite no-no. They would say that I was only looking out for myself without any regard for Tate's or Chasity's feelings. That couldn't be further from the truth. I wasn't only looking out for me. I was looking out for Tate, our future, and the future of our growing family. And with Chasity not being Tate's biological child, I knew that my baby and I could have him to ourselves.

I must have read those results at least a hundred times. When I was finally able to fully absorb everything, I made sure that I buried that envelope deep into my closet. Tate barely went through my things but I wanted to take extra precautions with the evidence. Now the only problem was how I was going to tell Tate the news?

Twenty minutes later, Tate walked in my house with his key. He gave me a kiss on the lips. I was feeling chirpier than usual, thanks to the DNA test.

"Damn, sweetheart! This pregnancy is really changing your attitude," he said. "You're happy, I'm happy. . . ."

I beamed with pride. "You really are, Tate?"

He lifted me off my feet. "Of course I'm happy! My sweetheart is having my baby! Why wouldn't I be happy?"

I let out a hearty laugh. He put me down on the couch. "Well, I feel amazing!"

He affectionately rubbed my face and pulled me up from the couch. "We need to go out and celebrate."

"Okay, where are we going?" I asked.

"Maybe we can grab a bite to eat at Night of the Cookers on Fulton Street. You like that place, don't you?"

"Hell, yeah! I love that place!" I said, shaking my booty.

Tate laughed at me. "Then that's what it is!"

As we made our way to downtown Brooklyn, Tate and I had a splendid conversation in the car about our baby. He even began picking out his own names—he wasn't really set on Tatum Jr. for a boy. He was being so wonderful to me that I actually felt bad about the whole DNA thing. Once we arrived at Cookers and were seated at our table, the guilt really began to wear on me. Tate immediately noticed the change in my mood.

Tate rubbed my cheek with the back of his hand. "Why are you so quiet all of a sudden?" he asked, with a look of concern on his face. "What's the matter? You have the first-time mommy blues already?"

I shook my head. "No, I'm okay. Just kind of nervous about what's in store for me, for us, and the baby, that's all."

Tate ordered our beverages from the waiter who came to our table. "Why are you so nervous? I'm right here with you and I'm not going anywhere."

I sighed. "I know, I know but I was just thinking about us. We're not married, Tate, and I don't want to end up being a baby mama like you know who."

Tate chuckled. "So what are you saying, Joi? Are you saying that you want us to be married before you have this baby?"

I frowned. "Yes, I do!" I was surprised that I was being so honest and frank about how I felt. "Do you want to bring another illegitimate child into this world?"

"So now you're calling my daughter a bastard," Tate said, giving me the evil eye.

I was beginning to get frustrated. Tate was using reverse psychology on me to get off the subject of marriage but I wasn't having it.

"I didn't say that, Tate!" I sucked my teeth. "I'm just saying that we are a couple and now that I'm pregnant, why wait? Let's just go ahead and make this official."

"But what if I'm not ready to get married?"

Now I was pissed. Enough was enough already. I slapped the menu on the table. A couple at the next table looked at me like I was crazy. I was about to unleash the fury but I caught myself and lowered my voice.

"What do you mean you're not fucking ready? After four years of fucking drama, you having this damn baby on me and—"

Tate stopped me from going any further.

He came closer to my face so that only I could hear him. "You know that I didn't have a baby on you, Joi. So I wish you'd stop throwing that shit in my face! Dara *was* my girlfriend—remember? That is, until I met you."

I narrowed my eyes. "Are you saying that it's my fault that you're not with Dara?" I asked, pointing at myself.

I could tell that Tate instantly regretted what he said to me. He attempted to explain.

"No, I'm not saying that," he said, not giving me any eye contact.

I took a deep breath. "Fuck this! I've been tolerating a lot of shit from you, Tatum Marshall! You've been protecting that ho from day one and rubbing this damn child of yours all in my face ever since she came into this world. And the sad part is that you don't even know that you're getting played by this trick!" I said.

"I'm getting played? What are you talking about?" Tate asked, with a confused expression on his face.

Just as I was about to tell Tate the results of the DNA test that I had taken, who walks inside of Cookers? Nobody else but Dara herself. She was with some guy and I couldn't take my eyes off him. He looked exactly like Chasity.

The entire expression on Tate's face changed when Dara walked into that restaurant. I'm not going to lie, it looked as if he was about to explode! It was the angriest that I had ever seen him. I prepared myself for the impending drama.

Dara spotted us and walked over to our table with her gentleman friend.

"Well, well, well!" she said, flinging her long weave over her shoulders. "If it isn't my favorite couple!" She let out a sarcastic laugh. "Hello, Jade," she said to me.

I smirked and tried hard to keep my cool. "Chick, you know my damn name. Don't play with me," I shot back.

Tate had a scowl on his face. "Yo, where's Chasity?" he asked, looking at Dara's male friend and giving him a quick head nod.

"It's obvious that she's not with you!" Dara rolled her eyes. "So don't worry about where she is. She's safe and that's all you need to know."

"Aren't you going to introduce us to your friend, Dara?" I asked, instantly putting the bitch on the spot.

Dara gave me this real nasty look. "Friend, Jill, Jill, friend," she said, purposely getting my name wrong again. "You already know the baby daddy," she said, fluttering her hands in Tate's direction.

I grinned. "You're such a deceitful little heifer. No shame in your game at all!"

"You must be talking about yourself, Boo," she said, flinging her weave again. "And as far as being a heifer? Child, please! I've been called worse! Ask my baby daddy—he knows!"

I had no idea what that meant and really didn't care. I just wanted her to go away before I blew her up.

"Anyway, I would love to sit around and play with you kids but me and my baby have a table on the good side of the restaurant. Toodles, suckers!" she said to Tate and I. Then she grabbed her guy friend's hand and sashayed away.

Tate still had that screw face as he watched them walk away. I could tell that he was burning up inside.

"That chick is so foul for bringing that lame-ass dude around me!"

I was confused. "What are you talking about, Tate?" I asked. Normally, I would have questioned him about his concern but this time, I didn't do that. From the looks of Dara's male friend, it wasn't hard to figure what the problem really was. I just wanted to hear what Tate had to say about it.

Tate cleared his throat then proceeded to fill me in on everything. "Did you see that guy with Dara?" I nodded my head. "His name is Haji. He was Dara's so-called best male friend before she and I got together. I met dude a few times, even thought he was cool. And if I'm not mistaken, Haji had a girlfriend at the time. Because of that, I didn't care about Dara being friends with homeboy. Then one day, I found out that Haji and Dara had been playing me and his girlfriend the entire time. Come to find out, they had been fucking each other, right up under our noses. That's why I end up cutting that chick loose."

Tate continued. "I found all this out around the time that I met you. I was on a rebound from Dara but sweetheart; you were like a breath of fresh air, something that I needed at the time. You helped me get back my mojo, you made me feel good about myself again and you were everything that I wanted in a woman. But even though I really liked you, I'm not going to lie; I still used to go back and forth between you and Dara. I couldn't continue to do that so I had to make a decision and I decided that I wanted to be with you."

I listened intently as Tate poured his heart out to me. "I admit that I gave Dara the ammunition to trap me off. I mean, damn, I was having unprotected sex with the woman. And contrary to what you may think, I wasn't too happy when she told me that she was pregnant with Chasity. Not only because it was a slim possibility that the baby was mine but I had fallen in love with you. So, sweetheart, I don't want you to worry about no Dara. Trust me, I am never, ever messing with her again and she knows this."

"Are you sure, Tate?" I asked, truly wanting to believe everything that came out of his mouth.

Tate held my hand. "Yes, I'm sure! I also had something to ask you."

I closed my eyes. My heart was beating ninety miles
per hour and I felt like I was about to faint. *Oh Lord,* I
prayed to myself. *I'm about to lose my . . .*

My silent prayers were interrupted by the red velvet
box in Tate's right hand. Inside of it was a beautiful
pear-shaped engagement ring. I instantly began crying
at the sight of it.

Tate's eyes got misty. "Joi, you've been through so
much with me. You've been patient with me and fiercely
loyal to me. You've put up with all my drama and you
stood up for me even though no one else thought that
I was the one for you. Because of that, I want you to be
my wife. Will you marry me?"

"Yes, yes!" I screamed out. "I will be your wife!"

We both got up and began kissing each other. The
patrons and staff began clapping and congratulating
us. There was such a commotion that Dara walked over
to our side of the restaurant to see what was going on.
When she saw the ring on my finger, she went ballistic.

"You're actually marrying this bitch?" she yelled,
pointing at me. "I don't believe this shit!"

Some people look confused and others were looking
like they were waiting for the drama to unfold.

Tate stood up. "Why are you even the fuck over here,
Dara?" he yelled back at her.

She put her hands on her hips and began swinging
that God forsaken weave all over the place.

She looked at me in disgust. "Why in the fuck are
you proposing to this man-stealing bitch when I was
the one that was with you first? I'm the mother of your
child!"

Tate laughed in her face. Sensing it was about to get physical, two burly men walked over to where we were standing.

"Excuse me miss," one of them said to Dara. "You're going to have to leave!"

Dara didn't budge. "I'm not going anywhere until this motherfucker tells me why he's marrying this skank bitch!"

I made a move to step to Dara's ass but Tate stopped me.

"No, sweetheart, I got this," he said, stepping directly in front of me. "You're pregnant. You don't need to get involved in this."

Dara really lost it when she heard "pregnant." Haji stepped in front of her and now he and Tate were face to face. I was afraid that they were about to turn Night of the Cookers out.

The burly men were insisting that all of us leave but we ignored them. I could have sworn I heard someone saying that they were going to call 911. But Tate had something to get off his chest and he made it clear that he wasn't going to leave until he said it. Haji quickly came to his senses and stepped to the side. Tate stared Dara dead in her face.

"I'm gonna say this to you and then me and my fiancée are outta here! I know that you've been playing me for a fucking sucker! Chasity is not my daughter!" Dara's eyes widened. "That's right! I took a DNA test about six months ago," he said. Tate took a folded piece of paper out of his back pocket, balled it up and hit Dara in the face with it. "I was just waiting for the right time to tell you to go to hell!"

Dara picked up the crumpled paper from the floor and looked it over.

"This beautiful woman right here," he said, pointing at me, "is having my child. Yes, my biological child! So what you may need to do is go home and introduce Chasity to her real daddy," he said, pointing at Haji. "Because I'm done with you!"

Tate grabbed my hand and we headed for the door. Just as we were about to walk through the crowd toward the exit, I stopped in front of the stunned Dara. I fluttered my left hand and the engagement ring in her face.

"Toodles! Sucker," I said, looking at her with a self-righteous smile on my face.

The expression on Dara's grill was absolutely priceless! It was definitely a Kodak moment and I would have loved to have captured the memory. Too bad I didn't have a camera.

Chapter 24

Let No Man Put Asunder

Ebony

After leaving the fight party that previous Saturday night, I went through the entire week tending to my daily activities and not talking to anyone. My friends had been blowing up my house and my cell phone for days. They were leaving all kinds of crazy messages on my voice mail but I was in no mood to talk to any of them. I just needed some time to myself.

Of course, I was still reeling from the episode between Phoenix and I.

One of the things that I always admired most about Phoenix was that she was a headstrong, confident woman who took no shit from anyone. Now she had finally met a man that she liked and was already morphing into an entirely different person. It was hard to believe that Phoenix had flipped on me, her best friend, for a guy. But that was something that she had to live with because I was over it and over her too.

Now it was a Friday evening. I had just gotten off work and I was on my way to pick up my son from his afterschool program. Shah was coming to get him for the weekend so I had to hurry up and get home. Speaking of Shah, he had been calling me every day since our rendezvous that previous weekend. He was acting like we were back together again but that so wasn't the case. And Shah just knew that he was going to spend another weekend with me but he was sadly mistaken. I immediately shut that down. I still needed time to digest everything that happened between us.

Twenty minutes later, I arrived at Kare's afterschool. The program was held inside of his school and they had a zillion different things going on. I had to maneuver my way through the crowd of children who were being picked up by their parents. I finally spotted Kare, who was standing a couple of feet away from me, talking to one of his friends. When he saw me, he immediately walked over to me and hugged me around my waist. I briefly chatted with Kare's afterschool counselor and signed him out. Three minutes later, we were in my car and on our way home.

After asking about homework and his school day, Kare and I went into another discussion. This one was about me and his father. Like I said, my son doesn't skip a beat. If Kare wants to know something, he was going to ask questions about it. How someone chose to answer those questions was purely up to them.

"Mommy," Kare called out to me from the back seat. "Is Daddy coming to live with us?" he asked, with no hesitation whatsoever.

I cringed as I envisioned Shah in my bed. The answer was hell no but I didn't dare say that aloud.

I took a deep breath. "Um, I don't know about that, baby. Why do you ask?" I asked him, while keeping my eyes on the road.

"Because that's what Daddy told me. He said that we were going to be living together as a family. Is that true?"

My jaw tightened. Why was Shah feeding Kare's mind with the propaganda? We were not getting back together. I was going to have a serious talk with this dude.

I gave Kare the best possible response that I could think of. "We will just have to wait and see what's going to happen, Kare Bear."

I thought that I was in the clear until Kare went into yet another topic.

"Ma, what happened to Dray and D.J.?" he asked.

Now I was completely speechless. "Well, baby, I—"

Kare quickly interrupted me. "I know, I know, Ma. Dray's not your boyfriend anymore. Does that mean that I'm never going to see D.J. again?"

I sighed. "No, baby. You probably won't."

It was no use in lying to the boy. I looked in the rearview mirror at Kare's facial expression.

He shrugged his shoulders. "I don't care. D.J. was just your boyfriend's son. It wasn't like he was my real friend anyway."

I held back my laughter. "Yes, Kare Bear, that about sums it up."

"Do you want another boyfriend, Ma?" he asked. I could feel him staring at the back of my head.

"For right now, I just want what's best for you."

"If you want what's best for me, Ma, why can't my daddy be your boyfriend?"

This time, I didn't respond. There were things that Kare was too young to understand and I damn sure wasn't ready to explain any of my personal business to my eight-year-old son. It was time for my baby boy to go back to being a kid and stay out of grown folk's business. I turned the radio to Hot 97 and listened as he sang along to one of the rapper Drake's songs.

We arrived home fifteen minutes later. Within the next hour, Kare was fed, bathed, all packed, and ready to go with his dad. Shortly after, Shah rang my doorbell. As soon as he walked in, Kare did his usual routine act when he saw his father. This time, I cut his greeting short. Shah and I needed to talk.

"Kare Bear, go in your room. I need a moment with your daddy," I said.

Kare didn't like that one bit but he did exactly as he was told. I didn't want him looking in my face while I set some things straight with his dad.

After Kare was in his bedroom, I invited Shah to have a seat in the living room. He sat on my couch. I remained standing.

"I'm going to get right to the point, Shah. I don't appreciate you telling Kare that you and I are getting back together. That was a discussion that you didn't need to be having with an eight-year-old child, especially when I never gave you a definite answer."

Shah leaned back on the couch. I could tell that he was slightly annoyed with me.

"I'm sorry that you feel that way, babe, but Kare is my son too. I can tell him whatever I want."

I felt myself getting upset. "No, the fuck you can't."

Shah hopped up from the couch and paced around my living room. "So, what was this past weekend then, huh, Ebony?" He looked toward Kare's room to make sure the coast was clear. "Didn't we spend time with each other? Didn't we make love to each other?"

I crossed my arms. "I don't know about you but I was just horny!"

I could tell that Shah didn't like that because he got all up in my face. "See, that's what I'm talking about!" he whispered through clenched teeth. I could see the fury and hurt in his eyes. "Here I am, fighting to get my family back and you still don't even know what it takes to hold a man down! I could see why that dude Dray left you!"

Now that was mean. I felt the tears forming in my eyes.

"You don't know a got-damn thing about me and Dray!" I said, whispering so that only he could hear.

Shah smirked. I could tell that he was getting a kick out of watching those tears flow down my cheeks. "Let's be real, Ebony! You're no fucking saint, babe!" he said. "And I know that you have to wonder why no one has wifed you yet. You're a professional side piece, a slide-off chick. A man may cheat with you, have a good time with you, but guess what? At the end of the day, he's going back home to his real woman. You heard me, fun-time girl! He's going *home* to the woman he really loves. With me being the father of your child, I wanted to make it right with you so that our son can have a two-parent home! But if you want to continue to be used and abused by these cats who don't give a fuck about you then go ahead."

I held my head down. When I didn't say anything, Shah stopped pacing the living room. He covered his face with his hands.

"You know what?" he began. "Ebony, I'm so sorry. I know that I did some pretty fucked-up shit to you in the past. I might have even turned you into the woman you are today. But real talk, I want you to give me another chance. I want to show you how it feels to be loved—unconditionally. I know what you need and, trust me, it's more than just sex. You need a man, a real man who's going to take care of you and Kare. I'm finally ready to be that man for you."

My mother always told me to make sure that the man that I ended up with loved me more than I loved him. Maybe Shah was the one I needed to be with after all.

Against my better judgment, the words that I never, ever thought I would say were coming out of my mouth.

"Maybe we can work on having something, Shah," I said. He went to kiss me but I stopped him. "But for now you're on probation."

"So are we going to still do it?" Shah snickered.

"I don't see anything wrong with that," I replied. "We always had good sex with each other."

Shah wrapped his hands around me and we shared a kiss.

"I love you, Ebony," he whispered in my ear. I didn't say a word. "Hey, let's get out of here, Twin!"

Kare came running out his room, gave me a quick hug, and followed Shah out the door. After I closed the door behind them, I stood there, with a dazed expression on my face. I couldn't believe that I had agreed to work things out with Shah. *Is this what my desperation has come to? What the hell was I thinking?*

Chapter 25

Get To Know You Better

Phoenix

I had made several attempts to reach out to Ebony during the week. She wasn't answering her cell or house phone and she hadn't returned any of my calls. By the time Friday rolled around, I was all dialed out.

It wasn't like I was calling Ebony to argue or fuss with her. I just wanted to apologize for hurting her feelings at the fight party the previous Saturday. After thinking about the way I acted, I realized that I was being silly and paranoid. Ebony and I had a friendship that spanned over the course of fifteen years and it would be effed up to lose a sister/friend over something so minute.

In the meantime, life went on as usual. I was definitely enjoying my companionship with Kevin. Thank God, he and I were on the same page. We both agreed that we needed to get to know each other better before jumping into something more serious. And more importantly, Kevin and I hadn't even had sex yet, which was a plus. Sex would only complicate things between us.

But man, was I anticipating rolling around in the sack with Kevin's sexy ass. I couldn't wait!

While everything seemed to be going well with my newfound blue-collar friend, I still had some nagging insecurities when it came to the whole commitment thing. In the back of my mind, there were the what-ifs. Like, what if I found out that Kevin had a girlfriend after all? Or what if some woman popped up from his past, claiming that he was the father of a child he never knew about?

The thought of these things happening scared me to death. But these fears were all me, Kevin had no part of them. Shoot, Brother Man was doing everything to make sure that I was more than comfortable with him.

While I still had my reservations about men in general, there was no way in hell I was going to tell him that I didn't believe that a monogamous relationship even existed. I wouldn't want Kevin to think that I was some emotionally disconnected freak.

It was Friday afternoon and I was at work, finishing up on some things when Kevin called me.

"Hey, gorgeous," Kevin greeted me as soon as I answered the phone.

"Hello, handsome," I replied, taking off my reading glasses. I leaned back in my chair.

"I can't talk for long," he began, "but I was wondering if we were hanging out tonight. It's Friday, baby!"

I swung around in the swivel chair at my desk. "Hey, why not? Let's do this!"

"That's exactly what I wanted to hear. My man Duke is having a party. It's his birthday."

"Oh, okay!" I said. "Taurus the bull! Happy birthday, Duke!"

"Yep, Duke is thirty-two years young today! Our boy, who is this big-time promoter, is throwing Duke a private party in the VIP section at this spot on Fifty-something Street. Forgot the name of the place. So I want you to throw on some sexy shit tonight, come through and hang out with your boy. It's gonna be off the hook!

My man Stu Childs always throws the banging-ass parties."

Did he just say Stuart Childs? I said to myself.

When Kevin mentioned Stu's name, I stopped breathing for a second. Then I got up from my chair and began air boxing like I was Sylvester Stallone in *Rocky*.

"Hello? Are you there?" Kevin said.

I was so quiet on the other end; he probably thought that the phone got cut off.

I plopped down in my chair. "Um, yeah, I'm here," I replied. "Where's this, um, place . . . Where is it again?"

"I'm going to hit you up with the exact name and address of the spot later. Just make sure you come out tonight, babe. I want you to meet Stu and some of my other friends, too. And Duke said he wants you to bring Ebony to the party. I think he likes your girl. I'll call you around six o'clock, okay?"

I put my head down on my desk. "No problem. See you later," I said, feeling sick to my stomach.

I hung up the phone. I must have been one dumb bunny to agree to go to a party that Stu, the best I never had, was throwing. Why on God's green Earth did Duke and Kevin have to know Stu? I had finally met a man who was everything that I wanted and needed and now this bullshit.

I put my phone away and glanced at my watch. It was 11:00 A.M. I only had a couple of hours to get in touch with Ebony, apologize to her, and then try to talk her into attending Duke's party with me. I damn sure didn't want to go by myself. And Ebony would definitely know what to do in this situation—she always had my back. I shook my head. Ebony always had my back and I had acted like a total jackass to her at that fight party. I just hoped that she would forgive me for not having hers.

As soon as I got home from work, I got on that phone. I let Ebony's phone ring but I didn't leave a voice mail. Then, fuck it, I decided that I would phone stalk her stubborn ass and call right back. The doggone phone kept ringing. Just as I was about to disconnect the call, she answered.

"What do you want, Phoenix?" she said, coming on the phone with an attitude.

I was so happy that Ebony picked up that her attitude did not faze me one bit.

I got straight to the point. "I'm so sorry, Ebony. I'm sorry for embarrassing you at the fight party, for the accusations, and I apologize for trying to chastise you. You're like a sister to me and I shouldn't have done you like that."

Ebony groaned. "Can you cut out all of the apologetic shit, please?"

I was confused. "Huh?"

She sucked her teeth then began laughing. I breathed a sigh of relief.

"Oh, Ebony, girl! I missed you so much!" I screamed.

"I missed you too, *chica!*" Ebony yelled into the phone. "Okay, blah, blah, blah . . . Now what's going on with you and Kevin?"

At this point, I didn't care what Ebony did, who she talked to, or how many men she chose to have sex with. I was just happy to be talking to my bestie again.

"Is Kare with his dad this weekend?" I asked.

"As a matter of fact, he is. They just left. Why do you ask?"

"Do you wanna hang out with me tonight?" I was hoping that she said yes.

"Wow!" she said. "So I'm good enough to hang out with the queen bee now?"

"I guess I deserved that."

There was a slight pause between us.

"So where are we going tonight?" Ebony asked.

I smiled. "Thank you, girl. Thank you!"

"Ah, shit, girl! It's no need to thank me. What are we getting into?" Ebony asked.

I filled her in on Duke's party and how he had requested her presence. Then I told her that Stu was Kevin's homeboy and that he was the one throwing the party.

"Bitch, shut up!" Ebony said loudly. "Herpes Stu is Kevin's homeboy? Did you tell Kevin that you and Stu knew each other?"

"Hell no!" I replied. "I ain't telling Kevin shit! Why do I have to say anything to Kevin about Stu?"

Ebony sucked her teeth. "Why do you have to say something?" she repeated. "Duh! Because Kevin is cool with him, that's why! Trust me, I'm sure that Stu is not feeling the way that everything went down between you and him. He's definitely gonna put Kevin on to you. You know that the men nowadays talk more than women—they are the new bitches! Are you sure you want to go to this party tonight, girl?"

I made a grunting noise. "Yes, Ebony. I have to go! Kevin wants to introduce me to some more of his friends, including Stu!"

"Okay, okay. Calm down, *chica*," Ebony said. "It might not turn out for the worst. Maybe Stu won't speak to you at all."

"I'm not worried about him speaking to me. It's him telling Kevin about us is what I'm worried about. I could see him putting a different spin on what really happened that weekend just because I dissed him. And I was the one that practically threw the pussy at Stu, remember?"

"Yeah, I remember, child, I remember."

I quickly moved on to the next subject. "Listen, you need to start getting ready and then come and pick me up at 10:30. We don't wanna be tardy for the party!"

Ebony chuckled. "Are you crazy, woman? It's only going on a quarter after six!"

"Exactly!" I replied. "I'm going to meet up with my future boyfriend and his friends tonight and we must get a head start in order to look the part, don't you agree?"

"You ain't never lie!" Ebony said. "Getting my shit together right now!"

We both laughed.

It was about 11:15 P.M. when Ebony and I walked into Libra Lounge on West Fifty-second Street. We were looking hot, if I might add, in our tight-fitting mini dresses and five-inch platform heels. Once we were inside, Ebony and I made our way through the throngs of partygoers and walked upstairs to the VIP area. The VIP was loaded with colorful cushy lounge chairs and a fully stocked bar. It also overlooked the crowded dance floor.

Kevin and a few of their friends were sitting in the far corner of the VIP area. They had various bottles of liquor and champagne in ice buckets on the table in front of them. Kevin spotted us and waved us over. I walked right over to Kevin and placed a sweet kiss on the lips in front of everybody. He wrapped his arm around my waist and pulled me close to him. I reintroduced Kevin to Ebony and he gave her a hug with his free arm.

"You ladies look good as hell tonight!" he said. "I'm glad y'all could make it to my boy's party."

I blushed. "You know that I was coming, babe," I said.

Kevin looked at Ebony. "Are you good, Miss Ebony?"

Ebony smiled. "I'm good, Kev. I'm good. I'm just rolling with my girl, that's all."

Kevin gave us the thumbs-up. "That's right. Y'all are like sisters. Make sure y'all stay tight with each other."

Kevin beckoned Duke over to where we were standing. He smiled as he approached Ebony and me.

"Look who the wind blew in, Duke," Kevin said, gesturing toward Ebony.

Duke started smiling. I hadn't noticed how attractive he was. He was definitely Ebony's type.

Duke gave Ebony a warm hug. Kevin motioned for us to have a seat near them. I looked at all of the alcohol they had but I had to refrain from getting plastered. Kevin and I were going home together that night and I wanted to be semi-sober when I gave him some for the first time.

Kevin introduced me and Ebony to his other friends. And what made the introduction even better is that they had already heard about me.

Everything seemed like it was going great so far.

Suddenly, Stu walked his ass into the VIP area. Of course, he was looking fine as fuck. He froze in his tracks when he saw me sitting there and he did not look happy. I felt like I wanted to pee on myself! Kevin didn't see the worried expression on my face but Ebony sure did. Only she had no clue as to who Stu was because she had never seen him before.

Ebony leaned over to me. "You all right, Phoenix?" she asked. "You don't look so good."

"Look over to your left. The guy wearing the grey shirt is Stu," I whispered.

I gave her a head nod in his direction. Stu was staring right at us.

"So that's Stu, huh?" she asked, giving him the evil eye.

I swallowed. "Yep. And I so hope that this dude isn't the bitch that I think he is."

"Well, you're about to find out," she announced. "He's walking his ass over here right now."

I looked in his direction and Stu was definitely coming toward our group. I tried to hide my face with my hand, like that was going to do something. He showed Kevin, Duke, and all of their other friends some love. Just as Kevin was about to introduce us to each other, Stu spoke up.

"What's up, Phoenix?" he said, with a smirk on his face. "How you doing?"

Kevin looked at Stu then looked at me. I took a deep breath. "I'm fine, Stuart. How are you?"

Stu reached for my hand. "Could I talk to you for a minute, please?" he asked.

I could feel Kevin grilling me but I didn't dare give him any eye contact. Another thing that I didn't do was grab Stu's hand; I just got up from the couch on my own.

"So you know my dude Stu, huh?" Kevin asked me, with this bewildered look on his face. Ebony was sitting on the couch, not knowing what to do next. Duke had a frown on his face and I didn't bother to respond to Kevin's question. Instead, I followed Stu to an isolated corner near the bathrooms to talk.

As soon as we were away from the others, Stu came right at me.

"Yo, what's up with you, B?" he asked, addressing me like I was one of his friends. "Why haven't you returned my fucking phone calls? And why did you leave my crib like that? What the fuck was that about, B?"

I felt my inner hood bitch about to emerge.

I frowned. "First of all, my name ain't B, *son*," I said, going right into gangster mode on him. "And it's obvious that I left your fucking house because I didn't want to give you any pussy! Does that answer your mother-fucking question?"

A few seconds later, Kevin appeared where we were standing. He put his arm around me and gave Stu a playful punch in the stomach.

"What's up, Mr. Childs?" he teased. "How you know my woman, man?"

Stu didn't even look at Kevin. He just stood there giving me the mean mug. "Yeah, I know your girl, man. Your girl knows me too. She knows me very well. Don't you, Phoenix?"

Kevin turned to me. "So how you know my boy?" he asked, pointing at Stu.

I crossed my arms. "I just know him," I replied not wanting to go into detail.

Kevin rubbed his chin. "When I told you to come out tonight, did I not mention that my *boy* Stu was throwing this party? Why didn't you say anything about knowing Stu then? You got something to hide from me?" he asked.

I rolled my eyes up in my head. "Kevin, me and Stu did hang out a time or two."

Kevin chuckled. "Oh, okay. But don't you think that's something I needed to know especially since he's my man and you're supposed to be my lady?"

I looked away from the both of them. "It was nothing, Kevin. That's why I didn't tell you about it."

Stu the hater obviously didn't like what he was hearing. "Oh, really? So I'm nothing now?" he yelled at me. "You weren't saying that shit when you invited me into your fucking house and got butt-ass naked in front of me! You were practically throwing that raggedy pussy at me!"

All hell was about to break loose but thankfully, Kevin pushed me to the side and got in Stu's face.

"Look, Stu," Kevin began, talking through clenched teeth. "I know that you're my man and everything but you're disrespecting my lady right now! Be easy, homie!"

Stu stepped back from Kevin and began pointing at me. "Your lady? Your lady was just throwing pussy at me, like, two weeks ago, B! Don't let her fool you. She ain't no fucking lady, man!"

At that moment, Ebony had walked over and decided to get in on the whole ordeal. She stepped in front of me. "Fuck you, Stu, with your herpes-infested dick! She didn't fuck you because you're a diseased, dirty-dick bastard!"

Now everyone who was in that VIP area was standing around, watching us make fools of ourselves and listening to the entire transaction. Stu and Ebony almost got into it too but Kevin stopped it. The whole spectacle was so embarrassing.

Kevin began pushing on Stu, gesturing for him to step outside of the VIP area so that they could talk among themselves. Duke went along with them. After the men stepped off, Ebony and I took the longest walk ever back over to where we were sitting. People were staring at us and whispering. I poured a full cup of Coconut Cîroc and guzzled it down. I was stressed out. Ebony looked at me and shook her head.

I frowned at her. "What?"

"Girl, you got some real fucking drama going on in here tonight!" she exclaimed, with this smug expression on her face. "You can't say shit about me no more!"

I took another sip of my drink. "I'm so not used to this shit, Ebony. Why did Stu have to put me on blast like that? Now, Kevin is not going to wanna mess with me anymore!"

Ebony turned around to face me. "You should have told Kevin the truth, Phoenix! You never had sex with Stu so what was the problem with telling your guy that you knew him?"

I rolled my eyes. "Because I didn't think that Kevin needed to know all that, that's why!" I yelled over the music.

"Okay, so that's why you got put on blast. Don't be mad."

Ten minutes later, Kevin and Duke walked back into the VIP area. Kevin had a smile on his face and was acting like nothing ever happened.

"You all right?" he said, resting his hand on my inner thigh.

I nodded my head. "Yeah. Are you all right?" I asked, with a suspicious look on my face.

Kevin took a swig of his drink. "Yep! I'm more than all right!"

Things had got off to a rocky start but the celebration finally begun. Stu gave me the side eye the whole time but kept his distance. Ebony and Duke looked like they were enjoying each other. About an hour later, the hostesses brought out Duke's birthday cake. Kevin and his boys gave Duke a toast before he blew out the candles. Considering everything that happened, everyone ended up having a really great time.

It was around three in the morning when the party ended. We were all standing outside of the lounge bar, saying our good-byes to each other and trying to figure out who was riding with whom. Duke wanted Ebony to come home with him but, surprisingly, she turned down his offer. I was definitely proud of her for that. I was anticipating on leaving with Kevin but I hoped that the situation with Stu didn't put a damper on our plans. I walked over to Kevin as he was about to leave.

I wrapped my arm in his. "I'm gonna tell Ebony to go on home so that I could ride with you back to your house," I said to him.

Kevin raised one eyebrow. "Nah, it's been a change of plans. I'm riding with Duke and my boy Ashton. Let Eb take you on home. I'm outta here," he said, pulling away from me.

I stood there with a stunned expression on my face. Ebony was standing right beside me, taking everything in.

I grabbed his arm. "But, Kevin, I thought that we were going—"

He snatched his arm from my grasp and cut me off. "And I thought that we were too, Phoenix, until my man Stu put me on to how you really get down!"

"Stu is lying, Kevin! He's lying!" I yelled.

Ebony tugged at my arm but I snatched away from her. I didn't mean to do that—I knew that she meant well. She was just trying to keep me from making an ass of myself. But I think she was too late.

"So you're going to believe that dude over me, Kevin?" I asked.

"Who am I supposed to believe? Am I supposed to believe you? You didn't even bother to tell me that you knew my boy Stu! And you damn sure left out the part about you and him hooking up two weeks before I started talking to you!"

Then Kevin walked away from me. Just as I was about to go after him, Ebony stopped me in my tracks. I was visibly upset. I stood there and watched him until he disappeared from my view.

As Ebony and I walked back to her car together, I began crying. Before we pulled off, she tried to comfort me.

"Don't cry, girl," she said, putting her arm around me and bringing my head to her shoulder. "Kevin is a little tipsy right now. He doesn't really know what he's saying. He's probably more pissed at Stu then he is you."

I looked up at Ebony. "He knows what he's saying, Ebony. I didn't keep it real with him and look what happened."

Ebony started the car up and we headed back to Queens. "Look, Phoenix, I know that you really like Kevin. You may have money, designer clothes, and good looks, but now you see that none of that shit can keep this man around if he doesn't want to be there. This is your first lesson in Love 101."

I was in another world. I heard everything that she said but I wasn't listening. All I knew was that I wanted Kevin back. I was not about to let things between us end before it even got started. That just wasn't going to happen.

Chapter 26

Love Is All We Need

Joi

I was the happiest that I had ever been in my life. Everything that I had aspired to have had been going as planned. I went from being that fatherless little girl, endlessly searching for that love that I had never had from a man. I went through relationship after relationship, determined to fulfill my childhood dream of being a wife and a mother. I yearned for that complete family structure. Now I was about to have all of that, thanks to Tate, and I was more than grateful for it.

The jealousy and contempt that I had for the women who had the life that I longed for were officially over and done with. I wasn't the most religious person, but many nights, I prayed for God to remove these feelings. Once He did that, my blessings were unblocked and now four years later, I was pregnant and engaged to the love of my life.

It had been about a week since Tate proposed and I still hadn't told anyone about the engagement. I was worried about the mixed responses. Honestly, I wasn't in the mood for questions like, "Are you sure you're ready for that?" and "Don't you think that if he cheats with you, he will cheat on you?" I didn't need that negative thinking around me. Tate and I loved each other—that was all that mattered.

Throughout the week, Tate had begun moving his belongings into my two-bedroom apartment. We both thought that it was a good idea to live there for a year or so after the baby was born. We wanted to save money for a home.

By Friday, he was completely moved in. We had to make room for his stuff and unpack boxes so we hadn't had a chance to talk about what transpired that night at Cookers.

To celebrate our new life together, I made a celebratory dinner for us. After the food was ready, I made Tate a plate. Instead of looking at the delicious dish that I had prepared for him, he was staring at me like I was the main course meal.

"Pregnancy really suits you, sweetheart," he said, with a horny look on his face. "Let me find out that I need to keep you knocked up all the time."

I let out a hearty laugh and waved him off. "Hell no!" I replied, in response to the idea of keeping me knocked up. "But we can definitely go half on a baby," I said, enticingly, while sliding into the seat next to him. "I don't mind that part of the baby-making process at all."

Tate put some shrimp linguini in his mouth. He nodded his head. "And this fine specimen of a woman can cook, too? Shit, that's what I'm talking about!"

I giggled. "Oh, boy, stop! You got me blushing over here."

Tate blew a kiss at me. "You've been through enough with me. The least I could do is make you smile."

I nodded my head in agreement. "Yeah, you're right. And I thank you for doing it, too."

We continued to eat our dinner. "You know that Dara tried to get in touch with me after our run-in at Night of the Cookers, right?"

I shook my head. "Yeah, I figured the bitch would try to reach you so that she could plead her innocence. What did she have to say about herself?"

"She wasn't saying anything that I didn't expect for her to say. She said that she was so sorry for lying to me, and of course, she had the waterworks going. Then she tried to blame you for my suspicions about Chasity."

I sucked my teeth. "Girl, bye!" I said, in response to Dara's accusations. "She's the one running around giving up her stink twat to any man she meets! If she hadn't had raw dog sex with different guys, she wouldn't have had to worry about paternity for Chasity." I paused. "By the way, was that guy she walked in Cooker's with Chasity's father?"

"Yes, he is!"

I put down my fork. "Wait a minute. How do you know that for sure?"

"Doesn't Chasity look just like him?" Tate asked.

I nodded my head. "Yeah, she really does but that doesn't mean anything."

Tate began to get choked up. "Honestly, I really don't give a shit who the father is. All I know is that I'm not Chasity's daddy. I finally come to grips with that."

I held my head down. "I understand, Tate. I'm sorry that I put you through so much when it came to Chasity. It was nothing against the little girl . . ."

"I know, sweetheart, I know. You didn't do anything wrong. I had my own suspicions. And to think that I didn't want to get a DNA test for Chasity."

"So are you saying that the results of this DNA test is what prompted you to propose to me?"

Tate shrugged his shoulder. "No, not at all. I proposed to you because I saw how much you had my back. It made me realize how much you love me and how much you were ready to go to bat for me. What man doesn't want a woman who can hold them down?"

"Aw, thank you, babe! I'm glad that you said that because I feel the same way about you. But it's just that I feel sort of bad about how I acted. I started off being so selfish. I wanted you all for myself, I wasn't happy about sharing you with Chasity and Dara. That's why I want you to be honest with me about something."

Tate gave me his undivided attention. "Shoot."

"Would you like to continue to have Chasity in your life? After all, you are the man who played daddy to her for three years."

Tate shook his head. "Nah, sweetheart, I'm good! I done closed that chapter of my life and I'm going to leave Chasity alone. It's time for her mother to do the right thing by her."

Now that those cards were on the table, I felt relieved.

Tate got up from his seat and walked over to me. He kissed me on the lips then kissed my baby pouch. Suddenly, tears began forming in his eyes. He knelt down and laid his head on my stomach.

"I love you so much, Joi. Thank you for giving me so many chances," he said.

I began crying too, and kissed him on the forehead. "When you love someone, babe, you are supposed to give them more than one chance."

Tate picked me up from the chair and carried me into what was now "our" bedroom. He laid me on the bed, pulled up my T-shirt, and began going down on me like I was the shrimp linguini we had just had for dinner. In between the sucking and licking, Tate kept telling me that my good pussy had him blinded with love. I wanted to laugh at that statement but I told him that I loved him back, while pushing his head deeper into me.

After munching on my good-good for like twenty minutes, Tate came up for air. His chin and mouth were glistening with my juices and I licked every bit of me off his face. He hurriedly undressed, anticipating on getting some good old pregnant pussy. But before Tate entered me, he hesitated.

"I don't want to hurt the baby," he whispered.

I pulled his face to mine and began kissing him passionately. "The baby is going to be fine. Let's make love, baby. Slide it in."

And he did. We made love for most of the night, with our dinner sitting right on the table where we had left it.

The next morning, I left Tate sleeping in the bed while I got up to make me some breakfast and a few phone calls. After having the talk with Tate that night before, I knew that it was the right time to spill the beans about my engagement to my family and close friends.

I told my mother first. I held the phone away from my ear as she screamed and cried tears of joy.

"I prayed for this, Joi, I prayed for this!" she said. "I just wanted the best for you. You deserve it!"

"Yes, Mommy, thank you. And thank you for having that talk with me that day. I really needed that."

"I know you did, baby. I know. And I apologize again for not being there when you needed me the most."

"Mommy, I need you now!" I exclaimed, with a laugh. "I don't know the first thing about no baby."

My mother chuckled. "You know I will be right there by your side."

"Do you know if Payne is home this morning?" I asked, looking at the clock on my kitchen wall. It was 9:15 A.M.

"Um, he should be. He has a set that he has to do later on this afternoon."

"I think I'm going to give him a call."

"Do that. I'll hang up now."

After I hung up with my mother, I dialed my brother's number. Payne and I hadn't spoken since the dinner at my mother's house.

"Oh, my goodness!" said Payne as soon as he answered the call. "If it isn't Miss Ser-ree," he added.

I laughed. Payne calling me Misery didn't annoy me as much as it would have before my mother and I had that talk.

"Hey, Payne!" I said cheerfully.

I could hear Payne tapping the phone. "Hello? Hello? Who is this woman and what has she done with my miserable little sister?" he asked.

I laughed again. All of these years and I didn't realize how funny my brother really was. "Oh, shut up, Payne! I just called to let you know that I love you very much. Can you forgive me?"

There was silence on the other end of the phone. It sounded like Payne was crying.

"Joi," he whispered. "I waited so long to hear those words from you! I love you too, baby sis, I always loved you. I just wanted you to love me back, love me for who I am. And trust me, girl, I want to be there for my niece or nephew, the same way that you have been there for Rayni."

I could hear Payne sniffling on the other end of the phone.

I began to tear up. "Don't cry, Payne! Please don't cry. I promise you that from now on, I'm going to be the best sister that I can be to you."

"And I'm going to be the best sister to you too!"

We both began laughing hysterically. We laughed so long and so loud that I awakened Tate from his restful sleep. He walked into the kitchen with only his pajama bottoms on and opened the refrigerator.

"Who are you chucking it up with early this morning?" he asked while yawning and pouring some orange juice into a glass.

I wiped the tears of laughter from my eyes. "I'm talking to my broster," I replied.

Tate frowned. "Your broster?" he repeated.

"Yes, my broster, Payne: my brother/sister!" I said, laughing again.

Tate laughed too and shook his head. "Y'all two are crazy! Tell my broster-in-law that I said what's up," he said before shuffling back into the bedroom.

"You heard Tate, Payne?" I asked.

Payne chuckled. "Yaaaaazzz!" he replied. "He be knowing what it is."

"Guess what, Payne?"

"Yes, my love."

"I'm engaged. I'm getting married!" I screamed.

"Wooooooooooooo!" Payne yelled into the phone. "My baby sister is getting married! Oh, Lord Jesus! I'm so happy! Child, we have to start preparing for this wedding now! I am going to throw you the most elaborate baby shower, the most elegant bridal shower and reception for a little of nothing! Don't worry, Boo, your big broster got you, honey!"

Payne and I ended up staying on that phone for three hours, prepping and planning my baby shower and future wedding. At one point, Tate joined in, giving Payne some ideas for the tuxedo that he wanted. I was so involved with what was going on in my life that I had forgotten to call my girls Ebony and Phoenix to tell them the wonderful news.

Chapter 27

Mr. Wrong

Ebony

I dropped Phoenix at home in the wee hours of Saturday morning. She was so distraught over Kevin that I offered to stay the rest of the morning at her house. She turned me down and insisted that I go home and have a relaxing weekend. I was worried about my girl but I left her alone. I made sure she got in her building safely and was on my way back to Brooklyn.

A couple of stoplights later, I realized that I was tired as hell. The alcohol in my system didn't help matters much. Phoenix was a bag of tears and regret so I damn sure didn't want to go back to her apartment. That was when I decided to call Shah up to see what he was doing. He didn't live too far from where I was at that moment so I figured that I would go to his house and crash there for the next couple of hours. I needed to sleep some of that liquor off.

"Hello?" said Shah when he answered the phone. It sounded as if he was wide awake.

"What's up, baby daddy? What are you doing up?"

"Um, I had just got up to use the bathroom when my phone rang. What's up?"

Little did Shah know, I was right around the corner from his house. I wanted to be nearby, just in case he invited me inside.

"I wanted know if could come by and crash. I've been hanging out with Phoenix tonight and I'm a little too tired and tipsy to be driving home. I'm parking my car in front of your house right now."

"You're parking your car in front of my house?" he asked, with some concern in his voice.

"Yeah, I'm parking my car in front of your house! What the hell is wrong with you, Shah? You don't want me to come over or something?"

While sitting directly in front of the house that Shah rented his apartment in, I spotted a chick sneaking out of his front gate with some high-heeled shoes in her hand.

I slowly put the phone down. "You have got to be fucking kidding me," I whispered to myself. "Who the hell is this?"

Before she could get out the gate good, I got out of my car. "Um, excuse you!" I called out to this mystery woman. "What in the fuck are you doing coming out of my baby father's house?" I asked, walking toward her.

The woman stopped in her tracks, obviously not expecting for anyone to be approaching her on the street at three in the morning. She immediately got on defensive mode and put her hands on her hips. "Oh, so you're the one that Shah warned me about! The question is what are you doing here? Shah said that you were stalking him but I didn't believe it. Now I know it's true! I'm looking at crazy with my own two eyes!"

I chuckled. "Is that what he told you?"

"Oh, there's more! He also told me that you're a desperate bitch and that you're still in love with him! He don't want you anymore, Boo! Like damn, get over it already!"

This broad was pissing me off but I was trying hard not to show it. I didn't want her to think that she got under my skin.

"Well, that's funny because this here is the same bitch that had his face embedded between her legs last week."

"Fuck . . .," screamed the female. Before things went from bad to worse, Shah ran out of his house. He quickly stepped in between us, and lucky for the chick he did. I was about to snatch those cheap-ass Outre weave tracks out of her head.

After me and Miss Thing managed to calm down, I got in Shah's ass. "So, I'm saying, Shah, what's really good with you? One minute you're proclaiming that you're all in love with me, and the next minute you're laid up with some trick," I yelled.

"Trick, I know you're not talking about me, bitch!" the woman screamed back.

"Who is this, Shah?" I said, pointing at her over Shah's shoulder.

"You're just mad 'cause you got dumped!" she blurted out.

Shah tried to shut us up but to no avail. I was sure that his neighbors were listening to everything that was going on.

"Yo!" he said. "You ladies need to chill!" He looked at the girl. "Look, Keira, go home. Call me when you get there."

Keira rolled her eyes at me and got into her Honda coupe. She pulled off in a matter of seconds, leaving Shah and me alone with each other. I was highly upset but I wasn't about to lose sleep over Shah. What I really wanted to do was kick myself for falling victim to his trifling ass once again.

"Really, Shah?" I said to him while he held his head down in shame. "Really? I thought that we were trying to work on getting back together."

"Look, Ebony, I've been thinking—"

"Thinking what, Shah? You told me that you wanted to work on getting your family back!"

Shah looked up and down the block. "I . . . I was just tying up some loose ends, Eb, I didn't expect for you to . . ."

I began walking back and forth. "Why in the hell do you keep doing this shit to me, Shah?" I asked, with a disgusted look on my face.

Shah frowned. "Doing what, Ebony? All I told you is that I was just tying up some loose ends! That's all!"

I slapped my forehead. "Oh, my God!" I exclaimed. "Like, I'm so sick of this! I'm so sick of the lying, the cheat . . ." I had to stop and think. "On second thought, you know what? You're not my man, you're just my son's father and I should have let you stay that way. Should have never let you gas me up and end up in my damn bed. Should have never listened to your lies."

"Ebony, what I said to you wasn't no lie! None of what I said was a lie!"

"Uughh!" I moaned. "I'm so stupid! Why do I keep letting these sorry-ass Negros into my life?"

Shah went to touch me. I pulled back from him and balled up my fist.

"Get the fuck off me, Shah! Don't you dare put your got-damn hands on me! From here on in, you are only Kare's father to me! There's not going to be any more sex and it damn sure won't be no conversation between us unless it's about our son. And that's all I want from you. The only thing that I want from you is to be a good father to our child. You and I don't have shit with each other."

"But, Ebony, me and Keira . . . I broke it off with her so that we could . . ."

I walked to my car and slammed my driver's side door. "Fuck you, Shah. Fuck . . . you," I said. Then I pulled off, leaving Shah's pathetic ass standing by the curb.

I rode back to Brooklyn feeling like someone had hit me in the chest with a roll of quarters. During the drive, I got to thinking about my luck with men. Once again, I wanted to know what was it about me that made a brother wanted to cheat and lie to me. I had a lot going for myself, at least I thought so, and I was a cool person with a happy-go-lucky spirit. Wasn't that enough for these men?

Then again, that could have been the problem. I had always been the fun girl, who was always down for a good time. I was the woman who the brothers called when they wanted to have great conversation and even better sex. I allowed men to treat me like a leased vehicle—at the end of the contract, they let me go and replaced me with something brand new. I had never been kept before. I was never that one.

I guessed that I had learned some hard lessons in the last couple of weeks, about men, about relationships, and about myself. I wasn't angry at Shah, Chase, Dray, or even Mateo. I was mad at Ebony. I had to claim responsibility for my actions, for putting myself in the position to get played. And as the old saying goes, "Fools rush in," and I was that fool. I couldn't continue to do the same thing and expect different results. That was insanity.

Truthfully, Phoenix had been on point when she told me about myself at that fight party. If she and Kevin were to get past that Stu fiasco, she didn't need me messing up her future with this man by getting fucked, lied to, and then dumped by her man's friend Duke. I wasn't sure if Duke was that kind of guy but it seemed like getting kicked to the curb had become a recurring thing with me.

Fifteen minutes later, I was parking my car in front of my house. When I stepped foot inside of my apartment, I undressed in the living room and then slid my naked body into my bed. The only sounds that could be heard in my quiet apartment were the sounds of me crying myself to sleep.

Chapter 28

In the Morning

Phoenix

Just when it seemed as if I was getting closer and closer to having a relationship with the man of my dreams, something, or rather someone threw a monkey wrench right in it.

I thought back to my chance meeting with Kevin. This man told me that he had been checking me out for months and had been trying to find the right words to say to me. Instead of being flattered with his efforts, I started off being a real jerk to Kevin. In turn, this wonderful blue-collar man turned out to have every one of the qualities that I wanted in a guy. And most importantly, he was feeling me.

Because of my dishonesty, it looked like I was about to lose Kevin for good. I couldn't say that I blamed Kevin for being upset with me. If the shoe was on the other foot, I probably would have reacted the same way.

I stood in my full-length mirror looking at myself. I had put a lot of money and effort into being a self-proclaimed fly girl, so to speak. I had made that fucking mirror my best friend but I only saw the beauty on the outside. I couldn't see how effed up I was on the inside.

Over the years, I was conflicted. It was hard for me to trust men. I felt that all men were like my father.

This was a man that I had trusted and loved dearly but he was also an admitted adulterer. His infidelity had changed the dynamic of our family structure because he had hurt my mother, a woman just like me. With this type of history, it was stressful for me to even date anyone. I damn sure didn't want to end up bitter and scorned like my mother. That's why I decided that the madness had to stop. It was time that I became less fearful and just let the chips fall where they may when it came to love.

I had been calling Kevin for most of the morning and he wasn't acknowledging my calls. But I wasn't going to give up that easily so I decided to call him back one last time. I hoped that he answered the phone because if he didn't, that was going to be the last time that he heard from me. To my surprise, he picked up.

"What's up, Phoenix?" he said.

"What's up, Kevin?" I paused for a moment then went into apologetic mode. "Look, Kevin, I'm so sorry that I didn't tell you about Stu and sorry for the spectacle at Duke's party."

"Don't ever lie to me again, Phoenix," he said in a stern voice.

"I won't," I replied, sounding like a six-year-old being scolded by her father.

"I don't want to sound crazy because it's so soon but you know that I'm feeling you, right?" he asked.

"I hope you are because I feel the same way about you."

"I think that you're someone I could build and grow with. That's why I was so upset about the Stu situation. I just knew that you and my man had something going on with each other."

"I am that somebody you can grow with, Kevin. And as far as Stu is concerned, I have no interest in being with him or any other man for that matter. I just want to be with you."

Suddenly, I began crying again. I hadn't cried this much in years. Kevin had me growing through these emotional changes. I didn't know what to do with myself.

"Come on, now, babe, don't cry," he said, comforting me over the phone. "I don't want you to cry."

I grabbed some Kleenex and blew my nose. "I just feel so embarrassed about the whole Stu thing," I said. "That's such a fucked-up way to start off with somebody."

Kevin sucked his teeth. "I ain't thinking about that shit anymore, Phoenix. Honestly, Stu gets all kinds of women but for him to go off like that, he must have really liked you. The only thing that he did was made me feel like I had someone really special."

I dried my tears. "Wow. I didn't think that you would say that."

"Phoenix, you are special! Let me tell you, all of my boys who were at the party that night gave you the seal of approval, even after that whole Stu mess went down. And my boy Duke seems to think that you're the one for me, who by the way, got on me last night."

Now I was starting to feel much better. Guys always listened to the advice of their friends and it looked like everything was working in my favor after all.

My eyes were wide opened. "What did he say?" I asked, with a hint of curiosity in my voice.

"He asked me why I didn't go home with you last night. I told him that you had me looking like an asshole at the party. We all know that Stu is a bragging dude and I damn sure didn't want him to be on my back about how he had sex with you. So Duke said, 'Fuck Stu!' And how am I letting Stu, of all people, dictate who I should be with? He asked me was I feeling you. I said, no doubt! Then he said, 'If you're feeling this woman, Kev, then what the fuck is the problem, man?'" Kevin said, imitating Duke's voice. "'You've been chasing Phoenix down for months, my dude, and now you're going to let that go? Are you crazy, boy?'" Kevin and I laughed. "Then he told me to make every minute that I imagined being with you a reality."

I smiled. "So what are we going to do, Kevin?" I asked.

"Why don't you come over here and find out?" he replied.

I was so excited! Finally, I had found that man who was worthy of having me.

"Where do you live again?" I asked.

Kevin gave me his address, which was located in Cambria Heights, Queens. I hopped in the shower, making sure that I smelled nice and fresh. Then instead of me taking hours to put on some makeup, I just settled for au naturale. It was the first time in a few years that I had done that one. I put my hair into a ponytail and threw on a pair of Nike leggings, some sneakers, and a hoodie. I grabbed my Yankees fitted baseball cap and put it on my head before I walked out the door. And, surprisingly enough, I didn't bother to do my usual routine of checking myself out in my full-length mirror.

About a half an hour later, I pulled up on 233rd Street. I got out of my car and stood by the curb, checking out Kevin's property. He lived in a four-bedroom house all by himself and, judging from the way that he kept his front yard, I was sure that the inside of his home was just as nice. I walked up to the door and rang the bell. Kevin appeared in the doorway in a matter of seconds to let me in.

As soon as I stepped through the threshold of the front door, Kevin began kissing me. Our kiss was so hot; it felt like our tongues were melting together. Then Kevin began peeling off my clothes. I took off his T-shirt and he stepped out of his sweats. There we were standing in the middle of his living room, stark naked. And his rod was thick as hell, too—it looked like a miniature tree trunk. Of course, I was very pleased at the sight of it.

Much to my delight, Kevin got on his knees and began servicing me by submerging his face into my freshly scrubbed box. His skills were out of this world! He sucked and licked on my clit until it felt like my legs were about to give out.

Right before I was about to cum, Kevin stopped munching on my carpet. It was obvious that he had other plans for me. He grabbed my hand and led me upstairs to his bedroom. The bedroom was painted bright white with a beautiful red, white, and black goose down comforter on the bed. Kevin dimmed the lights and turned back that comforter to reveal red sheets. I couldn't wait to lie on those sheets and consummate our newfound relationship.

Kevin and I fell backward onto the queen-sized bed. Instead of continuing our foreplay, he put on a condom and found his way inside of my steaming hot va-jay-jay.

"Damn, babe," he whispered in my ear. "It's so tight! Just the way I like it."

I was so turned on that no reply would come from my lips. I was too busy concentrating on Kevin's long stroke. My pussy was pulsating, eager for him to find that G-spot of mine. I wrapped my legs around his waist and began bucking wildly, as the pleasure began to heighten. Then Kevin started kissing me, like he wanted to suck the life out of me. And I nibbled on his skin, like I wanted to eat him alive.

"Kevin," I said, whispering my future man's name. Every syllable in that five-letter name sounded like music to my ears. I didn't know that making love to a man could feel so good.

After our hour-long hot and steamy interlude, Kevin and I lay in the bed together. He kissed me on the forehead and I smiled at him.

"Woo," I said. "That was so good!"

Kevin chuckled. "Not bad for a garbage specialist, huh?"

"No, not at all! Not to mention, I haven't had sex in nine months . . ."

"Nine months? But I thought that you and Stu . . ."

I held my head up. "You thought that me and Stu what?"

Kevin sat up. "Stu told me that y'all had sex with each other . . . I thought that—"

I frowned at him. "Oh, hell to the no! Stu is a lying sack of shit! I didn't . . . You know what, Kevin? Let me tell you what *really* happened with your boy that night. It sounds like I need to set the record straight."

So I told Kevin the truth about his boy. By the end of my story, he was cracking up. I did recap on what had occurred at Stu's condo.

"Damn, man! That's fucked up!" Kevin said. "Oh, well, you win some, you lose some. Guess Stu lost one."

I agreed. "Yeah, basically." I kissed Kevin on the lips. "And I'm glad he did. Lying on his penis and whatnot!"

"So are we going to do this, Phoenix?"

"Do what?" I asked, with a concerned look on my face.

"Spend this future of ours together."

My heart began racing. "You want to have a future with me?"

He shook his head at my silliness. "On second thought, maybe I should go find me another girlfriend if you don't wanna be with a garbage specialist!"

I jumped out of the bed, butt ass naked. "No, no, no!" I yelled, holding out my hands. Kevin started laughing at me. "I don't mind being with a garbage specialist, especially if his name is Kevin Wright!"

"That's me, babe! And I'm your man! Don't you ever forget that."

After we confirmed that we were going to take things to the next level, we made love for most of that Saturday afternoon and the night.

When I left Kevin's house that next morning, I was smiling all the way home. A few months before, I didn't think that I would be where I was at that moment. It was the happiest that I had been in a long time. No amount of material things or money could make me feel the way that I did. I thought that those *things* were all I needed to make me happy. It wasn't until I met Mr. Wright that I realized how wrong I've been.

Chapter 29

Searching

Ebony

It was a Sunday afternoon and I had just finished running my errands. I wanted to make sure that all of my laundry, grocery shopping, and cleaning was done before my Kare Bear came home from his father's house.

And as for my new attitude, I hadn't put much more thought to it. I just wanted to things to be normal again. I just wanted to be normal again.

I hadn't spoken to Phoenix since I dropped her off early Saturday morning and I hadn't seen Joi since we had lunch with each other the week before so I decided to call them up. I missed my girls. I called Phoenix first.

"Helloooo?" she said, answering the phone like she was on cloud nine.

"Hello to you!" I said, with a smile on my face. "Somebody is sounding hella happy this afternoon!"

"Yes, I am! I got in touch with Kevin. As a matter of fact, I'm just coming from his house this morning."

"That's what's up! I'm glad that you guys worked things out, girl."

"Shit, me too! And it feels damn good to be with my man and not someone else's."

"I know what you mean, girlfriend," I said beaming with pride. "I'm happy for you! Why don't you and Joi come over for lunch? It's almost twelve-thirty in the afternoon and I need the company."

"That sounds like a plan. Did you call Joi yet?"

"No, not yet. I'll call her on the three-way."

I dialed Joi's phone number. She picked up right away. "Hey, Eb," she said.

"Hey, Miss Joi," I replied. "Phoenix is on the phone, too."

"Hey, Boo," Joi said, happily greeting our friend. "What's up with you, sexy?"

"Girl, you're sounding like you're on top of the world right now!" Phoenix exclaimed. "What in the almighty hell is going on with you, child?"

We all laughed. "I'm gonna have to tell y'all that in person!" Joi said.

"Well, that's exactly why I called you, honey pie," I said. "I'm gonna throw some chicken cutlets on this George Foreman grill of mine, make a delicious tossed salad, mix up some fresh lemonade, and we can have some girl talk."

"Girlfriend, you know I love me some of your chicken salad!" Joi said. "I'm eating for two now so go extra heavy on the chicken!"

"I don't know about you, Joi, but I got my car keys in my hand and I'm walking out the door. See you in a few, ladies," Phoenix said.

We hung up the phone and I immediately began preparing the meal for my girls. There was so much that we had to catch up on and I couldn't wait.

Phoenix and Joi arrived at my house a little after one o'clock. We sat at the table in my kitchen and laughed about old times, good times, even the worst of times. Of course, I talked about men and how I was tired of going through the same bullshit with those assholes.

"That's why I have decided to become celibate," I said, with an earnest look on my face.

Phoenix dropped her fork on the table. "You decided what?" she asked in amazement.

"You heard me! I've decided to become celibate. And I'm going to see a therapist. I know that I have some deep-rooted issues and I refuse to allow another man up into my space until I get myself together. After breaking up with Dray, I saw how quickly I reverted back to my old habits. I can't allow myself to go down that road to nowhere again."

I began shedding some tears. Both of my friends hugged me at the same time.

Joi held my hand. "Girl, we are here to support you. You do whatever you have to do so that you can start loving Ebony, you hear me?" she said.

I wiped a tear from my cheek. "I will. You know I love y'all, right?"

We hugged again. Now it was Phoenix's turn to tell us her good news.

"Kevin and I are officially a couple now!" she said, clapping excitedly. We all screamed. "That's right, *chicas!* Mr. Wright is my man and I'm his woman. I'm in a re-lay-tion-ship!"

We all laughed.

"Yes, you are, girlfriend," I said. "Kevin is such a cool guy, he's hardworking and he's gorgeous, too. You have to meet him, Joi."

"Most definitely! Phoenix can bring him to my wedding next year," Joi said, before stuffing some salad in her mouth.

It got so quiet in that kitchen that we could have heard a pin drop. After everything had sunk in, I was the first to speak.

"Wedding?" I asked, with a bewildered look on my face. "Did you just say your wedding?"

Joi showed us her left hand. I couldn't believe that Phoenix and I hadn't noticed the sparkling two-carat marquis diamond and platinum masterpiece on her left ring finger. Phoenix grabbed Joi's hand so that we could get a better look at the impressive rock that she was wearing.

"This ring is the motherfucking truth!" Phoenix said, mesmerized by its flawlessness. "Got me cussing up a storm over here!"

"That is beautiful, Joi!" I cried out. "I'm so happy for you!"

Joi held her hand away from her face and looked at her own ring. "Yes, ladies, Tate proposed to me at Night of the Cookers last week."

Phoenix and I hadn't been big fans of Tate in the past but it looked as if he had proved us wrong. Not only was our beloved sister/friend knocked up with his child but he stepped up to the plate and proposed to her. Maybe that old Tate wasn't as fucked up as I thought he was.

Joi took a sip of her lemonade. "But that's not all. Tate took a DNA test for Chasity and he found out that that little girl is really not his daughter."

"Whoa," said Phoenix. "That's a big deal right there! I'm sorry to hear that. Feel bad for Tate and the little girl, too. Her mama ain't shit for that!"

Joi shook her head. "Yeah, I felt bad for the both of them too. It's so unfair to Chasity. I did ask him if he wanted to continue being a father to her. I wanted it to be his choice."

"What did he say?" I asked.

"He just said that he was going to let Chasity go and move on. He's cutting all ties with her and her mother. He was upset about it but hey, his real seed is right here," she said, pointing to her belly.

"Ah, phooey! Fuck his fake ass baby mama!" Phoenix blurted out with her cold-hearted ass. "That bitch, Dara shouldn't have lied! Now she's gonna have to find her illegitimate child another damn daddy! Man, I can't stand a trifling, scheming ho!"

Joi chuckled. "Girl, that ho, Dara has no one to answer to but God Himself. She knows who the father of her baby is and she did her daughter a disservice by lying to Tate. Hopefully, Chasity will grow up and won't remember a thing about Tatum Marshall, the man who was almost her daddy but then again not really."

There was more laughter. "You're right, girl," I said. "With a mother like Dara, Chasity is going to be another little girl lost. I can relate."

We finished up our lunch then took our chat into the living room, where we talked about Joi's wedding and her baby shower. Then we talked about the summer barbecues that we were going to have in Kevin's backyard. Too bad he didn't know yet.

The girls left my house at exactly four-thirty that afternoon. Joi had to meet up with Tate and Phoenix had a date with Kevin. I had to hang around the house because I was expecting Shah to drop off Kare Bear at five o'clock, like he usually did. As soon as the clock hit 5:00 P.M., my doorbell was ringing. It was Kare, standing outside of my door with his father standing directly behind him. I rolled my eyes when I saw Shah's pathetic mug staring back at me through my porch window.

As soon as I opened the door, Kare ran inside and gave me a big hug. Shah walked in behind him, dropping Kare's overnight bag near the front door.

"Hey, Ebony," he said, with a solemn look on his face.

"Hey, Shah," I replied, without one trace of anger in my voice.

Shah looked at me strangely. "Are you good?"

I raised my left eyebrow. "Of course I am. Why would I be anything else but good?" I asked.

Shah shrugged. "I don't know, just asking." He looked around my apartment like it was the first time that he'd been there.

"Okay, look Shah, you have to go now," I said. "Thanks for returning our little care package."

I held the door opened for Shah to walk out. He ignored the open door and stood there, staring at me.

"Can we talk?" he asked.

I threw my hands in the air. "Listen, Shah, you and I don't have anything to talk about. Right now, I'm in a great place and I want to stay there. No more of listening to your talk of how you're a better man, how you want us to be family again. I don't give a fuck about that and most of all; I don't give a fuck about you. We are done."

Shah frowned. "So is this what we're going to do? Act uncivilized and angry with each other?"

I laughed. "Honey, I'm nowhere near being angry with you. I was more upset with myself for allowing you back into my life. Now you and Keira can continue to do what it is y'all do."

Shah held his head down. "Keira decided to leave me alone for good."

I laughed even harder. "Welp! Good for her!"

Seeing that he was getting absolutely nowhere with me, Shah finally turned around to leave.

"All right, I'm out. I guess I'll be seeing you the following weekend when I come to pick up my boy."

I had the biggest smile on my face. "That's probably best." I looked toward Kare's bedroom. "Kare Bear?

You father is about to leave! Come say good-bye to him!" I yelled.

Kare came running out of the room and into Shah's arms. He gave our son a hug and a kiss.

"Daddy loves you, boy!" Shah said.

"Love you too, Daddy. See you later!" Kare said, jumping out of his arms and scurrying back to his room.

Shah looked at me with those bedroom eyes of his. "Daddy loves you too, girl."

"Well, we have something in common, Shah, because got-dammit, I love me too. Good-bye, Shah."

He stepped outside and I slammed my door. I didn't look back.

While I was cleaning, I turned on some music. One of my favorite songs, "Me, Myself and I" by Beyoncé, was coming through my radio speakers.

I sang along with Mrs. Carter. "'Me, myself and I is all I got in the end, that's what I found out . . .'"

Beyoncé had hit home with those words. It was time that I gave my heart to someone that truly deserved it. That someone was me.

"And it ain't no need to cry, I took a vow that from now on, I'm gonna be own best friend . . ."

And those were the words that Ebony Mahogany Brown was definitely going to live by.

The End.